River *of* Arpeggios

River *of* Arpeggios

GARY RUKIN

River of Arpeggios

For information about this title or to order other books and/or electronic media, contact the publisher:

GSRukin Publishing
ariverofarpeggios.com
gsrukinpublishing@gmail.com

ISBNs:
979-8-9852913-0-8 (softcover)
979-8-9852913-1-5 (eBook)

Printed in the United States of America

Cover and Interior design: 1106 Design

This novel's story and main characters are fictitious. While actual musicians are mentioned, the characters who inhabit this work of fiction are wholly imaginary.

Arpeggio:

A broken chord. The notes of a musical chord, played
individually, in ascending or descending sequence.

*This book is dedicated to my parents, Mel and Marion,
who fostered my love of music and gifts too marvelous
to repay, to all who came before me, to my
sister Barbara, and my wife Sherry.*

*I would be remiss not to acknowledge Les Urban
for his skills and support, the use of his recording
studio, his fine guitar work on Breakaway,
and his friendship for the past fifty years.*

*May you know the gift of music
and carry it in your heart.*

Contents

Prologue

I *am a musician.* The songs I play are memories. I play them by rote, my fingers choreographed with muscle memory. Each chord resonates within me, summoning ghosts.

The first ghost I summon is my father's ghost, playing his guitar. Gone from this world nine days before my eleventh birthday; he is my muse. His strings are my strings. His baritone is my voice.

The second ghost I summon is my attic room in our house. The slant of the roof cuts the ceiling of the room at the wall by the bed to my exact height at age eleven: five feet, three inches. When I inherited my father's guitar, its resonance in that room was hypnotic. Included in my legacy were a small tin of guitar picks, two sets of D'Addario guitar strings, a Mel Bay guitar book, and a silver Timex watch.

The third ghost I summon are his fingers. Mine imitate my father on his guitar, as best I can. This ghost binds me to him. Especially today. Today I am thirty-four years old, the same age as my father at his death.

I am holding his guitar, though it is no longer mine. The strings press into my fingertips as my fingers assemble themselves into an A minor seventh chord, which vibrates the tear ducts behind my eyes. I modulate to a C, which stays the tears, then to a G major, which places my father's face before me, so close I can smell the sandalwood of his aftershave and feel his mustache tickle my face. Then the E minor seventh opens my tear ducts, and I cry.

These are my ghosts, my memories. We are connected though the music. All ways. Always.

Unstrung

alance walked home from school on November 16, 1987, down Sacramento Avenue, still processing the news that a classmate, one he barely knew, one whose face he was startled to see clearly in his mind, had died in a plane crash on a flight from Denver to Boise. Principal Milikan called a school assembly, and Miss Gibson, the school counselor, passed around an appointment sheet. She explained that this was a time to grieve, that grief is normal, and we should feel free to discuss our emotions and concerns with her, our parents, or a favorite teacher.

Palance didn't feel any of this. He didn't miss Mark Blevin. His solitary memory of the kid was playing baseball during PE. Palance was pitching and threw him three consecutive strikes to end the game. That was back in April. They were in fifth grade. At that time, the leaves, now gone from the trees, were in bloom, with yellow buds, and he felt the elation of winning and spring and his teammates gathered around him. Now he felt numb, wishing he could grieve. He turned left on Fargo; there was a chill in the air and brittle leaves swirling at his feet.

Palance knew something was wrong before he walked into the house. Sitting on the cream-colored living-room couch, used only on holidays, were his mother, Aunt Sandi on her right, and Uncle Ross next to Aunt Sandi, staring into space. The lights were off. The vanishing sunlight illuminated their faces. They weren't talking. His mother was still. There was nothing on the coffee table, not even bridge mix. Aunt Sandi clasped her hands together. Her eyes were red. Palance's first thought was that they had heard about Mark. He deposited his backpack at the bottom of the stairs and waited for instructions.

"We need to talk to you," Uncle Ross said. Tears were evident in both women's eyes. Palance walked over, and Uncle Ross reached toward him hesitantly and guided him onto the couch between he and Aunt Sandi while his mother sobbed deeply. "There was an accident," Uncle Ross began, and Palance relaxed because he already knew about Mark. Then the door swooped open, and his sister, Jillian, walked in. Everything stopped, including his breath, as if someone had hit the "Pause" button. When the scene moved forward again, everything had unraveled, and his father was never coming home. Jillian was screaming, and Mom rested her head in Aunt Sandi's lap.

While Uncle Ross explained what happened, a vision appeared in Palance's mind. His dad was flying the plane that crashed with Mark inside, and the scene unfolded as a dogfight in a war movie. Enemy fire had crippled the plane, the engine buzzed, and blue-gray clouds filled the sky. The soundtrack was riddled with the rat-a-tat of machine-gun fire. Palance saw his father with aviator goggles and a determined look on his face. Mark appeared in the rear seat as the gunner, destroying the enemy, and victory in defeat was their final act of redemption. The engine stalled; the plane ignited and exploded in a fiery beacon.

Suddenly Palance heard his uncle fade, and his mother take over. She was sobbing about an automobile accident and a drunk driver running a red light. Slowly, he understood Mark was not the problem. He realized he would never smell his father's aftershave coming into the kitchen in the morning. His father would no longer be part of their nightly dinners. There would be no more car trips in the summer to small towns with beaches and swimming pools.

Thoughts and images flowed through Palance's mind in haphazard rhythms. It was a jangle of discordant sounds, the traffic outside, and the hum of the refrigerator. If he allowed this reality, he would snap like a twig. He recalled a guitar lesson from his father. He had tightened a tuning peg too far; the string snapped and slapped his face with a loud twang. It cut a red line in his cheek. Tears mingled with blood, salting the wound. His father removed the broken string, exchanged it for one that came neatly coiled in a paper packet, and let Palance tighten the new string until it resonated evenly. He longed for this contact, which would not come—not now, not ever.

The doorbell jarred him from his reverie. Palance's heart beat rapidly. The couch cushion shifted, and he watched his uncle shuffle toward the door, glancing back toward them. Palance's cousin Joel stood there, dressed in dirty blue jeans and an old leather jacket, arms limp at his side and a blank expression on his face.

"Got here as quick as I could," he said, with his head down, not looking anyone in the eye. Joel threw his jacket on a vacant chair, put his arm around Uncle Ross, his father, and walked him slowly back to the couch. Both used the same shuffling gait. Joel stopped to lay his arm on Palance's shoulder, let it slide off, and ran his fingers over Jillian's hair before taking a seat next to Uncle Ross. He kissed his mother on the cheek, ignoring Palance's mother, his Aunt Elaine, who'd buried her face in a pillow on Aunt Sandi's lap.

Jillian had red eyes but no tears. Joel looked pitifully at Palance. Palance held back the urge to punch him in the stomach. He moved to the other end of the couch to comfort his sister, his arms around her shoulders, his body tightening with the shallow gasps of her breaths, his sleeve dampening as her tears fell. Palance waited for his father to walk in, deposit his keys into the silver bowl on the fireplace mantle, and take care of things.

He could hear his father's voice: "Back home from the funny farm. How's the family zoo?" He could hear the crisp tapping of his father's shoes on the tile floor.

"Pal . . . Jillian," his mother said in a voice that resembled Jillian's more than her own, "I need to talk to you." His every muscle resisted, and yet he turned toward her, the scent of Aunt Sandi's lavender cologne enveloping him. Palance focused on the dampness of his shirtsleeve as Jillian continued to cry.

"Uh, huh," he said. Jillian was silent except for her tears.

"It happened this afternoon. Your father was on his way to a meeting," his mom told them.

"Uh, huh."

"The Rabbi's going to be here soon. The funeral," she began, "the funeral is . . . tomorrow."

"No," Jillian screamed, and Palance let go of her as she fell onto the floor, and his mind emptied.

"Can I go to my room?" Palance asked, the air thickening around him. "I have homework." His mother held him with her eyes but gave him permission. He grabbed his backpack and took the stairs two at a time to his room. He pulled out his science book and stared at the blue and red spheres on the cover. They represented atoms and molecules. He tried to understand the lesson they had today and all of last week. He remembered valence electrons and something about vibrations, but it didn't fit together. Nothing made sense.

Palance pressed his face against the bed, hoping for comfort, the rough fabric of the bedspread chafing his skin. He got up and walked to his dresser, opened the bottom drawer, and, from under a pile of underwear, took out a folded envelope. It contained three of his father's guitar picks. He stole them, only a few from a collection of dozens—nobody would notice—and felt the small weight of them in his hand.

He wanted to cry, but his eyes and mouth were parched, and he needed a drink. He walked to the bathroom, careful not to make a sound and draw attention from downstairs. He turned on the light. The blue and red towels were too bright for his mood. Palance turned on the faucet, splashed water onto his face, and felt it running down his cheeks. He filled his cupped hands and drank. After three handfuls, he buried his face in a towel and gasped hard. Turning around, he saw Jillian standing before him, staring at him, quietly waiting, and when he stepped out of the bathroom, she reached for his hand and led him back down the stairs. Her hands were cold.

Black cloth covered the mirror in the entryway, and a feeling of dread overwhelmed him. Uncle Ross, who had a belly laugh so infectious it could move a room to tears, was sitting quietly, holding Aunt Sandi's hand. Palance's mother looked young and small. He sat down beside her, and her tears infected him. He felt his own eyes welling up, until finally tears were wet on his face. He let them fall and knew everything had changed.

They all sat together on the couch, except for Joel, who spun aimlessly back and forth on the swivel chair, gripping its arms tightly. Palance felt adrift in this silent cacophony. He heard a few breaks in the stillness: his mother's breathing, irregular and shallow, his sister's nails against the fabric of the couch, the timid rustling as Aunt Sandi straightened out her shirtsleeves.

"I'll make some coffee," his mother announced. She patted Palance and Jillian's legs, peeling herself off the couch. "Anyone want anything?" she asked, crying on her way to the kitchen.

"Can I have a Coke?" Joel asked. Palance sneered. *He's been here a thousand times. He knows where everything is. He can get it himself.*

"I'll get it for you," Aunt Sandi said. She walked into the kitchen, taking Jillian's hand as she went. The women gathered in there, leaving the men in the living room, where the silence turned deadly. They heard every movement in the kitchen—the water pouring into the coffee maker and ice cubes clinking into a glass.

Palance walked into the kitchen, reached for a glass, filled it with water from the sink, and walked back into the living room, the world of men, where he felt equally alienated.

"How's school?" Joel asked.

Palance just looked at him and shook his head a little. Then he stared down at the carpet, hoping to discourage further conversation.

"It's been a while since we've seen you," Uncle Ross said to Joel.

"Just working," he said. Aunt Sandi came back into the room with Joel's Coke and her lavender scent. She handed Joel the glass and kissed him on the cheek.

"None of this makes sense," she said to no one in particular. "I don't know what Elaine's going to do." She looked back at Palance and took her seat in the middle of the couch.

Palance longed to flee, to get on his bike and ride to the beach. He wanted to feel the concrete fly beneath him as the wind and rumble of the cars drowned out his thoughts. He wanted to smell the popcorn by the Pickle Barrel and the dead alewives on the sand. Stand on the pier and stare at the water hard enough to feel in motion, gliding out to sea.

Palance knew two chords his father had taught him, the C major scale in first position, and how to strum. His father sang and played most of the songs from the '60's and '70's, and at parties, after a couple of drinks, he would take out his guitar. Lately his dad had been playing more jazz than the old tunes, and they'd allow him a few of these, but, soon, they'd clamor for the old songs.

Palance had always known he would follow in his father's footsteps. A feeling of loss washed over him. His body felt stiff and unwieldy.

"Pal," he heard, and resisted at first, searching for the trance that had taken him out of there.

"Pal." It was his mother's voice, but coming out of this meek, tear-stained mother, the one who sounded more like Jilly. "The rabbi's here."

Palance had missed a series of events. Rabbi Hornstein, tall, with slumped shoulders and a gray goatee, stood next to Grampa Ben and Nana Ruth, who kissed Palance on both cheeks, one on each side. Rabbi Hornstein handed his mother a small black ribbon, pinning one to Jillian's collar and another to Palance's shirt.

"This is a hard time," the rabbi said in a low, sonorous voice. He puts his fleshy hand on Palance's shoulder. "Tomorrow at the service I'm going to talk about your father."

Palance wanted to confront the rabbi. *Who is he to talk about my father? He never heard my father sing or play the guitar. He never sat in the back seat of our car on the way to some little town his dad wanted to see.*

"If there's anything either of you want me to say, you can tell me tomorrow morning at the funeral parlor," Rabbi Hornstein said, looking back and forth from Palance to Jillian. "Or you can write something down and hand it to me then."

"Say that he gave the best hugs and sang the best songs. All the best songs," Jilly told him before breaking into tears, folding into her mother's arms. "Daddy sang the best songs in the world."

Palance wished he could write a song for his father, a song that would carry itself up to heaven so his father could hear it. Palance knew he told his father he loved him, but only as an answer when his father would tuck him in at night and say it first, or when he got a present. He wished he could write songs and play them the way his father did. Songs to make people laugh or cry. Palance didn't know how to write music, or play songs—only two chords—and the tears flooded his face. He swore he'd write down some words. He would do the best he could to say something to his father that *meant* something. Someday, he would write songs and sing them for his father.

Everyone had gone home for the night. Palance occasionally heard sobs from his sister's room—they shared a common wall. His mother paced in the hallway. He couldn't sleep—he had to write words for his father. Words to tell what his father meant to him. The words he wrote were not about his father, what his father did or said or looked like, but what was gone. On the top of the paper, he wrote, "What I Will Miss." When he was done, he climbed into bed and gathered the covers around himself tightly, gazing at the ceiling until it glazed over. He lay there for hours, finally falling into a fitful sleep.

Palance sat in the front row at the funeral home, and a line formed out the door—first just trickling in and then building like a wave. They came up to his family—men in suits and women in dark dresses—and stooped to his level. Each insisted on touching him. They kissed his cheek or tousled his hair. His tie bit into his neck. Palance sat on the aisle, the first person they greeted, followed by his mother and sister, then Grampa and Nana. His aunt, uncle, and cousin had been relegated to the second row. The procession was endless. The women's perfumes overwhelmed him. He wondered who would buy Jillian roses on her birthday in five weeks, one month after his. His father always bought them for her. He didn't know how much roses cost, but he had a few dollars saved up and was determined.

He looked over at Jilly and stared at her to gain her attention. She rolled her eyes at him. The people kept coming: his father's entire office, people from temple, from the neighborhood, second cousins of second cousins, people who asked if he knew who they were. He smiled politely, nodding his head in ignorance.

Finally, the mourners passed, and the service began. Palance periodically checked for his father. It sank in—the reality that his father was dead. His mother's eyes were red and teary. Jilly whimpered, though her eyes were dry. He was ashamed to be able to sit without showing his emotions. He remembered the guitar picks he'd stolen. He would never be able to ask his father's forgiveness.

Palance listened to the rabbi without hearing his words. Periodically, people shrieked or shed tears, said prayers, shuffled papers, and mentioned names: he and Jillian, his mother, his father's name, especially, and now Palance began to feel too much. Every time he looked up, he felt a twinge in his stomach. The rabbi began to speak about his family as if they were close, personal friends. The rabbi was a presence only on High Holy Days and an occasional Friday-night service when they showed up. Until yesterday, he had never been in their home. When Palance heard the rabbi speak the words he'd written last night, they seemed unfamiliar:

Dad, I will miss the smell of your cologne, the special scent that says you're home.

The way you fixed our broken things, my X-wing, and the washing
machine.
We'll never know when it's dinner time. We always ate when you
arrived.
Music that once filled our rooms, now silent, empty, full of gloom.
My guitar teacher and baseball coach, every task that I approached
You helped guide me toward my goals, and now God holds tight
your soul,
Your voice and strings are quiet and still, a hole that I can never fill,
No hugs for Jilly, Mom, or me, like ships upon an empty sea,
Dad, every word I'll ever write, I'll write for you,
And every note, and every song I sing, I'll sing for you.

There was a hush in the room, and when Palance looked up, every eye was on him. His mouth was parched, and his legs were trembling. His mother's arm fell upon his shoulder, and a look of pride was on her face. Their eyes met and locked in the most grown-up encounter he had ever had with her, wordless and full of meaning.

Rabbi Hornstein called for them to stand, and the congregation recited the *Kaddish*, the Jewish prayer for the dead. Palance was swept away by the sounds of the Hebrew words he did not understand. In his desperation at the loss of his father, he brought to mind the pain he *could* bear—Mark Blevin dead in a plane crash. Palance contemplated Mark's family sitting in these same seats on another day, a similar arrangement of mourners and prayers. Palance wished he had not struck him out but allowed him a hit. Perhaps it would have meant something.

The service was over, and they were calling the pallbearers now. His uncle and cousin were siphoned off, along with his dad's best friends. At this moment, horns should have blared, timpani thunder, the heavens open and angels appear. Instead, his mother took Jillian's hand in her right and his in her left, and they walked in silence up the aisle through vast wooden doors, down concrete steps into a black limousine. Palance squeezed his mother's hand.

Palance, emerged from a daze sitting on a folding chair in the cemetery—again on his mother's left, Jilly on her right—with no knowledge of the journey. There was a crowd, a smaller version of the same people from the funeral home, standing around the gravesite. He, his family, and his older relatives were sitting on a few folding chairs placed directly in front of his father's coffin, which was held on a metal frame an arm's length away. Below the coffin was a deep rectangular cavity in the dirt. Palance heard the phrase *six feet under* in his head, and a man in blue overalls turned a crank, lowering the casket into the ground. Another man in overalls stood nearby. Words and murmurs, and a gust of wind temporarily distracted him from the wooden box. *When it's covered in dirt, this will be irreversible.* He watched the casket sink with every turn of the crank.

The coffin touched the ground, and the men in blue overalls shuffled the straps beneath it, jostling his father. Palance gasped as the container rattled in fits and starts, until the straps came free and the casket lay still. The rabbi distributed yellow roses to Palance, his mother, and his sister. Following their example, he dropped his flower on top of the coffin, his face vacant and numb. He watched it lie there. His mother, guided by the Rabbi's hand, shoveled a parcel of dirt from a mound near the grave into the hole, sprinkling the casket. She replaced the shovel into the mound of dirt, and nodded to Palance, indicating it was his turn. He trembled, afraid to defile his father's casket, and afraid not to do as he was told. Thunder rumbled in the distance, and he did the deed. He looked away before the dirt fell, and heard it splatter on the wood. He watched Jilly shovel a slight handful, staring into the hole until the Rabbi gently guided her toward their mother. Palance inhaled deeply, and then fought to exhale. When he caught his breath, they were back in the limousine.

Driving home, Palance focused his attention out the window, noting various landmarks: colorful shopping centers and chain restaurants; small stores set in strip malls and larger ones with giant parking lots. His mother and sister sat quietly, his mother's leg against his, while Jilly looked out the passenger-side window.

Palance watched clouds drift across the sky. A halo of sunlight broke through. It was too cold to rain and too early to snow. His sister sneezed. His mother withdrew a tissue from the box in the console and held it to her nose. Jilly grabbed it from her hand and blew her own nose; then leaned back on her mother for support. Soon Palance recognized the yellow-and-black street signs. They were back in the city, his neighborhood, and the limousine pulled up in front of their house. Cars were parked in front. For a full minute, none of them moved or even breathed; then the limousine driver opened the door, and Jilly, out first, yielded the lead to their mother, who ignored the pitcher of water and large bowl set outside the front door of their home as they stepped inside.

Aunt Sally and Aunt Lara, his mother's best friends, went on about their business without speaking to her. Normally, the three would unite like musketeers. Their husbands, Lee and Ralph, kept company on the far side of the room, speaking in hushed tones.

Palance took his place on his mother's left side as they sat on the couch. His mother's friends were setting up and serving food. Aunt Sally set a bowl of cashews on the coffee table in front of them and asked if they would like anything to drink.

"Coke," Palance said, unsure whether it would be more polite to get it himself. He looked at his mother, who was smoothing her dress and didn't respond.

"Could I please have some juice?" Jillian asked. Aunt Sally nodded and disappeared into the kitchen. Palance watched through the door as his Aunt Sandi and Uncle Ross arrived with Joel and headed straight to the kitchen. Joel took his place in the swivel chair and pivoted continuously left and right.

Freddy and Marcia walked up to them together. Freddy hugged Palance's mother, first tenderly, and then held her as she rose up and grasped him tightly. He stood back, and Marcia replaced him, patting her back and cooing in her singsong voice, "So sorry, Elaine, so sorry."

Freddy knelt in front of Palance and put his hands on his shoulders. "That was really beautiful," he said, "that poem you wrote. Your dad would be proud." He kissed Palance on the forehead. Palance wanted to rub away the moisture from the kiss, but it dried, and he left it alone. Marcia came over, sat next to him, and held his hand, not saying anything. Freddy sat next to Jillian, and his mother stared straight ahead.

Aunt Sally came back with Aunt Lara and their drinks. Palance was surprised to find ice in his glass. He noticed that any movement, his own shiver, or vibrations from the front door opening, tinkled the ice cubes like chimes and fizzed the Coke. When anyone talked, he vibrated his arm a touch to orchestrate their conversation, the way music in a movie fills in the background. For dramatic effect, he lifted the glass, tilting it to his lips, sending the ice cubes cascading into each other like billiard balls.

"That was a lovely poem," Aunt Lara said.

"Yes, it was. You have quite a way with words," Aunt Sally agreed.

Palance held his glass still, suppressing a belch, which dissipated in his belly.

"Elaine," Aunt Sally asked, "what do you need?" This question riveted Palance and Jilly's attention to their mother. They were not used to this blank, passive woman who was sitting between them. Palance dropped his glass. The Coke and ice splattered. The sound of the glass falling against the coffee table rang stridently. Everyone in the room turned, and Palance was horrified at the attention. His drink spilled on his pant leg and the carpet. His mother's eyes blazed.

"We'll clean that up, dear," Aunt Lara announced. She patted his mother's shoulder, kneeling in front of Palance, picking up the ice cubes and placing them back in the glass. Aunt Sally brought paper towels, which she handed to Aunt Lara, who pressed them into the carpet and the couch, soaking up the still-fizzing Coke. They proceeded with a series of wet cloths and paper towels until the carpet, couch, and

Palance's pant legs were clean and dry. Elaine broke down in tears, clutching her children to her, bumping their heads against each other.

Palance saw the terror in Jilly's eyes and tried to reassure her with his meager smile. He stood up to go to the bathroom. Nana grabbed him and held him in a bear hug, kissing him on the forehead and complimenting him on his poem. Grampa stood by silently, unable to reach in and break their bond. Palance murmured, "Bathroom," and she released him. A few steps later, he ran into Uncle Ross, who grasped his shoulders in his hands while Aunt Sandi told him he was destined to become, "a poet, a genius, a sculptor of words."

"We're here for you," Uncle Ross said.

"We are," Aunt Sandi reiterated.

"Bathroom," Palance begged. Six stairs down, Joel was blocking his path.

"I just wanted to let you know, Palance," Joel began, and Palance halted, because, in the eleven years he'd known him, Joel had never uttered more than two words in his direction. They were first cousins and complete strangers. "Uncle Alan was cool."

Palance listened closely, determined there was no more, and ducked under Joel's arm and down to the bathroom. Still, he was touched by those words, *Uncle Alan was cool.* In the bathroom, he peed, exhaling a slow, steady stream of air that relieved the pressure building inside him, and he belched.

Palance flushed the toilet, zipped up his pants, and lowered the lid. He sat for a moment, observing the weave of the maroon hand towels folded neatly on the rack. Gazing into the mirror, he searched his face for the image of a man. He was the man of the house now. There was no choice.

Palance stood ramrod straight, washing his hands, forcing his eyes to harden by splashing them with cold water. Lifting the towel to his face and pressing it tightly, until the moisture had been absorbed, he turned the doorknob, but instead of going back upstairs, he turned left and down the eight steps to the basement, his father's basement. He came to the long workbench that ran along the length of the back wall. He turned toward the shelf that held his father's guitar, in the bare wooden case that resembled a casket.

Though he knew he shouldn't, he unclipped the latches, lifted the lid, and gazed into the curved wooden body inside. Listening closely, he could hear his breath vibrate the strings and reverberate in the hollow wooden chamber of the Larriveé guitar. He hummed, with his head bowed, and for the first time today, felt he had uttered a prayer worthy of his father. He listened to the soft, echoing hum of the guitar. Palance heard the quick rhythm of footsteps coming toward him. He closed the guitar case, latched it, and turned to see Jason and Kyle walking toward him.

"Jilly said you might be down here," Kyle announced. "Sorry about your dad."

Jason nodded, and murmured, "Sucks."

"Yeah," Palance answered. "Anything happen in school today?"

"Test in math," Kyle said, "Lucky you . . . sorry."

"It's okay." The boys stood in a small circle, looking down. "How'd you get here?"

"My mom is upstairs," Jason said. "She drove us."

Palance squirmed in his skin. These were his friends, but, right now, he wanted to hold his father's guitar, and he needed to be alone.

"Pal," his father had told him, "for now, you'll have to wait until we're together to play. When you're thirteen, I'll buy you one of your own. Okay, Pal?" Palance remembered not only the speech but also the way his father sat him in the tall chair and placed the guitar in his hands. Palance recalled the first moment he held the guitar, the way it smelled, a mixture of sawdust and varnish with a hint of his father's aftershave. He was surprised how light it was and how well it fit him, the indented curve of the body resting against his leg. How smooth the wood felt as he moved his hand back and forth along the neck. How, when he plucked a string, the wood vibrated against his belly.

"Hey, I just got *Joshua Tree* by U2," Jason said. "It's pretty awesome. You heard it yet?"

"Not yet," Palance said. "I heard some cuts on the radio."

"I wanna get some sunglasses. The kind Bono has," Jason said, his eyes lighting up. "Maybe we could start a band."

"I wanna play the skins," Kyle said. "You know, the drums."

"Who do you wanna be, Palance?" Jason asked.

"I don't know. Maybe Springsteen." Palance knew what to say. A part of him *did* want to be Springsteen, but a bigger part of him wanted to be his father, to play songs at parties.

"Bruuuuce! Bruuuuce!" Kyle intoned. "He wants to be The Boss."

"Boys," Jason's mom spoke sternly, sticking her head down in the basement so they could see her. "Keep it quiet. This isn't a party. Jason, Kyle, two more minutes, and then we're leaving."

Jason's mom pulled her head back up the stairs, and the boys stared at each other. All three shuffled their feet from side to side. Jason put his hand on Palance's shoulder and bowed his head. "I liked it when your dad would play for us," he said.

"Yeah," Kyle said. "When are you coming back to school?"

"Probably next week, I guess. Did we get any homework today?"

"Just a math worksheet," Jason said. "I'm sure they'll let you skip it."

"Hey," Kyle said, "'Vector' Veckhart isn't likely to let anybody skip anything."

"Can you bring home a copy of the worksheet?" Palance said to Jason. "I'll come over to hear U2 on the weekend and pick it up, maybe. If I can."

"Sure. Hey, I'm serious about starting a band," Jason said. "I'm thinking about the bass. You know, boom, boom, boom." Jason closed his eyes and played an imaginary bass. His fingers moved spastically while his head tilted back.

"You gonna take lessons?" Kyle asked.

Palance listened but couldn't process it; he was focused on his father's guitar. He wondered if his mom would let him have it. He wondered how he would learn to play, now that his father was gone.

"Boys!" Jason's mom called. "We're leaving."

"Keep the faith, man," Jason cautioned.

"Yeah," Kyle added. They both looked at him pitifully as they walked up the stairs.

His mind was still on the guitar. He walked over to his father's workbench and picked up a screwdriver, letting the handle roll back and forth in his hands. Down here, he felt comfortable. It reminded him of his father, the soft, stern timbre of his voice, the shuffle of his walk. The size of his hands. He'd always admired his father's large palms and long, tapered fingers, so deliberate in their movement.

The guitar called to him, sitting in its coffin-like case, seated in velvet, its strings under exquisite tension. Palance remembered the day his father bought it, trading the deep cherry wood of his old Guild for this blond Larriveé from Canada adorned with mother-of-pearl inlay. When he'd brought it home, he'd placed the case in front of the family and opened the lid. Palance remembered gasping at the beauty of the instrument.

Even before he turned, before he knew he was going to open the guitar case, he could feel the weight of the wood in his hands, hear the vibration of its strings and smell its scent. He could feel the spiraling bass strings indent his fingers, and the thin, straight treble strings cut into them. Palance fought the urge. *Today should not be the day. I should be upstairs with my mother and sister.* Palance gathered the guitar tuner and string winder that his father had left on the workbench, and held them in his hand.

The tuner and the string winder belong in the guitar case. Palance followed his legs as they carried him to the shelf where the guitar sat. Palance ran his hand along the top of the case and flipped down the latches. The case gasped from the inrush of air. Palance stood a moment before he lifted the lid, held and raised the neck to allow access to the storage compartment in the case. He slipped the tuner and string winder in. Palance needed to close the case and go upstairs, but he couldn't. He rested his hand against the strings and then slowly pulled away. They vibrated with a gentle shimmer. Lightly, he patted the strings with an open palm, and they responded with a sparkle of harmonics. Swallowed up in the sound, he struck the strings again, this time harder. The sound engulfed him in waves.

Palance plucked the thickest string. The sound rumbled and settled in his belly. He felt his stomach expand, the tightness dissipate. The sound of the next string opened his chest. His heart swelled inside him. The next string resonated in his throat, and he breathed deeply. The next string was sharp. He felt a presence and turned to see his mother behind him, hands on her hips. Her eyes were cold and hard.

"What the hell," she said.

"Mom," Palance said, but he had nothing to follow it up with. The steel of her eyes penetrated his.

"What the hell do you think you're doing?" she said. It was not a question. Before he could turn around to close the case, she slapped him on the cheek. He stumbled back into the guitar, which radiated dissonance as it rattled on the shelf. "Take the strings off," she said.

"Huh?"

"You heard me. Take them off, now," she ordered, and walked back up the stairs.

Palance didn't breathe.

"*Now*," she said, turning around before she had cleared his line of sight.

Palance, trembling, went to the closet and removed the two towels, placing them on his father's workbench. He carried the guitar to the workbench, cradling it in his arms. One by one, he removed the strings, unwinding each tuning head with the string winder, and then using the same tool to remove the bridge pins. The guitar groaned throughout the process. Carefully he wound each string and hung them on a hook in the pegboard behind the workbench. When he had removed all six strings, he looked at the guitar, naked and bare, and then cautiously transferred the voiceless instrument back to its case. He felt numb as he ascended the stairs.

The guitar remained unstrung for eight years.

Too Old to Be So Young

The air blew briskly on the eighth day of February of Palance's first year at Mather High School. It was unseasonably mild. Gray and windy, the temperature hovered near fifty. Adults marveled at the lack of snow and ice, speaking about it endlessly, as if some miracle had blown across the lake and into Chicago. Walking out of Mather through the brown grass, up Lincoln Avenue toward the river and the bus stop, Palance wished for spring and especially summer, when the grass would be green, classes and homework banished, and the days would lay empty before him. He used his fingers to form chords on his right arm as if it were a guitar neck and practiced the change from D-major to B-minor, working up the strength in his thumb and index finger for his first barre-chord. Palance was humming "Walking in Memphis," hoping he and Jason would be able to figure out the correct chords tonight. There was something not quite right about the D-major in the bridge.

Palance had too much homework for a weekend. He had a poster board for Earth Science on the phases of the moon and their relationship to the tides, a book report, and a chapter's worth of trigonometry. He wanted the Seagull guitar he received for his last birthday to sound more like music, and less like a cheap, dissonant ukulele. His fingers were sore, and he sounded nothing like the CDs he played over and over. At Peterson Avenue, he waited for the light to change and glanced toward McDonald's, but let the money in his pocket jingle, saving up for the new R.E.M. CD. He loved the way the singer's voice growled and sputtered. Palance glanced enviously into the window of Coconut's Music, where the rows of CDs called to him. They mocked the poverty of his wallet. His mom made ends meet, but he had to earn his own spending money. His prospects were meager without snow to shovel, and it was too early to mow lawns. His grandparents bought him the guitar for his last birthday, and he was beyond grateful.

Past Peterson, Palance cut up Troy, where apartment buildings provided shelter from the wind, and started walking home. If he saw the bus before Devon, he'd take it; if not, he'd walk. On Troy, the traffic noises dimmed. A crumpled piece of paper blew down the street, careening from curb to curb. His mom dismissed his music and his request for a metal stud in his ear. The girls in school fell for guys brazen enough to get an earring. Girls didn't look at him that way. Especially not Alanna Shaw.

In his mind, Palance saw Alanna the way she looked today in English class. In morning homeroom, her light-brown hair fell straight past her shoulders, but, in the afternoon, after P.E., her hair, still damp, tumbled in waves and ringlets. She took her seat one row in front and one seat to the right, close enough to touch. Her aroma was intoxicating. At the end of the class period, she came up to him in the hallway, asking what the homework was. She had drifted off in class, she said, and, with a minimum of stutters, he was able to identify the chapters and problem sets that would be due on Monday, but that was all. He felt young and foolish.

Troy dead-ended at Hood Street. Palance walked east and then north onto Kedzie, where the trees rose and hid the sewage canal. When he was young, he would tie a string to a branch and a piece of bread to the string and go fishing in the canal, as if he were Tom Sawyer off on an adventure, his pant legs rolled up. The canal flowed into Lake Michigan, out through the St. Lawrence Seaway, and east into the Atlantic Ocean. When the bus went by, he let it pass, his mind attempting to memorize the definitions for trigonometry. Mr. Ogbert loved to give pop quizzes, bringing them out from a locked desk drawer, the way bullies on the playground sneak from behind corners. Sine: opposite over hypotenuse. Cosine: adjacent over hypotenuse. Tangent: opposite over adjacent. He remembered these were functions, waves like in the ocean, the various rhythms of life and nature, rising and falling in regular, predictable, patterns.

Palance felt these rhythms as he walked. The sky brightened, traffic noises became part of a glorious symphony, punctuated by his footsteps, and he matched his footsteps to the patterns in the concrete sidewalk, so that he took two steps in the square and then stepped over the line and sang the rhythm, "Ba..ba..pa, ba..ba..pa," on and on while the wind through the trees joined in, adding a *whoosh* at the end, and the rhythm became, "Ba..

ba..pa..whoosh, ba..ba..pa..woosh." The traffic modulated into a backbeat. Palance walked briskly. The apartment buildings turned to bungalows. The wind blew discarded paper cups and cigarette packs beside him, and the brickyard replaced the river on his left. His mind was locked into Ba..ba..pa..whoosh. Palance felt lifted, like the tides, and saw his poster board already created in his mind. He celebrated the freedom to spend the weekend making music; there was relief in the air. Alanna seemed more approachable, and maybe there was hope for his ragged guitar playing. Palance arrived home and bounded up the single step to the back door and into the kitchen.

"I'm home," he yelled, to no one in particular. He saw Jilly's books on the table and knew she was home, too. This year, she was in seventh grade and thought she was a big deal. Palance understood the knockdown that is freshman year, when you have to try out for everything, and you need a signed pass just to pee.

"Just a sec," his mother called from the living room. She was on the telephone, pacing in her beige slacks and bare feet across the gray carpet. Palance opened the fridge and made himself a turkey sandwich. He had skipped lunch to save up for CDs. He found a bag of potato chips in the cabinet and added a few to his plate.

"You eat like a pig," Jilly told him, walking into the room with her silver headphones on over her new purple-streaked hair.

"Mom let you do that?"

"I pick my battles with you kids," his mother said, walking into the kitchen. Jilly stuck her tongue out at him.

"What's next," Palance asked, "a tattoo?"

"Why don't you worry about you," his mom answered. "Try doing your homework."

"It's Friday."

"And you'll be playing your guitar all weekend. You are so much like your father. Did you know he went to Mather? Just like you. Start your homework now."

"Yeah," Jilly added, "start your homework."

"Both of you," his mom said. "*Now!*"

"Jason's coming over after dinner," Palance told her. "I feel bad Dad suffered through Mather." He looked over at Jilly. "You're next."

"Ha, ha," Jilly said.

"I'm at the hospital tonight after six, so you're in for the night," their mother told them. "I'll be home at one."

"Okay," Palance conceded, and pulled out his trig. He stuck his tongue out at Jilly on the other side of the kitchen table and then started his homework. "Oh, Mom."

"Yeah."

"I need a poster board for science."

Dinner was Chicken Parmesan with spaghetti and a green salad. Palance slurped his noodles. His mom ate silently and glared at Jilly when she chewed with her mouth open. Ever since Jilly's last birthday, she'd been even more annoying. Mom called Jilly her in-between daughter. *In-between* seemed to cover their entire lives—everything had been makeshift and haphazard since their father died. The ceramic bowl in the hallway still sat empty, waiting for his keys.

"You kids are in charge of the dishes," his mom said, and walked off to get ready.

"Wash," Jilly claimed. "You dry."

"Okay. How'd you get Mom to let you dye your hair?"

"I asked her to let me pierce my eyebrow."

"There's no way."

"I know," Jilly smirked. "But I got what I wanted."

Palance knew Jilly did better with Mom than he did. She could charm anyone, even when she was being a brat. She always got what she wanted. Palance listened to the rush of the water in the sink and the circular rhythms of Jilly's sponge while she danced with her headphones on. *Even though she listens to that god-awful Duran Duran, at least she loves music,* Palance thought. The dishes were almost finished when the doorbell rang.

"It's Jason. Any way you can finish up yourself?"

"No," she said, not bothering to look up.

Palance answered the door and let Jason in. He was carrying his bass in one hand and a brown Pignose amp in the other.

"Hey, man," Palance said to Jason. "You ready to jam?"

"More than you know," Jason answered. "Much more." Jason looked weird, even for him—something about his eyes—and Palance wondered what was up. He knew better than to ask with his mom in the next room and his sister standing next to him.

"Finish the dishes," Jilly yelled.

"Jillian Heller, you are a complete and total . . ."

"Palance," his mother stopped him, walking in with her work clothes on, "You're too old to be so young. Finish the dishes."

Palance did not have to look at Jillian to know her tongue was sticking out at him. "I gotta finish these," he said to Jason.

"Be nice to your sister," his mom said, as she moved toward the door. "Jillian, lights out at ten. Palance, you have until eleven. Don't call unless it's an emergency."

Palance finished drying the dishes and put them away before his mother's car pulled out of the driveway.

"Come on," Jason said, "I've got something righteous to share. We might want to check it out in the garage." He put his bass and amp on the kitchen table.

"Just a sec," Palance said, flicking the dishtowel at Jillian. "Stay out of our way, and I don't care if you're up all night."

They stepped down to the family room and into the garage. Palance closed the door and pulled the string to turn on a bare light bulb. Jason reached into his shirt pocket, took out a folded piece of paper, and unwrapped a jagged little cigarette. Palance took in the pungent smell, and his eyes widened. He'd always wanted to try smoking weed, but he didn't know if he had the nerve. He still wasn't sure. Jason pulled out a Bic lighter, and Palance knew he was going to try it.

"Hold on a second," Palance said, locking the door to the garage. He looked around and made sure they were away from the gas can. He took an empty tin from a shelf and set it on a box between them. "For an ashtray."

Jason snapped the lighter on, and a two-inch flame rose. Jason explained that he got the pot from his cousin Lee. He and Lee had smoked it before, and this was primo. Palance was not clear what that meant but was too embarrassed to ask for clarification. Jason brought the flame close to the end of the joint, and Palance watched as it caught fire and crackled. Jason blew out the fire; the tip glowed red, and he took a puff off the other end, gasping as he held his breath. Jason passed it to Palance, exhaled a cloud of smoke, and coughed as Palance held the joint tentatively between his thumb and index finger.

"Just breathe in a little, and hold it," Jason said.

Palance put the joint to his lips. He tasted Jason's saliva and a sweet, sticky odor. He worried about Jilly, though she was probably in front of the television. Jason said he'd done it before, so Palance inhaled and held the smoke in his lungs for a second, until it grated on his throat and a coughing spasm left him breathless.

"Just take in a little at a time," Jason said. "It's worth it. Man, is it worth it."

Palance pulled two bottles of water from a case in the corner, took a drink from one, and handed the other to Jason, who took a second puff. When he exhaled, his eyes grew happy and distant, the corners of his mouth turning up. Palance took the joint, put it to his lips, and inhaled. His throat itched, but it was just a tickle, and he passed the joint back to Jason. Palance took another sip of water.

"It started with jazz musicians," Jason said, taking another toke. "This is how they got their cool."

"Cool." Jazz reminded Palance of his father, and, for a moment, he was ashamed. He wondered if his father ever got high—and then he wondered if *he* was high. He seemed okay—no hallucinations, no urge to rip off his clothes. Jason passed the joint back to him, and, this time, Palance took a deeper toke, looked Jason in the eye, and said, "Really cool," as if that were something profound, and then, for no reason at all, started laughing. Palance leaned back on a stack of boxes and watched the lit tip of the joint pass back and forth between them. The air filled with smoke. *This is sacred, something Native Americans might have done in the old days, when they lived in teepees and hunted buffalo,* Palance thought.

"How are you doing?" Jason asked.

"Pretty . . . wow," Palance said, unable to express himself any further.

"You good for now?" Jason asked.

"Good," he said. "Really good."

Jason took the piece of paper from his pocket, and put what was left of the joint on it, folded it up into a small square, and handed it to Palance. "For you. For later."

"Thanks, man," Palance said, pushing the paper into his right-front pants pocket. Palance had difficulty speaking or controlling his widening smile. He nodded up and down, and giggled, feeling the rhythm of his head bob. They both laughed in fits. Palance felt lightheaded and enlightened.

"Open the garage door," Jason said. "To get rid of the smoke."

"Okay," Palance answered. He pressed the button and heard the motor whirr and the chain grind. He worried about Jillian coming out, but he could always say they wanted privacy. He watched the door climb up in sections, each panel bending on its hinge and raising like a curtain.

The two of them walked outside, where the clouds had dissipated, revealing stars and a full moon rising. He twirled in the cool night air before realizing Jason was right there—then he struggled not to fall and landed with his back against the maple tree in the front yard.

"Yeah, man," Jason said, smiling broadly, looking fuzzy and wise.

Palance looked him in the eyes and said, "Let's play some music."

"Cool," Jason said, and they walked back into the house. Palance saw that Jilly was unconcerned. She was watching TV in the family room.

"Basement?" Jason asked.

"Let's go to my room," Palance answered. Someday he would be ready to play music in the basement—but not tonight, not yet. He hadn't made peace with those ghosts.

They walked down the hall to Palance's room. He tried not to giggle or look suspicious as they passed Jillian. She turned but didn't seem to notice anything. "Hey, man," he asked Jason, "didn't you leave your bass in the kitchen?" They both started laughing, and Jilly looked disgusted. "You want a Coke?" Palance asked Jason.

"Un-huh."

They walked back into the kitchen. Palance took two glasses out of the cabinet, held one under the icemaker, and listened to the high-pitched *clink* as the ice cubes hit bottom and then the lower-pitched *thunk* as they hit each other, and before he realized, the ice cubes had overflowed the glass and fallen, clacking on the floor.

"I think that's too much ice, dude," Jason said, and they both started giggling again.

"What are you doing in there?" Jillian yelled.

"Pop," Palance yelled back. "You want one?"

"No!"

Palance picked up the ice cubes from the floor and dumped them into the sink, chasing them around the room as they skidded across the tile like cartoon props. When he finally had them all, he poured half the ice out of one glass into the other and added Coke to both.

Palance needed to play music, to feel his guitar vibrating against his belly. He picked up Jason's amp, and felt his smile widen until his jaw hurt. "C'mon," he said. "Let's play."

Jason grabbed his bass, and they walked in stride. Palance put the amp down on the floor of his room and plugged it in. He took his guitar case from the corner, and opened it, pulling out the mahogany and spruce Seagull guitar and his father's tuner. He brushed the low E-string with a pick, and it reverberated in a way he hadn't heard before.

Jason plucked the E-string on his bass, and the two notes blended and beat against each other, pulsing in and out. Palance turned on the tuner, and, carefully, the way his father taught him, adjusted each string in order, first loosening and then tightening to pitch, and, finally, returning to the bottom string and starting over.

"Can I borrow the tuner?" Jason asked, reaching for it.

"Careful," Palance told him, "it was . . ."

"I know," Jason said, and Palance could tell by the way his face softened that he meant it.

Palance listened to the deep tones of the bass strings as they loosened, stretched, and filled the room. Even with the tiny Pignose amp, the sound rumbled. "Key of D," Palance said, and strummed a D chord, but that sounded too strident, and so he played a pattern with his fingers he'd learned from a Mel Bay Book. Jason started a run from D to A, and, when he got to the A, Palance switched to an A-major chord. Jason and Palance had played together before, but this was different. The sound expanded and flowed. The two of them fed off each other, taking turns leading and following. Palance's fingers moved in new combinations. The sound twisted and flowed.

When they finished on the same note at the same time, they looked at each other in amazement. Palance reached for his Coke and drank it to soothe his dry throat. He put down his drink, hit an A-minor chord, and they were off again. Palance picked out patterns that reminded him of his walk home from school, of the wind and the sidewalk, the paper blowing, and the river. Jason guided the music with a steady booming resonance. Palance countered with a ripple of melody. Palance listened as the music diverged from the lessons he had taken. He heard his whole life in the music. He heard his father. He and Jason complemented each other, and the notes bound them together. Their eyes locked. They had to start a band.

When the music faded, Palance felt unusually tired, more drained than sleepy, and Jason had his head bowed, with his bass resting on his knees. Palance still heard the sound rever-berate around him.

"Can you hear that?" he asked Jason, his body moving to the rhythm he was sensing.

"What?"

"I hear a song."

"Cool," Jason said. "I knew you'd like getting stoned."

Palance did not want this feeling to end. "Hey, Jason."

"Yeah?"

"Wanna start a band? For real?"

"Hell, yeah."

"Let's do it," Palance said. "Let's freakin' do it."

"We need a drummer. Kyle plays in the band at school. He plays the drums."

"Cool. We need a singer. Can you sing?"

"I dunno," Jason said. "Can you?"

"I dunno," Palance replied, and they both started laughing.

"Try it," Jason said. "Sing something. Anything."

Palance played a D-major chord and launched into U2's "I Still Haven't Found What I'm Looking For." He belted it out, all of his natural shyness and inhibition gone. He felt his whole being expand and got through a couple of verses and a chorus before the shyness seeped back in. He looked at Jason. "Your turn," he told him.

Jason told Palance that his voice had soul, and he'd better start learning lyrics, because he was going to be a star. They were going to get the band together, and, if Kyle wouldn't play drums, they'd find someone who would. "You're the man," he said to Palance.

Palance started playing the introduction to the same song again, and he stared back at Jason, letting him know he could start whenever he wanted. Jason began singing. It was a little weak, but sounded good to Palance until Jason hit the chorus and his voice cracked. They both laughed so hard they had to put their instruments down on the bed, as they rolled onto the floor.

"We need a name," Jason said. Something cool."

"Maybe that could be the name. We could call ourselves Something Cool."

"More cutting-edge."

"Whispering," Palance said, unsure why that would be cutting-edge—it just flew out of his mouth.

"Screams," Jason countered.

"Whispering Screams," they cried together, and Palance and Jason declared in unison, "The Whispering Screams."

"That is so cool," Jason said.

Palance started playing *Walking in Memphis*. It was rusty, but coming together. His left index finger strained at the barre-chord, the B-minor, but he managed it with a little string buzz.

Palance sang the lyrics, slowly at first, getting stronger, and he saw himself getting off the plane, wearing blue suede shoes. He saw himself in Memphis, at Graceland. When he got to the bridge, he played the D-major chord, and without thinking, dropped his pinky finger on the third fret of the first string, and it sounded right. When the song was over, he wanted to play it again.

"What about girls?" Jason asked.

"What about 'em?"

"Do you think if we're in a band, we can get girls to come?"

Palance thought about Alanna Shaw, and he couldn't see asking her out. He could see himself asking if she wanted to see his band—or at least handing her a flyer. "Let's call Kyle," he said. "We need to get this going."

Palance guided Jason toward the kitchen. The phone was there, and he needed a refill on his pop. His mouth was dry, and he had a taste for something sweet. Already the Whispering Screams seemed a concrete reality, the Garden of Eden he longed for. He saw an audience that included Alanna Shaw. He clinked the ice cubes into the glass, and the phone rang. Palance waited two rings, hoping Jillian would answer. Then, he picked it up.

"Uh-huh," he said into the phone. His mom was reminding him that it was nine o'clock. He could stay up until eleven. He had his guitar lesson tomorrow at eight-thirty in the morning and then brunch at Nana Ray's. Jason could stay until nine-thirty tonight. His mother would want him home by ten. She was certain of that. Palance was grateful she was doing all the talking. He was afraid he would start giggling, and she would know. He was more grateful when she asked to speak to Jillian.

"Jillian," he yelled, "Phone. Mom." Palance sat down and breathed a sigh of relief; then he filled his glass. "More pop?" he asked Jason.

"Yeah."

Palance filled both glasses, handed one to Jason, and then drained and refilled his own.

"It's too late to call Kyle," Jason said. His mom freaks out if you call after eight-thirty.

"What'd Mom say to you?" Palance asked Jilly.

"I dunno. Brunch tomorrow. She was her usual hyper self. Oh, and Pal . . ."

"Yeah?"

"Don't do anything stupid. I know you're up to something."

"Isn't it past your bedtime?"

"Just don't get caught."

Her warning evaded him. He was in love with music, with Jason, Alanna, the band, and his guitar. His head felt won-drously dizzy. "Do we need a keyboard or another guitar?" he asked Jason.

"I think we're good. What do you think?"

"My dad had some records of a group called Cream from the old days. They just had bass, drums, and guitar, and they were awesome."

"You need an electric, man," Jason said.

"An electric guitar," Palance exclaimed, his eyes exploding in fireworks while Jason's head nodded. "How much do they cost?"

"My bass was about a hundred fifty. But I'm gonna need a bigger amp."

"How much is a decent amp?" Palance asked.

"I think a Peavey is between a hundred and two hundred."

"We gotta figure out a way to make some money."

The two boys looked at each other blankly. Finally Jason formed his hand into a fist and raised it, saying, "Gotta have faith. It'll come."

"Faith," Palance said, mimicking Jason's words and his gesture.

"Faith," they said in unison, and the music played in Palance's head.

Jason left. Jillian turned off the TV and headed for her room, her eyes half closed. "Night," she murmured, passing him. Palance rinsed Jason's glass in the sink, poured himself more pop, and sat quietly, listening to the ice cubes clink and the fizz shimmer. It was only ten-thirty. He had more than two hours before his mother arrived home. Palance felt the folded packet in his right-front pants pocket, the key to this new and startling universe. He felt dull and wanted to be shiny again. If he walked out by the brickyard, he would be alone. The neighbors were in for the night, and they never wandered out there. He was drawn outside, as if, outside, he could expand into infinity.

Palance went to the junk drawer; he pushed aside fast-food menus, scissors, and tape, and found a pack of matches next to an almost-empty box of birthday candles. He stuffed the matches into his pocket, walked out through the door to the garage and then out the other side, feeling like Alice through the looking glass. He stood on Kedzie in the night air, relishing the cool quiet. Palance crossed Kedzie and walked to the chain-link fence, leaned against the metal grate, and heard it rattle. He removed the folded paper and pack of matches from his pocket. Palance placed what was left of the joint in his mouth and struck the match. He burned his fingers, singed the tip of his nose, took a puff, and drew smoke into his lungs. The marijuana affected him differently without Jason there. The air sparkled. Waves formed within him and ran up and down his body. He finished what he could before the joint burned his fingers and he tossed what remained over the fence into the brickyard.

A cool breeze blew the few wisps of clouds through the sky. The stars glowed vibrantly and guided him back toward the house. His feet sailed along the sidewalk, back through the garage, and into his room. He cradled his guitar in his arms and floated down the steps to the basement, turning left, toward his father's guitar, still unstrung in its bare wooden case.

Palance slipped the strap of his guitar over his neck and stood in front of his father's guitar. He laid both hands on his father's guitar case and closed his eyes, not knowing what to expect or why he was doing this. His mind emptied and then filled with ethereal sounds. At first barely perceptible, they grew louder, formed patterns, and distilled into melody. He stood with his hands on the case and listened.

Palance recalled his mother's words, "Too old to be so young." The words blended with the music. He removed his hands from his father's guitar case and placed them onto his own instrument. His hands made the changes, D-major to A-major, back to D-major and then to E-minor, and then G-major to A-major. He closed his eyes, played them repeatedly, and felt a presence beside him.

Palance watched his fingers move. His eyelids sank, and he melded into the music. Patterns wove into melodies, formed rhythms, and doubled back into harmonies. Palance knew he was not this good. He let that feeling pass, and the music enveloped him. He felt an ache for what had been lost. A cleansing ache that yearned for a life not yet his.

"*Too old to be so young,*" Palance sang, "*Too young to be so wise,*" and he knew the song. All he had to do was sing it, play it, and write it down. The music and lyrics flowed into his mouth and fingers. As he sang, Palance felt his inner child meld into a grown-up self. He felt his whole being transform, the way a chrysalis becomes a butterfly. "*Too wise to be a child, you are as ageless as the tides.*" Palance saw himself up on stage, lights surrounding him. He saw himself with auras of purple and blue, nearly blinded, the audience in shadow. Alanna gazing at him in wonder and adoration.

The music carried him to the top of a cliff overlooking an ocean, a shimmer of stars in a black sky pierced by a full moon. "*And when the moon is holding water and the tides are rising high. The waves are pounding, crashing in your mind.*"

A storm rose, and ominous dark clouds obliterated the stars and moon.

On the ocean below him, Palance saw a small boat with Alanna in it. He sensed her fear and built a bonfire on the beach. Its flames flickered and rose to guide her to shore and rescue her. *"Do not weep into the ocean, or seek shelter from the storm, there is a fire on the shore to keep you warm."*

Palance's consciousness fell back into the basement. His fingers on the guitar bathed him in the music. The words poured liquid from his throat: *"Too old to be at home, too young to be away."* Palance dreamt of a life he had not yet lived. He could see it in the distance. *"Far from the home you know and from the home that you'll create."*

Palance ached from the pain of being a kid, of knowing what should be, what could be, and not knowing how to get there. *"Too old to never know, too young to have your way."* He longed to be the person he was meant to be. *"You walk the path that Eden lost somewhere along the way."*

Palance saw himself as he should be—free, clear, and wild, charging through a glorious wilderness, the ground green and lush, the sun overhead in an azure-blue sky. His heart was full of love, and he was running to meet it, far from home, school, and the chores and ties that bound him. *"Too old to be so young, too young to be so tied."* He was running toward the ocean. The water, only a few feet away, was a perfect reflection of the sky. The sand was white and warm on his bare feet. The water welcomed his body as he entered. Sound engulfed him: the surf, circling seagulls, blood pounding in his veins, and the splash of his feet as they entered the water. All of this and the music of his guitar as he heard himself sing, *"Your mind is on that other ocean, spirit clear and wild."*

Too late, he heard the key in the door, his mother's footsteps above him, and the sound of her feet on the stairs. Falling from intoxication, each footstep plunged him lower. He was groping through the fuzz of his brain for an excuse or an explanation. The song occupied the totality of his mind. He shuddered.

"Palance?"

"Mom?"

"It's after one. What are you doing up?"

Palance should have apologized, but he was glowing, proud and shimmering with hope. "I wrote a song," he said. "My first song."

Palance saw the exhaustion in his mother's eyes, the droop of her shoulders. He was amazed when she sat down on the stepstool. "Can I hear it?" she asked.

Palance brushed aside his fears and sang her the song.

When he was done, she asked,

"What do you call it?"

"I don't know."

"Your father wanted to be a rock star," she said. "Look where it got him."

"Mom?"

"Go to bed. You should have been there hours ago."

Palance took his guitar by the neck and walked up the stairs, glancing back to see his mother with her narrow eyes focused angrily at the wall. Her energy had zapped his, leaving him plodding and tired. Each stair was an effort, each step an accusation. The stars had winked out and left a deep blackness.

Once the door to his room closed, some of the joy returned. Palance carefully put his guitar away, refusing to dwell on his mother's anger. He lay down in bed, and his song played endlessly in a loop in his mind. He remembered bonding with Jason, the unrestrained flow of their music, and his first song. Palance treasured this moment and curled into it like a ball, and, for the rest of his life, pursued it like any mythical chalice.

Too Old to Be So Young

Too old to be so young,
too young to be so wise,
too wise to be a child you are
as ageless as the tides

C   *And when the moon is holding water,*
H   *and the tides are rising high,*
O   *and the waves are pounding, crashing in your mind—*
R   *Do not weep into the ocean,*
U   *or seek shelter from the storm,*
S   *there is a fire on the shore to keep you warm.*

Too old to be at home,
too young to be away,
far from the home you know and from
the home that you'll create.

Chorus

Too old to never know,
too young to have your way,
you walk the path that Eden lost
somewhere along the way.

Chorus
Too old to be so free,
too young to be so tied,
your mind is on that other ocean,
spirit clear and wild.

Chorus

Chapter Three

Breakaway

Palance *walked to Nana's* and Grampa's house. His mother and sister drove the three blocks. His mind ricocheted from one thought to another. "I've got a gig." It was only a stupid sweet-sixteen party, but it was their first gig, and his fingers didn't stop moving. They tapped on his legs as he walked. First day of April, warm and bright. Flowering lilac bushes framed the yards and filled his nostrils. The sun was blinding. Palance's thoughts rattled. He wished his hands were on his new cherry-red Ibanez electric guitar. He'd worked, scrimped, and saved for that guitar. The lyrics of his new song ran through his mind: *I don't know, it seems so slow, my head is aching, heart is breaking.* Palance was seventeen and spent his free time alone in his room, with that guitar, playing scales and arpeggios.

Palance was proud of the hard calluses on his fingertips and desperately wanted a girlfriend. He envied Jason's relationship with Traci and was jealous of the dates Kyle seemed to scare up. He could count his on the fingers of one hand—and those boring school dances. Even Jilly was starting to go out with guys. Alanna was way out of his league.

The wind picked up, a warm breeze, and he passed the familiar landmarks between the two houses. Crossing Francisco, Palance saw Scott from English class on the other side of the street, bouncing a tennis ball between his house and the next. Palance nodded his head toward him, listening to the rhythm of the bouncing ball, pop-pop-pop: three-quarter time. Scott nodded back without breaking the rhythm, and Palance walked down three more houses and opened the door. Nana came and kissed him on the cheek, looking him up and down. She rubbed his arm with her open palm, as if polishing him.

"How is school?" Grampa asked. "You apply to college yet?"

Palance put his arm around Nana and kissed Grampa on the forehead. "Next year, Gramps. Still a junior." Palance's mother and Jillian were sitting on the couch under the acrylics his mother had painted when she was in college, ominous sea-scapes with tumbling waves, stormy skies, and fragile wooden boats. Framed by her work, she seemed more at home here than in her own house. She was braiding Jillian's hair into a rope down her back.

"You look skinny," Nana said to Palance, patting his belly. "Come eat something. Elaine, don't you feed him?" The look of contentment washed from his mother's face.

"Never," she answered.

Palance wouldn't admit it to his friends, but he loved these Saturday brunches. They began after his father died. Nana put out enough food for an army: lox and bagels, tuna salad, rye bread, three kinds of cheese, corned beef, pastrami, tomatoes, carrots, cucumbers, onions, and crackers, as if she were trying to wipe out memories of hardship with food. She knew hardship. She and Grampa had escaped Russia in their twenties.

Jillian created the same plate each week. One scoop of tuna salad in the center of the dish, topped with three cherry tomatoes, an egg bagel with plain cream cheese, one leaf of lettuce, and two cucumber slices, the sandwich cut into four even parts, and placed evenly around the mound of tuna salad. Nana called it "The Jillian Special," and often asked Jilly to make one just like it for her. Palance's mom and Nana, her mother, vied for the smallest possible portions. They would continually ask for, "just a little bit" and then balk at whatever portion, no matter how small, only to ask for another moments later. Only Palance ate greedily, often neglecting to wait between mouthfuls, or keep his elbows off the table.

"Watch your manners," his mother said, even while Nana was smiling in encouragement and placing additional serving platters before him.

"He's a growing boy," Nana said.

"What's new, kids?" Grampa asked, chewing a piece of carrot with a loud, rhythmic crunch.

"I am going to be a psychologist," Jillian said with an air of authority and a piece of tuna salad on the right side of her lip.

"Decided when?" her mother asked. "Last week you were going . . ."

"Decided yesterday. I saw a movie . . . about Sybil. I'd be good at it."

Palance did not offer information until confronted directly, not now, not ever. He knew he would likely be judged wrong.

He stuffed his mouth, partially from hunger, and partially to avoid conversation. Excited as he was about the gig that night, he was reluctant to share his news. When he couldn't eat another bite, his hands fell to his side, and his fingers again tapped against his legs. He knew better than to tap on the table.

"What's new with you, Pal?" Grampa asked. His mother's eyes were riveted on him.

"Got a gig tonight. My band is playing . . . at a party."

"Beth Howry's sweet-sixteen party," Jilly snickered.

"Kyle got us the gig," Palance said. "His folks know her folks."

"I'm sure it will be lovely," Nana said and began clearing dishes. Palance was puzzled that neither one pushed for more information or looked him in the eye.

"I've heard rock music can damage your hearing," Grampa said. "How loud do you play your music?"

"Very loud," Jillian answered.

Palance's mind drifted to his new song. The chorus played through his mind: *Break away, break away, now.*

"Dessert?" Nana asked, looking down at him severely to let him know this wasn't the first time she'd asked.

He was tempted to ask for *just a bit* but didn't want to get on Nana's bad side. He'd been there before, and it was no fun. Palance nodded his head and was rewarded with her specialty, a slice of homemade apple strudel.

"You're the best, Nana," Jilly said.

"Excellent," Palance added, feeling the need to say something. Nana beamed and watched her grandchildren eat. The adults drank coffee from china cups, and Nana put a sugar cube in her mouth to sweeten the coffee.

"You've been working a lot lately, Elaine," Grampa said.

"I haven't won the lottery yet."

"No good ever came of gambling," Nana said forcefully.

Palance noticed the same look of removal on his mother's face that he practiced daily. He'd always thought of himself as his father's son: same face, hair, walk, and mannerisms, but looking at his Mom, he saw it for the first time. He was struck with the horrifying possibility that the two of them might not be so different.

Palance took a bite of the apple strudel. Still warm from the oven, it slid effortlessly down his throat. Looking around the table, he noticed everyone was chewing.

"How do you make this so good?" Palance asked.

"It's a secret," Nana whispered. "I'm getting old, so soon I'll teach your sister. Your mother," she said, glancing in her direction, "has no interest in baking."

"Will you show me?" Palance asked.

"You. You're going to bake?" Nana laughed, and Palance laughed, too, at his own image in an apron covered in flour.

"It's better to be a girl," Jillian said. "Girls can do anything now. Right, Nana?"

"You can do anything," Nana said. "Maybe someday you'll be president."

"Maybe I will."

"I've got to get going," Palance said. "To get ready." Palance kissed Grampa on his cheek and gave Nana a tight squeeze. "Everything was delicious. As usual."

"Did you get enough to eat?" she asked, and Palance laughed.

He kissed his mother on the cheek and patted Jillian on the head, in part to show her affection and because he knew it annoyed her. "I love you," he shouted by the door, suddenly frozen by their tight faces and narrow eyes, looking at him as if he were a soldier headed to war.

Palance shut the door and crossed the street to where Scott was still playing with the tennis ball. Palance held up his arm, and Scott threw it to him. He threw it back to Scott, who asked, "Did you write your paper yet? *The Lady and the Tiger.*"

"Sunday," Palance answered and turned toward home, where the Ibanez waited for him. Sunday was what his regular life would have to wait for, when the gig was over. On the walk home, he ran through their set list: fourteen songs—thirteen covers and one original, tapping out the beat to each. Kyle was a pain in the ass, but he was a good drummer, his time as steady as he was annoying.

Palance glanced at his watch. One-thirty. Two hours to practice, one hour to nap. Then it would be time to shower, dress, and set up. Everything had to be perfect. They were supposed to be there by six, but Kyle insisted on picking them up at five-fifteen, because he had a drum set and sound system to assemble.

Palance saw Jerry and Joey, the young twins, out playing Cops and Robbers, dressed up with their badges and toy guns. Joey turned his rifle in Palance's direction. Palance held up his hands. "Don't shoot. I surrender."

"Can we listen to you practice this weekend?" Jerry asked.

"No practice this weekend. We've got a gig."

"Are you famous yet?" Joey asked.

"Not yet. Maybe next week."

"Okay," he answered, nodding his head. Palance nodded back.

Palance waited outside for Kyle to pick him up. His guitar, amp, and music were with him. He checked the guitar case twice for his strap, cord, and tuner. He heard the purr of Kyle's blue Toyota Tercel Wagon before it came into view. Jason was riding shotgun, so Palance got into the back seat, with his amp next to him and the Ibanez across his lap. In the hatch, Jason's amp, Kyle's sound system, and drums were stacked tightly. Microphone stands rolled precariously back and forth on top. It occurred to Palance that if the car stopped suddenly, his head would be in jeopardy. Fortunately, Kyle was as cautious driving as everywhere else. He stayed at or below the speed limit.

The mood in the car was somber, like a final exam. Even Kyle was silent, and Jason's head was bowed. Palance thought about his father, who played in a band in college. He wondered what his father would say to him before the gig. The microphone stands clanged against each other. Palance put up his hands to stop them, but they stayed in back.

"Bungee cords," he said. "We need bungee cords."

"Yeah, man," Jason said, looking back. Palance saw his bloodshot eyes and knew he was stoned. He told himself this was only a sweet-sixteen party, but he knew it was more. Their reputation, his reputation at Mather, would rise or fall on their performance tonight. There would be twenty sophomore girls there, and he might have a shot with one of them.

Kyle pulled up in front of Beth Howry's house and parked the car. Palance and Kyle both looked at Jason's eyes and decided they'd approach first. Palance carried his guitar, and Kyle grabbed two microphone stands. They walked up the steps to the front door and rang the bell. Mrs. Howry answered, in blue jeans and a t-shirt, and let them in.

"You boys can set up downstairs," she said. "I'm going to change, but I'll have some sandwiches ready in the kitchen when you're done. I know how you kids eat." She led them through the living room, with its intricate oriental rug and dark wood. The living room melded into the wood-paneled dining room, and Mrs. Howry led them into the kitchen. "You can bring the rest of the equipment in through the back door," she said, and took them down the stairs to the basement. It was dark, with a low ceiling and tile floor.

"The Beatles started in a place like this," Kyle said. "In Liverpool. It was called *The Cavern*."

"Leave the girls room to dance," Mrs. Howry said. "That corner would be a good place to set up. And please keep it to a dim roar."

Kyle and Palance dropped their things in the corner and went to get Jason and the rest of the gear. Palance noticed pictures of the family, of Beth and her brother at descending ages from the basement to the kitchen, so that the trip up the stairs represented a journey backward in time. He observed the family becoming younger and younger. A quick glance into the kitchen revealed a ceramic plaque hanging on the wall, with tiny handprints pressed into it. There were purple and blue crepe paper strands hung on the walls and doorways throughout the house, and a photograph of Beth pasted onto a posterboard on a wooden easel in the basement, with markers in the tray for guests to write messages to her. Mylar balloons floated listlessly. Looking out for parents, Palance punched one and watched it bounce against the wall and then back to him. Outside, Jason was still sitting in the car.

Kyle turned to Palance and said, "This may get ugly."

"Maybe he's not as stoned as he looks," Palance replied.

"Hey J-bird," Kyle yelled. "Showtime."

Jason stirred while Kyle lifted the wagon hatch and started pulling out their equipment. Kyle grabbed the bass and snare drums and carried them into the house. Palance grabbed his amp and one of the speakers from the sound system.

"What should I get?" Jason asked.

"Your bass and amp might come in handy," Palance answered, turning toward the house. He looked back to see Jason still struggling to pull his amp out of the back. He shook his head and figured he'd get himself set up before he focused on Jason. Going back up the stairs, he ran into Jason on his way down and told him to set up down there. He didn't want him running into Mr. or Mrs. Howry and getting them kicked out before they started.

"Let's set up and then get some food into him," Kyle said. "That usually helps."

Palance nodded in assent. He had never seen Jason this bad. Back in the basement, Jason was moving on his own. He had his bass and amp plugged in and ready to go.

"What can we do to get the sound system ready?" Palance asked Kyle.

"I can take care of that. Why don't you two run through a couple of tunes?"

Palance set up his guitar stand, took the Ibanez out of the case, and pulled out his strap, cord, and a chamois cloth. He put the guitar around his neck and used the chamois to polish the wood, carefully running it along the neck, back, and front. Then he plugged one end of the cord into the Ibanez and the other into the tuner. He flashed back to his memory of his father showing him how to tune a guitar and followed those instructions.

"Hey, J-bird," Palance said. "'Still Haven't Found.' One, two, one, two, three, four . . ." Jason managed to play the song flawlessly. His eyes sharpened and cleared. He was showing off his rock-star moves. His head tilted back, and he rolled his shoulders. They ran through a couple of songs, and Kyle, who always looked too nervous to be happy, nodded as they played. He assembled his drum kit like a kid on Christmas morning. Palance plugged his guitar into the amp and put it back on the stand. He started plugging cords into microphones and the mixing board. Kyle eyed him suspiciously.

"We've been practicing with this setup for weeks now," Palance said to him. "I won't screw it up." Kyle didn't answer; he just kept watching. Palance turned the power on, just to piss him off. "Testing," he spoke into his microphone. "Testing 1, 2, 3, testing." His voice boomed over the speakers. Kyle had a look of horror on his face. Jason was nodding absentmindedly, and Palance realized how much fun tonight might be. "Boys," he said, "Let's get something to eat before we rock this joint." Then Beth Howry walked in.

"Hi, Kyle," she said, softly, almost a whisper. She was wearing a shiny blue dress, and her light-brown hair was curled. She looked like a child playing dress-up, in silver high heels. Her makeup was thick, and her fingernails were painted pink; one was bitten down. "I'm glad you're playing at my party."

"Hey, Beth," Kyle said. "Do you know Palance and Jason?"

"Seen them around school. And I've seen Palance at the Bunny Hutch," she said, biting another fingernail and grinding her toe into the floor.

Palance nodded, and Jason grunted in her direction.

"Sixteen, huh? You ready to party?" Palance asked. He noticed a slight bump on her nose and bright green eyes that made her look shy and bookish.

"Do you guys play anything we can dance to?"

"We'll have you on the floor all night," Kyle said. Jason giggled, and Palance turned away to hide the grin on his face.

"I'll let you set up. Can you start at seven-thirty?"

"Sure," Kyle answered.

Looking at Palance, she said, "Play something special for me." She leaned toward him coyly. "It's my birthday."

"Are there sandwiches for us yet?" Kyle asked.

"One second," Beth answered, and climbed the few steps into the kitchen before coming back halfway, awkwardly, in her heels. "Come and get it."

The boys went upstairs and stuffed down a couple of sandwiches each before Kyle herded them back downstairs for a final run-through. "They might have requests," he said. "If we can manage, we should fake it."

"I'm not playing *Achy Breaky Heart*," Jason told Kyle.

Palance launched into a laughable falsetto version of *I Will Always Love You*. Jason sat on the floor, laughing.

"Okay clowns, for real," Kyle insisted. They ran through a few songs. Kyle got up to turn a couple of knobs on the sound system.

Palance glanced at his watch and announced, "Ten minutes." He heard the muffled sound of footsteps, voices, and laughter from upstairs as the doorbell rang every few minutes. Mrs. Howry came down the stairs.

"Almost showtime, boys," she said. "Low roar. We've still got eight years left on the mortgage, and we need the foundation to last." She chuckled, noticed the boys weren't smiling, and stopped.

"Can I get you kids anything?"

"Coke, please," Kyle said.

"Me, too," Palance added. "Please." Jason nodded.

She pulled three cans out of a cooler at the other end of the room and handed them one each. "Break a leg," she told them, walking up the stairs. "I'm sure I'm going to need a drink, too."

"Okay," Kyle said, "we've all got the set lists. We'll start with "Smells Like Teen Spirit," and then the U2 song."

"We can read, Kyle," Jason said. "We're not stupid."

Palance heard footsteps and turned to see Beth stepping down the stairs, uneasy in her heels. He was startled to see Alanna Shaw walking behind her, radiant in a white blouse and lavender skirt.

"Do you guys know my cousin?" Beth asked. "She's in your same grade."

Jason nodded and mumbled, "Hey, Alanna."

Palance didn't understand why motion did not cease in her presence, why all eyes didn't automatically turn her way, and why other boys didn't kneel and bow their heads to her, although he had never been able to express any feelings at all in her presence.

Kyle waved from behind his drum kit. Palance kept his guitar on as a shield but walked toward Alanna until the cord was stretched taut and jerked him back. Jason, who knew about his crush, giggled into his microphone. Palance turned red when a smile formed on Alanna's face, and he was startled when she walked up to him. "I didn't know you played the guitar," she said.

Too tongue-tied in her presence to form words, Palance played *Too Old to Be So Young*, the song that had always been hers. He even managed to sing a few of the words, realizing he was going to have to perform in front of her in a few moments. Beth put her hand on Palance's right arm, squeezed it and said to Alanna, "I told you they were good." Then, turning to Palance, inches from his face, her hand warm as it slid down his arm, she said, "I'm so glad you're here for my party."

Palance could smell her perfume. The scent put him in a frenzy. He wanted to pull her to him. For a moment, he forgot Alanna was there, even though Beth was too young, too straight, and too awkward. His thoughts were jumbled. Her scent and his frenzy remained. Out of the corner of his eye, he saw Alanna smiling directly at him. Their eyes met and locked.

Like a flood, the other girls came pouring down the stairs, loud and raucous. One of them yelled, "Let's party" and looked toward Palance and the band, commanding, "Play some music. Now."

Palance turned around to face Jason. Kyle counted out, "One, two, three, four," and started the introduction on the tom-toms. Palance banged out a power chord, stepped on the compressor pedal to sustain the sound, and lifted his guitar into the air, letting it reverberate throughout the room. He'd practiced this move for hours. The girls stopped in their tracks, every head turned toward him. He raised the volume and did it again, watching the pictures on the wall vibrate and Beth smile. Alanna looked amused. Palance dropped the guitar back down into playing position; then he jumped into the air, his landing a signal for Jason to come in, and there was thunder in the room.

Kyle provided the power, the deep bass drum resonating in their stomachs, moving the girls to the dance floor. The chiming of the high-hat locked them in a trance. The pounding of the tom-toms moved their feet and arms. The cymbals wrenched their heads with each crash. Palance felt it, too. Jason's bass notes were thick and expansive, encompassing the room and setting heartbeats into rhythm with the music. The girls moved and breathed together as one. He poured everything he had into the music, and it engulfed him.

When the song ended, Palance went into the next one, not pausing a beat, which threw Jason and Kyle off. He wanted to ride this feeling like a wave. He caught a glimpse of Alanna, her cyan-blue eyes bright as the mylar balloons around her. Her blond hair swayed as her head shook, back and forth, until her eyes met his. Palance sang as the drums pounded behind him and the bass thumped his chest. He leaned into the microphone and roared out the song.

Before he could begin another, Kyle was announcing the next song, "Sweet Little Sixteen," for Beth. It was Kyle's only vocal, and Palance was unhappy to lose the microphone, even for a moment. Kyle invited Beth up with the band. She stood next to Palance, swaying a bit, leaning in and rubbing up against him. He felt her hair soft against his arm. She put her arm around his waist. When the song was over, he was tempted to pull her to him, but Alanna was in the corner of his eye.

He started the next song, searching through it for that elusive power. He looked at Jason, locked onto the bass line, and lost himself in the beat. His guitar chords floated on top of them in waves, and the words flowed above the chords. Palance drove his gaze into Alanna and felt her body shift toward him, undulating with the music. Not satisfied, he looked at Beth, inviting her closer. Still not satisfied, he lowered his voice and guitar, and whispered the lyric, gently strumming, signaling Jason and Kyle to lower their volume, drawing everyone's attention. When the dancing stopped and all eyes were on him, he banged out the rest of the song, projecting his voice in rich, deep tones, and watched the girls stand mesmerized, as he basked in the glow.

This is better than being stoned, Palance thought, and he imagined larger crowds, stadium gigs, cameras flashing, and running into waiting limousines, where guards struggled to contain a barrage of fans begging for an autograph. When the song ended, Palance saw Mrs. Howry walking toward them. His mind soared. He tried to come down, but this high was not responsive to his will, so he braced himself for whatever she had in store, but it was not him she was after, only his microphone.

"It's time for a special treat," Mrs. Howry began. "Mr. Howry," she said, pointing to her husband in back of the room by a television set, "has put together a video montage of Beth's life, and many of you are in it."

Palance felt a hand on his arm and turned to see Alanna pulling him away from the band. He lifted his guitar over his head and set it on the stand, following her out.

"Do you get high?" she whispered.

Palance nodded and watched her lip curl. They walked up the stairs and out the back door, where she pulled him to her and kissed him on the mouth. His first real kiss. Her hands moved to his butt, and their tongues intertwined as she guided him into her car. He was sitting in the passenger seat of her red Celica, looking up through the moon roof, while she rifled through her purse and pulled out a small pipe and a cigarette lighter shaped like a lipstick holder. She put the pipe between his lips and flicked on the lighter. He inhaled and turned the pipe back toward her. Alanna took a hit off the pipe, put her hand behind his head, and pulled him to her, breathing the smoke into his mouth.

"You were amazing in there," she said, her voice gasping and harsh from the smoke. "How long have you been playing?"

"Since I can remember. I started taking lessons when I was eleven. My Dad taught me since I was old enough to hold a guitar."

"I think you're going to be famous," Alanna told him. "Very famous." She turned the pipe back to him and relit it.

Palance was more interested in Alanna than the weed, and he trembled when her tongue slipped into his mouth. He couldn't believe this was happening and felt his eyes lose focus. Alanna kept pressing her lips to his. He was unable to break away. Each time he tried to tell her they should go back inside, her lips were on his, and there was more smoke. Her mouth was wet and delicious, her scent mingling with the pot. Her tongue was in his mouth; she was wilder and more beautiful than he imagined. He was dizzy. She took his hand, gazed at him with her blue eyes sparkling, and told him it was time to go back.

Alanna took a comb and makeup from her bag, fixed herself and, with a few drops of spit on her hands, pushed down Palance's hair and stroked it. Each trace of her fingers sent chills through his body. He reached toward her hair, but she intercepted his hand, smiled wickedly, and told him not to mess it up.

"Beth will see and be jealous. She likes you, you know."

"Huh," Palance answered.

Walking back to the house, Palance's feet barely touched pavement. Alanna pulled out a small tube of mouthwash spray, used it, and then sprayed the peppermint mist into his mouth. They stumbled through the back door, into the kitchen, bumping into chairs and stumbling down the stairs, almost falling into Kyle at the bottom.

"Not you, too?" Kyle asked him.

"Hey, man," Palance answered, "don't harsh my buzz," and he pushed Kyle away more forcefully than he meant to, causing him to stumble.

"You're late. Let's play," Kyle said, his face red and hard as he walked back to the drum kit. Jason was standing in place with his bass on, ready to go. Palance put on his guitar. He felt elated, yet annoyed, as if he'd lost something. An anger settled in him, an anger he needed to channel, and Jason and Kyle played "Losing My Religion," by *R.E.M.* He looked out at the girls, who were scattered, and tried to remember his part. Alanna was nowhere to be seen. Beth was holding court in the middle of the room. Palance struggled to keep up. He stumbled as Beth walked toward him. He felt no inspiration from the pot. He longed for the energy he had before the break.

Suddenly the song was over, and Kyle banged his sticks together eight times. He played two measures of the relentless beat to the song Palance had written. Palance snarled out the lyrics, *I don't know, it seems so slow, head is aching, heart is breaking* and watched as the girls began to pay attention. He had to make this song work. He had to feel it in his gut. *Mood is low, thoughts don't flow, mind is breaking, heart is raging*, and even as his dream was coming true, the world of possibilities closed in around him. Beth seemed unreasonably alluring, only a few yards away.

Blow by blow and toe-to-toe, ground is quaking, body's shaking. Beth was standing before him now, dancing to the song, his song. Palance felt both trapped and enthralled, unfaithful to Alanna in a way that thrilled him. *Heart and soul take their toll, sleeping, waking, seems like faking.* The words and music lifted him. The band was playing *his song*. The girls were dancing, their eyes on the band, on him. He crouched down before the chorus exploded, *Break away, from the chains that bind you, break away from the pain inside you*; he watched as they gyrated and spun, and he felt power once again surging inside him. *Break away*, he screamed, *from the shame that hides you, keeping you down, keeping you down*. He tried one of his signature jumps but caught the guitar cord with his foot coming down, and tripped. He fell on his knees, wincing in pain. The plug remained halfway in, and his amp began buzzing and screeching, finally stopping when he pulled the cord out. While he was horrified, some of the girls screamed, and Beth's eyes grew huge. He grabbed the microphone and finished the chorus, *Break away, break away now*, and plugged his guitar back in.

Beth's eyes were on him, and Palance grinned widely at her. *I don't know as changes go, there's ups and downs and 'round and 'round, yes and no, lock and load, run aground, tossed and bound.* He could feel the ground shifting beneath him. Alanna walked down the stairs, balancing a cup in one hand and holding onto the handrail with the other. In one night, his goddess had shifted from pedestal to flesh, and now she was stumbling down the stairs. *Rock and roll, bend and fold, pound for pound too tightly wound, so many pows right here and now. Time to get down to the sound and break away*, the chorus began, just as Alanna's feet touched the floor and Palance caught a defiant glance between Beth and Alanna. They were vying for him.

Break away from the fear, break away far and near, Palance sang. It amazed him how much these words meant now; *break away from the dream, break away seldom seen. Break away to the clear, break away I'm still here*. Beth danced exuberantly. Alanna seemed removed. He tried a more guttural voice, *Break away, born and bred, break away, burned and bled*, his voice foreign and strong. Alanna walked to the punchbowl, unsteady, this muse who'd stirred him for years and had finally granted him a taste of her favors.

Palance sang, *I don't see who I can be. I don't hear, my head ain't clear. I don't feel and I can't heal, out of gear, it's too severe, and out of touch it's too damn much.* Now the song was all there was; the girls faded, the way smoke leaves a room, so you never notice until it's gone.

Palance narrowed his eyes, and the girls came back into focus, vibrant and lithe. Beth appeared graceful before him. Alanna was stiff and wavering in the distance; *Sharp as steel, it's too damn real, out of luck and in the clutch, get that deal signed and sealed, but break away,* he sang, *from the chains that bind you, break away, from the pain inside you, break away, from the shame that hides you, keeping you down, break away, break away now.* The girls cheered and squealed.

Jason grabbed his microphone and announced, "Hey, party people," his eyes still glazed over, "that song was written by our own Palance Heller. Take a bow, man."

The girls cheered. Beth chanted, "Play it again," and the girls joined in, "play it again," until it grew into a roar. Palance watched Beth sway toward him. She handed him a plastic glass, some kind of punch. He gulped it, reeled from the alcohol, smiled, and watched her saunter away. Then he began the song again, this time everyone singing along on the chorus: *Break away from the chains that bind you, break away, from the pain inside you.* Everyone was singing *his song.*

Alanna drifted back toward the band. Palance watched her lips mimic his own. She pushed back her mane of blond hair and raised up her arms, striking a pose; twirling and transformed into the image Palance once held in his imagination, false and sensuous as a fairy tale. Beth was dancing near him on the left, young and seductive, while Alanna mirrored her on his right, aloof and self-absorbed. As the song ended, *Break away burned and bled*, Palance recalled the story from English class, *The Lady and the Tiger*, and wondered which gate to choose.

Both girls moved toward him. His heart palpitated as the light flickered on and off like a strobe. At the light switch, Mrs. Howry announced that parents were upstairs waiting to take their children home. She walked toward the punch bowl, scooped out a cup, and held her nose to it; then pushed her lips tightly together.

"Winston," she called, once quietly and then again more forcefully, "would you come down here, please?" He did, and they conferred, whispering back and forth with concerned looks on their faces. Mr. Howry approached the band and pulled the microphone out of the stand to make the announcement that, since there had been drinking, no one who drove to the party on their own would be allowed to drive home. The Howrys would assist them in getting their automobiles and persons where they needed to be.

"Uncle Win," Alanna said to him, "I can help get everyone home safely." She flashed a wicked smile toward Palance.

Kyle spoke up. "Mr. Howry, sir," he said, "I haven't had anything to drink besides water and Diet Coke, and I need to get the equipment home."

Mr. Howry leaned toward Kyle's mouth and sniffed, looked carefully into his eyes, and said, "Okay. You can drive home with the band and equipment. Start packing up now." Looking toward Alanna, he said, "Lannie, I think it would be best if you stayed in the spare room tonight."

"But, Uncle Win."

"I need to call your folks one way or the other," he said. "This way, I can tell them it was your decision to stay overnight."

"Overnight sounds good," she said, her words slow and mechanical, trying hard not to slur her speech.

"Come on, guys," Kyle said. "Let's pack it up."

The girls streamed up the stairs, and Palance felt the energy drain from him. The alcohol, pot, and excitement of the evening had taken their toll. "I need to sit down a minute," he said. "How 'bout you, J-bird?"

"You two just get your gear packed up," Kyle said. "Then take a break until we're ready to head up the stairs."

Palance managed to cram his cords and music into his guitar case, and when no one was looking, snuck another cup of punch from the bowl—and one for Jason. "Sorry, man," he said to Kyle, "designated driver." Kyle looked at the two of them, shook his head, and went back to disassembling the sound system. "Man, we were awesome tonight. Don't you think?"

"Totally," Jason said. "We had those girls in a frenzy. I was so high."

"You two get any higher, and we'll be busted," Kyle told them. "Can't you control yourselves?"

Jason started laughing, and Palance joined in. "Yes, Dad," Jason said. "We'll behave." Kyle rolled his eyes.

"What can I do to tear down?" Palance asked. "I can wrap mic cords."

"Fine."

Palance wrapped the microphone cables into coils. "Was I okay?" he asked.

"Primo," Jason said.

"You were a little shaky after the break," Kyle said, "and you were late."

"We need more gigs," Palance declared. "This was a blast."

"Palance, are you okay to carry the mic stands upstairs?" Kyle asked him.

"Sure," he said, grabbing one in each hand and heading out to the car. As he climbed the stairs, Palance caught Jason pulling a vial out of his pocket and holding something to his nose. He knew Jason smoked too much pot, but he never thought he'd be this stupid. He looked back over his shoulder and saw his friend, the vial still in his hand, sitting cross-legged on an empty floor, staring into space.

Kyle loaded the gear in a prescribed pattern only he knew. Palance put his hand on Kyle's shoulder and said, "Thanks, man. For everything."

"You were outstanding," Kyle said. "Just a little more discretion next time. Okay?"

"You've got it. I'll grab my amp and guitar."

All that was left of the glory were their guitars and amplifiers. Palance looked around at the torn crepe paper and empty punch bowl. It seemed like a dream, the screaming girls, the dancing, all of it. He looked down at Jason, and an overwhelming feeling of sadness came over him. Jason's bass lines drove home, and his voice felt right on the harmonies, but Jason was somewhere else. He reached down to help pull him up and grasped his arm tightly.

"We were something, the three of us," Palance said. "We were something."

Jason threw his arm around Palance's shoulder and pulled himself up the rest of the way. "Yeah, man. We were."

"Can you get your stuff out to the car?" Palance asked.

"Yeah, man. J-bird's cool."

Palance grabbed his amplifier in one hand and guitar in the other. He made his way up the stairs. Behind him, Jason's footsteps were clumsy and erratic. The outside air was cool. When Kyle finished loading the car, it was exactly as they arrived.

"Let me settle up with the Howrys," Kyle said. Palance was amazed they were getting money for this. Jason got into the car, calling shotgun, and Palance didn't want the night to end.

Kyle came out of the house with a twenty-dollar bill for each of them. Palance folded it and stuck it into his shirt pocket.

"Time to go," Kyle said.

Palance spotted Beth Howry, sitting on her front steps, changed into sweatpants and a t-shirt. "Hey, man," he said to Kyle. "You mind taking care of my stuff for tonight? I'll pick it up in the morning. I'm going to walk home."

"You sure?"

"Yeah."

"Okay."

"Thanks," Palance said, and waited until they drove off to walk toward Beth. "Hell of a party," he said to her.

"Yeah, sweet sixteen. Like in the movies."

"Your dad seems pretty pissed."

Beth let the corners of her mouth pull up a bit. "He'll get over it. He still thinks I'm twelve."

"I know the feeling." Palance saw the sadness in her bowed head and slumped shoulders, and hesitantly put his hand on hers.

Beth looked at him, hard, but before he could remove his hand, she leaned into his chest, and he heard her sob. "It's just . . ."

"Just what?"

"Not good enough."

"What?"

"Me," she said. Her tears stopped, their residue streaking down her face. "Me."

Palance didn't know what to say. His mouth was parched from the alcohol and pot.

"My brother," she sputtered, "is like Magna-cum-fucking-everything, and my cousin Alanna is, well—you drool over her. I saw you."

"I," Palance began, certain that, as soon as the single word left his lips, it was a mistake. Beth's eyes narrowed and her head slanted, as if to say, *Don't you dare.*

"I've seen you," she repeated. "And she goes for guys like you. Guys that other girls want. I know you don't want to hear it, but she knows she's pretty, and she's so coy, and she takes what she wants because she can, and . . ." Beth pulled away from him, looked straight at him, silent tears running down her face, and she got up, put her hand on the doorknob, and mumbled, "because she knows I like you. And I'm some hideous thing with freckles."

"Don't," Palance said, "Stay. You're not some . . . you're very pretty."

"I saw you sneak out with her," she said, "and I saw you kiss her."

What Palance wanted was to deny it ever happened, to take Beth in his arms, and declare his love for her. He didn't know when this shift occurred. This girl in front of him was crying for comfort and pushing him away at the same time. While a part of him still worshiped Alanna, the memory of her lips pressed against his and her tongue in his mouth, Beth seemed more real. He blurted out, "What do you want from me?" knowing that his misspoken words hurt her. He had to do something. He leaned down and kissed her, not hungrily, as with Alanna, but softly and tenderly. Beth didn't pull away, but when Palance moved back, she stared at him.

"What do you want from me?" she asked and held his arm as if to prevent him from running away.

"I don't know," he said, and, although it was, again, the wrong thing to say, it was the truth.

"Well, figure it out!" Beth shouted at him, and suddenly she was back inside the house, out of reach.

Palance rose to his feet and steadied himself. He had never been on such lofty and shaky ground. The wind picked up and billowed his shirt. He took a step and stumbled but did not fall. He walked backward with his eyes on the house. When he reached the sidewalk, he noticed one window was open, and a light was on in the room. Alanna leaned out the window in a loose purple t-shirt. The curve of her breasts was in clear view.

"Goodnight, Pal," she said with a thin smile and a tinge of mischief in her eyes. "See you in school."

Breakaway

I don't know, it seems so slow,
Head is aching, heart is breaking,
Mood is low, thoughts don't flow,
Mind is breaking, heart is raging,
Blow by blow and toe to toe,
Ground is quaking, body's shaking,
Heart and soul take their toll,
Sleeping, waking, seems like faking.

C   Break away, from the chains that bind you,
H   Break away, from the pain inside you,
O   Break away, from the shame that hides you,
R   Keeping you down, keeping you down,
U   Break away,
S   Break away now.

I don't know, as changes go,
There's ups and downs, 'round and 'round,
Yes and no, lock and load,
Run aground, tossed and bound,
Rock and roll, bend and fold,
Pound for pound too tightly wound,
So many pows right here and now,
Time to get down to the sound, and

Chorus

Break away from the fear, break away far and near,
Break away from the dream, break away, seldom seen,
Break away to the clear, break away, I'm still here,
Break away, born and bred, break away, burned and bled.

I don't see who I can be,
I don't hear, my head ain't clear,
I don't feel and I can't heal,
Out of gear, it's too severe, and
Out of touch, it's too damn much,
Sharp as steel, it's too damn real,
Out of luck and in the clutch,
Get that deal signed and sealed, but

Chorus

Break away now (3 times)

Where Do We Go From Here?

Palance fumbled with his tie. The weight of his father's absence settled deeper with each unsuccessful attempt. He pulled and tugged at it several times before settling for adequate. The caps and gowns were waiting at the high school. His mother came into the living room and adjusted his tie, pinching the corners until the knot was a perfect triangle, set at his collar.

"Your father could never get this right, either. You look very handsome," she said. "I'm proud of you."

Palance wasn't sure why she was proud. He had always done well in English and Social Studies, but his grades in other subjects left him a C average. Combined with his financial situation, his college choice was limited to Northeastern Illinois University, fifteen minutes away, or one of the Junior Colleges. He envied Kyle, headed to Cornell, and Jason going to Southern, proud of its status as the number-one party school.

"I've always been proud of you," his mother said. "I hope you know that."

"Mmm-hmm," he said.

"Your father would be proud," she said. He wondered what his father would really think of him now. Maybe they could start a band together—if he were still alive.

"First time in forever I've seen you with a tie," Jillian said, walking into the living room. "Are Nana and Grampa coming?"

"Yes, and Aunt Sandi and Uncle Ross are going to meet us at the restaurant afterwards. Best behavior, both of you."

"Yes, Mommy," Jilly said mockingly, and slipped next to Palance. "I'll keep an eye on this one. You know he's trouble."

"Five minutes," their mother said.

"Yes, ma'am," Jilly replied. Palance rolled his eyes.

Palance got out of the car near the school entrance. His mother and Jilly parked the car and headed to the football field for the ceremony. He walked to the gym and up to a folding table with caps and gowns. Even now, the room smelled of humiliation and sweat. The attendant examined her list and put a check mark near his name. She handed him a cap and gown in a plastic bag; then she instructed him to sit in one of the folding chairs and wait. He put the cap and gown on over his street clothes. Alanna walked up to him, moving forward as if to kiss him, before gently stroking his face.

"Oh," she said, "better not." Then she smiled furtively and shifted away before turning back, kissing him wetly, her lips parted and her tongue darting into his mouth. "Just reminding you what you gave up," she said. Alanna walked backwards and smiled at him, the same exquisite look that first drew him to her. For the past year, she alternately tempted and tormented him. He often thought, *If they weren't cousins*, but they were, she and Beth, and he didn't dare.

"Your loss," she added, wetting her lips and turning to take her seat. Palance was grateful Beth was a year behind, and not in the room. He turned to find Jason sitting in the back row with some of the stoners he was hanging out with more and more.

"Big day, J-bird," he said, disturbed at the degree to which his friend reeked of pot at ten-thirty in the morning, and how well he fit in with the stoners.

"Bring your axe to Kyle's party tonight," Jason said. "We're going to rock the joint. Get it? Rock the joint."

"Got it. You bringing full gear or just the Pignose?"

"I'm minimizing, man. Just the essentials. It's a small, small gig. Kyle said he's not even setting up the whole kit. I'll believe it when I see it."

"I'll bring the acoustic."

"Unplugged," Jason said. "Cool," bobbing his head with his eyes half-closed. He looked ready to nod off.

This night would be bittersweet. Kyle had an internship set up that left him little, if any, time for the band, and Jason was increasingly unreliable. Palance wondered if this would be their last gig. It was less of a gig than a jam session; more *requiem* than anything else.

"Ladies and Gentlemen," Vice-Principal Elkin said over the microphone, "when I call your name, please line up in front of the room. Mrs. Owen will walk the first set of graduates out to the football field. Anyone who doesn't cooperate won't graduate."

Mr. Elkin spoke without a pause, and though Palance tried to concentrate, this seemed like a final exam he was doomed to fail.

"Do not throw your caps up in the air. This is not a movie, and you will need to return both your cap and gown to receive your diploma. For that reason, and to avoid error, you will receive your diploma binder on stage, but you will come back here after the ceremony, turn in your cap and gown, and receive your actual diploma."

Mr. Elkin read off a list of names. Palance spaced out for the next ten minutes, until he heard his own, after Sonya Halloran, and lined up to take his place in a procession that would lead him out of the school and into the vast unknown he kept hearing described as his future. He had not so much achieved as endured.

They walked single file across the asphalt parking lot, onto the grassy field, and into the stadium. The spectacle of the day, the mortarboard caps and black flowing gowns, the grandiose cacophony of the marching band in their robin's-egg blue uniforms, and the blue-and-white bunting on the stage unexpectedly filled Palance with awe.

Ms. Delaney called them to attention. "Look at me," she said, approaching an empty row of chairs. "When the row is full, I will sit down, and then you will sit. Not a moment before, not a moment after." She taught freshman algebra in the same unforgiving manner.

Palance saw Kyle on the inside aisle of the row across from him, ramrod straight in his chair, eyes forward. Ms. Delaney nodded in their direction and took her seat. Neat as soldiers they sat in formation.

Palance scanned the bleachers, finding his family directly across from him, seven rows up. Jillian was on his mother's right, Nana and Grampa next to her. The seat on his mother's left was empty. For a moment, he waited for his father to appear.

"Ladies and gentlemen, parents, teachers, relatives, and friends," the principal began. "Today is a momentous occasion for the Stephen T. Mather graduating class of nineteen hundred and ninety-four. Please give them a hand." Palance closed his eyes, basking in the glow. The field smelled of grass and dirt. The speeches were long and arduous, and the sun was hot. The moment finally came when Ms. Delaney stood up, beckoned them to rise again, and led them across the fifty-yard line to the foot of the stage. Once on the stage, a woman Palance had never seen before shook his hand theatrically. Principal Milikan handed him a cardboard binder, and Palance followed Sonya to the other end of the stage and down the stairs, where Ms. Delaney waited to guide them back to their seats. She told him politely, for the last time in his high school career, to sit down and shut up. Palance enjoyed the pomp and circumstance, and wondered if, like the binders, life was a game of bait and switch. He watched the rest of his class flow across the stage in an endless stream, the sun beating down this windless day, until Wayne Zylinski was handed his empty cardboard binder, and Lin Foon began her valedictorian address, *We Are the Future*.

The rest of the afternoon blurred with the tedium of Lin's speech, the sun's heat, the shuffling of gowns, the irritation of a necktie, and the boredom of sitting next to strangers. Four years at this school, and he had no idea who they were. Up in the stands, even his grandparents looked apathetic, a word that described his attitude in school so well he felt an affinity toward it.

The last paragraph in Lin's speech finally captured his attention—and completed the song he had been working on. He needed an ending to the chorus, and Lin gave it to him. "Where do we go from here?" she asked. Lin concluded her speech, and the stadium broke out in applause.

"I'm applauding because it's over," Sonya Halloran whispered.

"I won't miss this place," he told her.

"Ladies and Gentlemen," Principal Milikan announced over the loudspeakers, "this concludes our ceremony. We ask that you keep your seats while the graduates file out."

"You will wait for my signal," Ms. Delaney said to the row, her manner stern and unyielding, "which will come immediately after the row behind us files out."

Eventually she stood and lifted her arms, as if conducting an orchestra, and they obediently stood and followed her back into the gymnasium. Palance turned in his cap and gown, retrieved his diploma, and, two feet from the exit, turned around and yelled, "So long, you sons of bitches. I'm outta here," raising his fist in triumph. He enjoyed the looks of consternation on the faces of the adults, until a hand grasped his arm. He turned to see Mrs. Braimer, the dean of students, who escorted him toward the door, saying, "It will be a pleasure to remove you permanently from the building." Palance mockingly bowed to her from outside and then turned to find his mother, sister, and grandparents inches from his face. His mother shook her head and gave him a look.

"Way to go, sport," Jillian said, wearing an alarmingly accurate imitation of their mother's face.

Lunch at Lou Malnati's was strained, and Palance wished his grandparents had not borne witness to his defiant departure. He sank his teeth into the thick delight of the pizza, the buttery dough, and thin slices of pepperoni. Aunt Sandi and Uncle Ross gave him a two-hundred-dollar savings bond, for which he thanked them profusely. Nana and Grampa gave him a hundred dollars in cash and an old pocket watch.

"It was my father's," Nana said. "From Russia." Jillian looked wide-eyed at this shiny prize, and his mother's eyes teared up a bit. "It's a family heirloom. We know you'll take good care of it."

Jillian unexpectedly handed him a wrapped package. "I had it made special for you," she said. "You can't return it, so you'd better like it."

Palance unwrapped the package to find a leather guitar strap with his name embossed.

"It cost me two nights of babysitting," she said.

"Thank you," Palance told her, putting his arm around her and kissing her on the cheek. "It's cool. Really cool. Thanks."

"You're gonna make me cry," their mom said, "both of you. I wish I had a camera. You're going to have to wait until tomorrow for my present," she told Palance. "I'll have it early in the afternoon."

"Sounds mysterious," Jillian said. "She won't even tell me what it is."

"I'm not telling a soul. Now who's up for a second slice?" she asked, placing one on Palance's plate before he answered.

Palance packed his Seagull acoustic guitar and laid the copy of his new song in the case. He stole the title and chorus from Lin Foon, "Where Do We Go from Here?" His mother was letting him borrow the car. He'd pick up Jason and Beth on the way to Kyle's house. Jason was screaming for a designated driver these days, even if he never asked for one. Palance tried to get himself up for the party. He was not happy about his friends leaving town in the fall. At least Beth had to stick around for another year. He was secretly glad to have Jilly around the house. She hadn't been so bad. Last week, they went out to lunch together. He couldn't get over the guitar strap. He opened his case and placed it inside.

"Bye, mom," he said, kissing her on the cheek as he walked out the door.

"Home by one."

"It's graduation. And it's Kyle's."

"One-thirty at the latest. And Palance."

"Yeah?"

"If you drink or smoke, or whatever, don't drive. Take a cab."

"Whatever," Palance said and walked out before she could continue the conversation. It was like she was giving him permission. In the car, he slid Bon Jovi into the CD player and listened to "Bed of Roses," trying to shake off the funk he'd been feeling. Maybe this summer would be special. Maybe it wouldn't all turn to crap. Palance drove to Beth's house first. He wanted her next to him. He saw Beth in the window, waiting. Her hair was in a ponytail, and she was wearing jeans and a pink pullover.

Mr. Howry opened the door, looking as stern as ever, and greeted Palance with a firm handshake and a wary eye. "Good evening, Palance," he said, leaning in to examine his eyes. "Beth needs to be home by one o'clock. Earlier, if possible." Mrs. Howry kissed Beth on the cheek and pulled out a camera to take their picture. Palance dutifully stood and waited for Beth to join him. This had become the ritual. The Howrys had photographic evidence of every occasion.

"I'll have her home by one, sir," Palance said to Mr. Howry. As they walked toward his mother's car, he felt the man's eyes following, and it wasn't until they were two blocks away that he dared put his arm around her. A moment later, he pulled over.

All day, he had waited for the feeling of her body pressing against his, her smell, clean with a hint of lilac, her lips wet and pliant, her mouth barely opening, the tip of her tongue wiping against his, then withdrawing. He'd spent hours staring at her freckles, faint and reddish brown, like constellations in an oddly colored sky, and listening to her sonorous voice. He wished she would sing with him, but she refused.

"We should get Jason," she said, pulling away from him.

"We should," he repeated, pulling her back.

"Later," she said, her eyes full of mischief as she pushed lightly away from him. "Later."

Palance complied and drove to Jason's house. Jason was waiting on his front steps, smoking a cigarette, his bass and amp next to him. He looked lost and abandoned. Palance shut off the engine and walked toward Jason, who nodded his head with his eyes closed.

"Hey J-bird. How's it going?" he asked.

"Big day, big buzz."

"You ready to roll, J?" Palance asked.

"I'm ready for whatever you got."

"Just Kyle's party. What've you got?"

"Nothing you want to mess with."

Lately Jason scared the hell out of him. He picked up Jason's bass. Jason hadn't moved yet. "Time to hit the bricks," he said, and Jason gripped the Pignose amp, swung it back and forth, and walked to the car. Palance put the bass in the trunk and then opened the rear car door for Jason, who fell into the seat, pulling the door shut behind him.

"Should we pick up Traci?" Palance asked, but Beth was shaking her head "No."

"She was too straight for me," Jason said. "I'm free and clear."

"Free, maybe," Palance replied. "I don't know about clear."

"Drive, old Pal of mine." Jason said, "Drive," and he did.

"Hello, Mrs. Brendicki," Beth said as she opened the door. "Congratulations for Kyle. Cornell's a great school."

"We're very proud," she said, "of all of you." She tightened her lips when she saw Palance and Jason with their guitars in hand. "We're pleased that Kyle will be occupied with more serious matters." Jason took a step forward, and Mrs. Brendicki stepped out of the way.

"Basement?" Palance asked, and she took another step back.

"Yes, Kyle's downstairs. You know the way, dear." Jason looked at her and smiled. She shuddered. There were plastic covers on their furniture. The living room resembled a museum, with three glass cabinets of Hummel figurines neatly arranged.

In the basement, two of Kyle's cousins were talking to Melody Dibbs, who played French horn in the school orchestra and had narrowly beaten out Kyle for salutatorian, leaving him with no title, but a full scholarship to Cornell. Kyle's cousins, Tyler and Skylar, looked eerily like him, more like bankers than kids.

"Thanks for keeping the gear down to a minimum," Kyle said to Jason and Palance. "My parents would have a cow if we rattled the Hummels. Hey, Beth."

"Hey, Kyle. Congratulations."

"You bring your horn, Melody?" Jason asked, smirking.

"Do you see my horn?"

"Anyone else coming, Kyle?" Palance asked.

"Wendy and Ashley. They should be here soon. Ashley might bring a date."

Wendy and Ashley were in Beth's year and had been following the band since last summer. Palance didn't mind them. Wendy had a thing for Jason.

Mrs. Brendicki clip-clopped down the stairs carrying a tray filled with neatly cut sandwiches and a stack of plastic cups. Mr. Brendicki followed, carrying two bowls of chips.

"Man, this is lame," Jason said to Palance, loud enough everyone could hear.

"Hi, Melody," Beth said, looking awkward as she huddled near Palance.

Wendy and Ashley came down the stairs giggling loudly, each with a two-liter bottle of Coke.

"Thanks for the help, girls," Mr. Brendicki said, setting down the snacks.

"Enjoy, graduates," Mrs. Brendicki announced, "and future graduates." The two of them tiptoed up the stairs, as if undercover.

"So, Kyle," Ashley asked, "what are you going to be?"

"I think he's going to be," Wendy began and then paused, "an . . . executive for some computer company . . . and play drums on the side."

"I'm," Kyle began.

"You go last," Ashley ordered. "That's the game. First everyone says what they think, and then you go at the end. Okay?" she asked, looking around the room. "I think he's going to own a music store. And give lessons."

Tyler and Skylar both grinned.

"I think he's going to work at McDonald's," Skylar said.

"Fry cook," Tyler said, and they fell down laughing.

"Play for real," Wendy yelled.

"Okay, for real," Beth said, "I think Kyle will own his own business and do really well."

"Why don't we play some music," Jason said, unpacking his bass.

"Okay, we can finish up later," Ashley said. "And be more serious about it."

"Ashley, what happened to your date?" Kyle asked.

"Never mind."

Palance unsnapped the lid on his guitar case. He'd had enough childish games, too many tests, too much of Kyle's parents and adults like them. He looked at his Seagull acoustic and wished he had his electric and a stack of amps behind him so he could blow off some steam. He wanted to pull out a joint, get them all stoned, and play loud enough to set the whole neighborhood vibrating. He wanted to have his way with Beth right there and then. This seemed like some damn Amish party, like they were going to start churning butter or something.

Palance saw Kyle taping up the bottom of his snare drum to keep the sound down, and anger fermented inside him. "Come on, man—make some damn noise."

"Can't," he said, and, after making certain his parents were nowhere within hearing range, he added, "Norm and Shirley."

Wendy and Ashley sat up, clapping their hands like children. Palance pulled Beth toward him, took her face in his hands, and kissed her passionately. Beth looked surprised and pleased. He whispered in her ear, "One more hour, and then we split this pop stand."

"Whatever you say, cowboy," she whispered back and playfully flicked her tongue in his ear. Palance could feel the itch in her, too. He took out his guitar. He didn't wait for Jason or Kyle—he just started with "Breakaway." While he played, Beth held onto him tightly, and when he sang *Break away now,* she nuzzled his neck and whispered, "Let's do it, soon."

"We've got to go," Tyler said to Kyle when the song was over.

"Yeah," Skylar said. "You guys are great, but the big hand is spinning, and . . ."

"We've got plans," Tyler finished. "Happy graduation one and all." They skipped up the stairs as if they'd been waiting to leave since they arrived.

When they finished the song, Jason said, "Let's jam," and started with a slow rambling progression, somewhere between a blues and a shuffle. Kyle joined in. Wendy and Ashley got up and danced with each other. Melody sat close to Kyle. She watched his hands, got up, and walked to the far end of the room, where Mr. Brendicki had an old-fashioned roll-top desk with small cubbyholes and drawers. Palance watched her as he chunked chords, his interest in the music waning. He was waiting for an opportunity to exit gracefully.

Kyle watched Melody. Each time she picked up a pen or some other artifact, he tensed, and his tempo increased. Palance was amused and started making up lyrics to what they were playing, first in his own head, and then out loud. *She's making you nervous, you're feeling on edge, if she turns on the calculator, you'll walk off the ledge.* Kyle glared in his direction at first, but then saw the humor in the situation, because he made up the next verse, *That stuff is my father's, he can't stand it touched, if you put down the pencil, I'll say thanks very much.*

Palance sang, *Everything in its place, every dog has his day, that paperclip, baby, is making me crazed. I've got the blues, from my head to my shoes, enough is enough, please don't touch that stuff,* and even Kyle was laughing now. Wendy and Ashley were bumping and grinding. Melody walked back toward Kyle with an exaggerated sway in her hips. She was holding a paperclip between her thumb and index finger and waved it at Kyle.

"I'm a naughty, naughty girl," she told him.

"Whatever," Kyle said.

"Did you tell them your news?" she asked.

"Let's play another song first."

"Hey, Jason," Wendy asked, sliding up beside him, "have you written any songs? Maybe I could inspire you."

"I'll work on it," Jason said, arching his eyebrows. "Maybe you and Ash can work on me later."

"We'll see," Wendy said.

"No, we won't," Ashley told him.

"Let's play," Kyle said.

"Hey, what's this?" Wendy asked, pulling the piece of paper out of Palance's guitar case. "It looks like a song."

"Hey," Palance yelled. He was usually calm, but felt angry. Beth walked over to Wendy and held out her hand, glaring, until Wendy handed over the piece of paper. She glanced at it, walked back, and handed it to Palance.

"New song?" Jason asked.

"Let's play something," Kyle said, trying to diffuse the tension in the room. No one seemed happy.

"Kyle's going to New York. Ithaca, New York," Melody blurted out, looking proud of herself.

"Yeah," Jason said. "We know. In September. Cornell."

"No, next week," Kyle said. "Wednesday. I've got an internship lined up at EMF. My dad knows someone who works there. I'm going to stay with them for the summer and then move to the dorm in September."

"So, is this is our last gig?" Palance asked.

"Maybe next summer," Kyle said.

Palance fooled around on his guitar, not playing a song, just a few notes; then he chunked out a chord. He couldn't even get it together to play an actual song. Jason tried to follow him, but after punching a few notes, he gave up, asking Ashley and Wendy if they wanted to go outside and take a walk with him. He held his thumb and index finger together up to his mouth and sucked in a breath. Kyle got up, saying he'd be right back.

Kyle walked up the stairs, and Beth asked if anyone wanted a Coke or a sandwich. Instead of answering, they walked over to the trays and started eating. Melody poured drinks, and

Palance started on the chips; then he rummaged through the sandwiches and picked one.

"You're good," Melody said to Palance. "I saw you guys play. Last month in the park."

"Thanks."

"He doesn't know how good," Beth said. "Except when he's stoned. Then he's full of himself."

"Trying to cut down," Palance said.

"What about Jason?" Melody asked.

"He's always stoned," Beth said.

Palance shrugged his shoulders and lifted his hands in frustration. Kyle came back down and joined them. He and Palance looked at each other for a long time without saying a word.

Palance finally said, "I'm gonna miss you, man."

"Yeah," Kyle said.

"Boys," Melody said, shaking her head. "You guys have been friends for how long?"

"Second grade," Kyle answered.

"And this is how you say goodbye?" Melody asked.

"I'm not the one who's leaving," Palance said, finished his sandwich, and walked back to his guitar. Beth shrugged her shoulders at Melody and sat next to him.

Jason, Wendy, and Ashley stumbled down the stairs, laughing and giggling.

"There's the prodigal son," Palance said, disgusted and jealous, even though he knew he had the better deal with Beth. J-bird had two hot-looking girls hanging off him, and they both looked like they were ready to do his bidding. He longed to party like Jason sometimes.

"What was that game we were playing?" Ashley asked. "Oh, yeah. I think that Kyle's gonna be . . . a drummer," she said, and literally fell down, laughing.

"Why don't you get some food in you?" Kyle said, causing Wendy to fall over in a fit of hilarity.

"We'll eat," Ashley said, "if you play," attempting to point at Kyle. She twisted a bit, as if she had been spun around and was having a hard time finding her balance.

"One last time?" Kyle asked Palance, looking apologetic.

"One last time," Palance replied. "You up for it, Jason?"

"I'm always up," he said.

"A little too high," Palance muttered and put his arms around his two bandmates as they walked back to their instruments. "One last hurrah for The Whispering Screams."

Jason began playing, and Palance followed Jason. The bass lines were solid and melodic. Jason's eyes were locked on Palance. In this journey, they traveled together. Kyle, for all his stiffness, was as determined on his instrument as he was in life. He guided them home.

Wendy and Ashley applauded unreasonably. Melody glared at them as if they were misbehaving children.

"Play that 'old and young' song you wrote," Beth said. "If that's okay."

Jason and Kyle began, and he had little choice but to join in. *Too old to be so young, too young to be so wise, too wise to be a child,* he sang. Palance didn't feel old or young or wise—he felt abandoned. They finished the song. So much more had ended.

"J-bird," Palance asked, "what do you want to play?"

Jason started playing "Cocaine Blues." Kyle raised his eyebrows toward Palance, who looked a bit uncomfortable, but played along, half-heartedly joining in on the chorus. Palance didn't like the increasing role drugs had taken in Jason's life. He was no saint. He'd smoked his share of weed, but he'd always *maintained*—Jason's word—which is more than he could say for his friend.

"So, what are you going to major in?" Melody asked Jason.

"Sex, drugs, and rock 'n roll."

"I'm majoring in . . ." Kyle started to say.

"Business." Jason and Palance both finished his sentence together. Kyle let a smile creep onto his face.

"We'll probably all work for him someday," Palance said affectionately.

"Speak for yourself," Jason told him. "Hey, Pal, you never said what you're going for."

"I'm gonna try a couple of things. Music, communications, maybe even drama. To help with the stage act. So," he said hesitantly, "when are we going to get together again? We should make plans. Thanksgiving? Winter break?"

"We'll get together, man," Jason said.

Kyle looked uncomfortable. Beth moved closer to Palance and leaned against him.

"One more song, guys," Jason said. "Then these lovely ladies have plans for me."

"Yeah," Ashley said, "to take you home."

"Take me home and have your way with me. Yeah, I know that's what you girls want."

"Yeah, like my folks would be cool with that," Ashley said.

"Yeah, right," Wendy said and laughed. "But maybe we could make a stop."

"Okay, Kyle," Jason said. "You're blowing town first—you pick."

Kyle looked at Palance, and said, "I defer to our leader."

"I always thought you were our leader," Palance said.

Kyle shook his head and said, "It's you, man. It's always been you." Jason smiled at Palance and nodded.

"Then let's jam," Palance said, all the while thinking, *This may never happen again. Kyle may sell his drum kit for a calculator and Jason pawn his bass for drugs. This is real, the three of us.* Jason came out of his stupor long enough to guide them. Palance might be their leader, but it was Jason who kept the music together.

Palance and Jason locked eyes, and though Jason wasn't leaving yet, it was Jason he would miss the most. It was only the gigs that kept them together now, and saying goodbye to Jason would be painful. So, they played, and when there was an opening, Palance took the music back, back as far as he could remember it. Back to "Walking in Memphis," the first song he and Jason ever played together. When they finished, Palance put his guitar on the stand. Jason put a hand on his shoulder in a rare moment of compassion.

Palance managed a smile, and said, "Thank you, man," to Jason, who smiled at him the way he always did, like a boy perpetually caught with his hand in the cookie jar, too cute to be punished. They clasped hands, reluctant to let go.

"Forever, man," Jason said back to him. "I'll be in touch."

"Do that," Palance said. He was grateful when Jason turned his attention to Kyle and he was left in the shadows formed by

Kyle's drum set and his guitar. He observed his two bandmates saying their piece and clasping hands. Beth exchanged words with Wendy and Ashley. Palance packed up his gear. Jason gave Beth a kiss on the forehead and told her to watch out for his friend. Palance said goodbye to Wendy and Ashley, who wouldn't hear of it. They told him they'd see him around, at his next gig.

"You okay to drive?" Palance asked Ashley.

"I'll manage, Dad," she said. Palance held onto Beth as Jason walked up the steps and was gone.

Palance and Kyle gazed at each other in silence. Beth walked over to Melody. Palance had always thought of Kyle as a pain in the ass, but now it felt as if he were losing a part of himself. He was angry with Kyle for leaving like this. He wanted to tell him to get the fuck out of here, him and his set of rules and what he would and wouldn't allow, but instead, he said, "Have a good summer."

"Yeah, I guess."

"It's been . . . it's been great."

"Thanks."

"For what?" Palance asked.

"You kept the band together. You kept Jason together, at least this far. I'll miss you."

"You too, man." Palance shook his hand, but it seemed too little. He pulled him in and hugged him. Kyle slapped him on the back three times. "You always did like waltz time," Palance said.

"Keep it steady," Kyle told him.

Palance turned to walk out. He grabbed his guitar and stand. Beth walked with him as he wished Melody a good summer. Halfway up the stairs, he turned around. Kyle looked familiar and tragic, sitting at his drum set, not even the whole kit, no other instruments around him.

"Don't forget my number," Palance told him.

"Oh, I've got your number," Kyle said.

Palance raised his fist halfheartedly. "You're a pain in the ass," he said.

"You, too."

"I'm gonna miss you."

"You, too."

Beth held the door open for him and let him through, out into the night, and gazed back before stepping out into the darkness. He opened the car door and popped the trunk, carefully laying his guitar and stand in there. He closed it carefully, just a click as it shut, and opened the passenger door for Beth. He didn't even turn on the radio.

"What time is it?" she asked.

"11:30," he said. "Early. Any ideas?"

"Yeah, let's go by the school."

"Rogers?"

"Yeah."

"Okay," he said, and drove west on Jarvis, turning right onto Washtenaw. The sign in front of Philip Rogers Elementary School told him to *Have a Great Summer*, and he pulled into the parking lot.

"Take your guitar," Beth said, walking into the park, ahead of him, the crickets chirping. "Meet me by the icehouse," she called over her shoulder, and began skipping toward it.

Palance flashed to winter days, when they would flood the depression in the field and turn it into an ice-skating rink. There was a little green shack with a potbelly stove inside they called "the icehouse." Palance lugged his guitar out of the trunk and walked toward Beth, following the sound of her steps in the grass. She was twenty yards ahead of him.

"What's your hurry?" he asked, catching up to her at the door of the icehouse, padlocked shut. She placed her hands on either side of his face. She kissed him and told him to open his guitar case. Palance took out his instrument.

"Play the song in your guitar case for me."

"It's too dark to see."

"You hear a song on the radio once or twice, and you can play it," she said. "You can play this."

Palance tuned the guitar. In the distance, he could see shadows and movement in the cars parked on the street. They were not alone, but the shadows hid them. Beth's green eyes were bright and softly focused. He saw the frame of her hair and felt her breath when she exhaled. She sat close enough that their knees touched. A car drove by. Palance waited for the droning engine to fade and sang to her softly.

My ships are torn and tattered, my cities are in flame, the sky is dark and shattered, and turned to rain. At night my dreams are scattered, awake I feel the pain, my soul is burned and battered, all that remains.

He felt adrift. *So when the battle's lost and the end is near, who pays the cost, who stays the fear, who'll raise a hand, who'll shed a tear, on shifting sand in the new frontier.* Then, he sang the line he stole from Lin Foon, *Where do we go from here?*

The hero always goes home at the end of the book, but home was childhood, and he couldn't go back. *Nothing left behind me, no direction home, no one left to guide me, I stand alone.* Palance looked at Beth. He wanted to tell her she was the one, shining piece of his life that remained. He had a moment before the next line, and kissed her gently, as if her lips were gossamer. *Many roads to travel, many rivers run, and many paths unravel before they're done.*

He played the chorus again, *Where do we go from here? When the journey fails and the angels wail, and the shadows blend and the night descends.* He finished the last bit of verse. *North Star still to guide me, wind to fill my sails, I know what's inside me, I'll brave the gale.* Palance sang the chorus again, ending with, *Where do we go from here?* He put the guitar back in its case. Beth was silent in this moment when he felt so vulnerable, and then leaned into him, laying her head in his lap. He stroked her hair gently. She rose onto her knees and kissed him full on, stroking his hair and caressing his face. She looked into his eyes as if they held the answer to some mystery.

"That was," she said, "so beautiful."

"It's not a band song," he said, accusing himself.

"It's your song," she said. "It's real."

He blushed.

"You're not alone," she said. "I'm here." She stroked his hair, kissing him gently on the lips. She took his hand and placed it over her heart, against her breast. "I'm here."

Palance left his hand on her breast and guided her tenderly closer, returning her kisses, first gently, and then more passionately. Beth looked around and, seeing no one near, hidden among the bushes and shadows, lay down on the ground, pulling Palance with her. There, on the grass, in the shadow of his childhood, they made love for the first time.

River of Arpeggios

Where Do We Go From Here?

My ships are torn and tattered,
My cities are in flame,
The sky is dark and shattered
And turned to rain.
At night my dreams are scattered,
Awake I feel the pain,
My soul is burned and battered,
All that remains.

C   *So when the battle's lost, and the end is near*
H   *Who pays the cost, who stays the fear*
O   *Who'll raise a hand, who'll shed a tear*
R   *On shifting sand*
U   *In the new frontier,*
S   *Where do we go from here?*

Nothing left behind me,
No direction home,
No one left to guide me,
I stand alone.
Many roads to travel,
Many rivers run,
Many paths unravel
Before they're done.

Chorus

When the journey fails,
And the angels wail,
And the shadows blend,
And the night descends,
North Star still to guide me,
Wind to fill my sails,
I know what's inside me,
I'll brave the gale.

Chorus

Beth's Song:
No Words to Speak

*P**alance didn't know how long** it had been miss-ing.* His mother went into a cleaning frenzy for Thanksgiving, and when he went down to the basement for a screwdriver, his father's guitar was gone. It had been years since she'd forced him to take off the strings, but he always touched the case for luck, and today, on his birthday, it was gone.

He didn't want to confront his Mom. She bought him the used Honda Civic for graduation, his birthday, and Hanukah. They'd been getting along, and everything was going great with Beth. Even school didn't bum him out. Did she toss it? Could she do that?

Palance went upstairs and found Jillian in her room. He leaned in. "Hey, perfect child, do you know what Mom's been up to?"

"What do you mean?"

"Anything weird?"

"It's Mom. Be specific."

Palance hesitated. He didn't want to upset her by bringing up Dad, and he was afraid that saying the words would make them true. "Dad's guitar is missing. She's on one of her benders, and she's tossing stuff left and right. She wouldn't throw it out, would she?"

"Don't know. Did you ask her?"

"You know how she gets."

"Ask her."

Palance decided to wait a day or two.

Thanksgiving, last night, was okay, but he missed Dad. Really missed him. He wanted to play him the songs he'd written. That was never going to happen.

Mom yelled, "Lunch is ready," and he walked down the stairs with Jilly behind him. On the table was a rehash of yesterday's dinner, without the fancy presentation. The turkey carcass was half gone, and the marshmallows had been surgically removed from the sweet potatoes.

"Anything new, Mom?" Palance asked.

"Not really, Pal, but thanks for asking," she said, looking quizzically at him. It was not a question he asked much. "What's new with you? I can't believe you're going to be nineteen." She took a few pieces of turkey and small portions of the side dishes.

"I'm not expecting anything," he told her. "I know the Honda's for my birthday, too."

"You're a lucky duck," Jillian said.

"What are you up to today?" his Mom asked.

"Beth's coming over, and we're going to Jason's. He's in from Southern." Kyle was staying in New York. Whenever he called, Kyle didn't have time to talk and rarely called him back.

"You two serious?" his Mom asked.

"Palance is never serious," Jilly said.

"You're a busybody," Palance told her, scooping cranberry sauce onto his plate.

"Serious?" his Mother asked.

"Hard to tell," he answered, not wanting to give anything away.

"Get through college," she told him. "It's important to have a diploma."

Jillian cut off a few slices of white meat, took a Kaiser roll, and made a sandwich with the cranberry sauce. "You're the best cook," she said to Mom.

"Do you have homework this weekend?" Palance's Mother asked him.

"I'm in college."

"I have a paper due on Monday," Jillian announced. "*Hamlet*."

"I know you're in college," his Mom said. "Why is everything a struggle with you?"

"Why doesn't anyone pay attention to me?" Jillian asked, spooning mashed potatoes onto her plate.

"You get good grades," their Mother answered. "I don't need to worry about you."

"Oh, so I'm the fuck-up," Palance said. "Happy damn birthday to me." He heaped a mountain of sweet potatoes onto his plate.

"I want you to do well," she said. "I'm not The Inquisition. But you're in college now, so it's your business."

"Sorry."

"I have to go to work soon, but there is one birthday surprise left for you. It's not from me, though."

"Who's it from?"

"You'll see. When I get home."

"And I'm taking you out to dinner next week for your birthday," Jillian said. "I think it's time we started communicating as adults."

"You're an odd one," Palance said to his sister, picking up a drumstick and taking a bite. "But I won't trade you in. Yet."

"How's Jason doing?" his Mom asked.

"Not sure," Palance said. "You know J-bird. He's a man of few words. How come you have to work today? It's a holiday."

"Hospitals don't close for holidays. I was lucky to get yesterday off. I should be home by midnight."

"But you're not a doctor or anything," Palance said.

"Takes more than doctors to run a hospital."

Jillian shook her head, looking supremely annoyed. "Don't you know anything?" she asked him.

"I know I have a date tonight, and you don't."

"I am so jealous," Jillian said, rolling her eyes. "I'm going to get my homework done."

"Are you really taking me out to dinner?" Palance asked his sister.

Jillian waited until she was finished chewing to answer him. "You have your choice of Kow-Kow or Barnaby's. Those are both within my budget. How is Wednesday?"

Palance stood up and kissed the top of her head. "You're the best," he said. "Kow-Kow on Wednesday is perfect."

"I wish I could bottle this moment," their mother said, smiling. As she opened the door to leave, Beth was standing there, about to ring the doorbell. "Come in, dear," she said.

"Hello, Mrs. Heller."

"You can call me 'Elaine,'" she told Beth. "We're not very formal around here."

"Thanks, Elaine," Beth said. It sounded odd to Palance. He called his mother "Elaine" when she wasn't around.

"Don't do anything I wouldn't do," his mother said. She started out the door, turned around and added, "I mean it."

Palance watched as she backed out of the driveway before he put his arms around Beth's waist and pulled her to him. "I missed you," he said.

"I didn't miss you at all," she said, kissing him. "I don't even like you."

"Liar."

"Maybe," she said. "Maybe I missed you a little."

"You two are disgusting," Jillian said, walking out of the room. "But cute."

"Stay straight tonight," Beth said to Palance.

"Straight as an arrow. Straight as the crow flies."

"I mean it," she said. "Jason's a great guy, but he's a bad influence."

"I thought I was the bad influence."

"You are," she said. "That's why I'm driving. But I'd still like you to stay straight."

Palance told her, "One second," kissed her, and went back for his guitar. "I have a surprise for you," he told her. "Maybe we could stop at the park afterward."

"I can't stay out late," she said. "And it's cold."

"Just for a few minutes."

"Promise?" she asked him.

"Promise," he said.

Beth's car was her Mom's black Camry. It was showroom clean and smelled of lilac and pine from the scented air freshener that hung like an icon from the rearview mirror.

"What should I do with my life?" Beth asked, out of the blue. "I might want to be a teacher . . . or an editor."

"A teacher? Why would you want to do that?"

"I think it might be fun."

"Just stick with me, baby," Palance told her. "When I'm rich and famous, we'll party with the stars."

"I think the stars are all in your head."

"Don't you think I have what it takes?"

"I think you're wonderful. I'm not sure you know what's important."

"I do, too," he declared adamantly, wondering what that was.

"What?" she challenged.

"You are," he told her, a wry smile lighting his face.

"And what else?" she asked, pulling up to Jason's house.

"Later," he told her, kissing her on the lips and then leaping out of the car.

Beth caught up to him at the front door, where they heard Jason ranting at his parents. Jason's mother was sobbing, and his father was shouting in between Jason's claims of innocence and slander. They stood back from the door as they heard it rattle and pop. Jason, in only his shirt and jeans, erupted forcefully and looked startled to see them on his front steps. He quickly recovered his composure.

"Aren't you a sight for sore eyes," Jason exclaimed. His eyes were wide. "Cold for Thanksgiving," he said.

"Especially without a jacket. Or shoes. How's school?" Beth asked. Jason looked frightened.

"Sex, drugs, rock 'n roll," he said. "All good. Classes suck."

"So, I guess we're not going to hang out at your house," Palance said.

"The environment is not quite suitable at the moment," Jason answered. "But I have an idea. How do you feel about beatniks, Old Bean?"

Palance bristled at the nickname, but let it slide. "I have no idea what you're talking about," he said.

"I heard about this coffeehouse a few blocks from here. Like where the beatniks used to hang."

"Who's there now?" Palance asked.

"Let's find out," Jason said.

"Okay with you?" Palance asked Beth, who was shivering in her thin coat.

"If they've got heat, I'm in," she said.

"One second," Jason told them, listening at the door. When he didn't hear anything, he ran back into his house.

"Man. I thought my Mom . . ." Palance said, shaking his head.

"I don't want to party with the rich and famous," Beth said. "Huh?"

"The Wizard of Oz," she told him.

"The Wizard of Oz?"

"Watch it with me sometime. It'll tell you where to find what you need."

The shouting started again. As if someone had hit "Rewind," the door exploded, and Jason propelled himself outside, slamming the door behind him and breathing heavily, this time holding his jacket and a pair of sneakers.

"What the hell is going on?" Palance asked.

"Forgot something," Jason said.

"What?"

"Pipe dreams."

"Follow the yellow brick road," Beth said. Palance wasn't sure who she was talking to.

"I'll be over the rainbow as soon as we're in the car," Jason said.

"Not in my mother's car, you won't," Beth told him. "No smoking. Anything."

Jason put on his coat, not bothering to button it, and then his shoes – no socks.

"So, where's this beatnik place?" Palance asked, getting into the front passenger seat.

"Man, I'm always riding in back. I don't get no respect," he said.

"Coffeehouse?" Palance said, looking directly at Jason, watching him drift into space.

"East on Touhy to Ashland, then right on Ashland to Lunt," Jason told him.

Beth drove past the school, along the circumference of the park. She squeezed Palance's hand as they passed the grove of trees that hid the icehouse. On Touhy, the houses gave way to storefronts and bars, turning into apartment buildings as they passed Ridge, and curved to the right past Damen.

"You missed it," Jason said, as they glided past Ashland.

"I want to see the lake," Beth said.

"You afraid they took it away?" Jason asked.

"I like the water," she replied.

At Sheridan, she turned right, then left onto Greenleaf, and the lake appeared. She pulled the car as close as possible, and parked with an unobstructed view of the water. Beyond the patchy grass and the golden sand, the water was grayish green, and the shallow waves were choppy. The horizon emerged with little contrast, making it hard to tell where the water ended, and the sky began.

"Another gray day in Chicago," Jason moaned.

"Shut up," Beth said, surprising them. "It's a miracle," she said, and the three of them sat in silence as she gazed out at the water, her hand clasping Palance's hand. He knew better than to interrupt. After a few minutes, she turned to the back seat and politely asked Jason where to drive. He directed her back onto Sheridan, left to Lunt, then right on Lunt to Glenwood.

"There are two Glenwoods," he said.

"Two Glenwoods?" she asked.

"One going north and one going south."

"Like life," she said, and Palance smiled at the way she kept him off balance.

"Go south," Jason said.

"Don't you always?" she replied, and drove through the old-world streets where the shops had been integrated into apartment buildings, dark-brown brick with European-style courtyards. The streets were dark and narrow.

"Here's Glenwood," Jason announced. The 'L-Tracks' loomed above them, and underneath, bright graffiti lined the walls. Two men were standing, smoking cigarettes. "Left after the tracks."

They parked down the street from The No Exit Café and Gallery, ancient music resonating from the fogged picture window. Their footsteps on the pavement echoed against the concrete as they entered the coffee-infused room. Brown wooden tables and rickety chairs huddled around a stage inside the window well, where a woman played a beat-up Stella guitar and sang, while a man accompanied her on a banjo. The woman fingerpicked patterns Palance hadn't heard before, singing about Barbr'y Allen, witchcraft, and unrequited love. The L-train roared past, drowning out the music; then a roaring *whoosh* from the espresso machine drowned out everything.

A woman in tight pink pants and purple tie-dyed t-shirt told them there was a five-dollar cover charge and let them know they could sit wherever they'd like. They moved cautiously, strangers in a foreign land, careful not to bump people or furniture. When they found a table, Palance sat facing the stage, Jason to his left, and Beth on his right. Palance ordered an espresso, and they brought it in a thick white mug. Jason ordered a cappuccino that overflowed with steamed milk, and Beth chose hot chocolate.

Jason patted his pants pocket, said he had to expand his mind, and headed to the washroom. Palance followed with his eyes, while Beth shook her head. If Palance was going to get high tonight, he'd have to be discreet.

The man on stage was singing an old blues song about horses and crossroads in a deep growling voice. Palance held Beth's hand and watched the woman on stage. Her fingers dipped and bent. She used the high string for the melody while her two middle fingers clawed at the top strings in an oscillating drone. Palance leaned in to kiss Beth, and their lips pressed together.

"Do you like this?" he asked her, but before she could answer, Jason came faltering out of the washroom and steered himself back to his chair.

"Like hep-ville," he said after he had settled. His voice was loud, and the couple on stage looked over. He hunched his shoulders and lowered his head in mock embarrassment.

"I like it," Palance said.

"Me, too," Beth added.

The L-train rumbled, and the café rattled and hummed. The espresso machine *whooshed*.

"So, what's Southern like?" Beth asked. "I've got to figure out where to go next year."

Palance had assumed she would stay in town with him.

"It's okay," Jason said with a shrug, turning his head so that his eyes disappeared from view. "It's a little small for me. I don't think I'm going to stay."

The woman on stage sang something old and British, four women named Mary and one of them about to die. Palance attended to each note. The chords were simple and plaintive, and the harmony alluring.

The waitress chewed gum and asked if they needed anything. Beth nodded and Palance asked for another espresso and a hot chocolate. Jason said he'd try an espresso.

"Maybe Pal and I could visit you downstate sometime, if that'd be okay," Beth asked Jason. "We'll see," Jason said. "Pretty amazing place."

"Southern?" Beth asked.

"No, here," Jason snapped.

"I love this," Palance said, sincerely. "Man, I wonder if I could play here sometime."

From behind, Palance heard a man say they had an open mic on Monday nights. "Come early," he said. "The signup sheet fills quickly."

Palance pictured himself on the stage. He'd need a younger crowd in here. He could put up flyers around school. He felt lost since the band broke up. The songs he had been writing were quieter. This would be a good place to try them out. If the open mic went well, he might be able to get a gig here. He imagined himself like the old folksingers his father listened to, Bob Dylan and Dave Van Ronk. He wondered how it would feel to command the stage on his own.

Palance took a sip of the espresso and felt a rush. Beth and Jason glared at each other.

"Been playing any music, J-bird?" Palance asked.

"Music, yeah," Jason said, and the anger washed from his face. "Been hanging with some older guys downstate. Heavy, heavy dudes."

"What are they majoring in?" Beth asked. Jason looked at her without answering.

"What kind of music?" Palance asked Jason.

"Grunge and metal, man. A lot heavier than what we were doing."

The words stung. Palance felt replaced—and more determined to branch out on his own.

"Good players?" Palance asked.

"The best," Jason said. Palance grew quiet, and his eyes lowered. Beth put her hand on his. She could sense the rage burning inside him. He wanted to accuse Jason of being a traitor.

"I'm thinking of going solo," Palance said.

"Man, I envy you," Jason told him.

"You *envy* me?" Palance asked. "Why?"

"Ever try going solo with a bass? You're a great songwriter."

"Thanks," Palance said. "There are guys in my classes who wish they could play half as well as you."

"Classes," Jason answered. "There's a concept."

"What do you mean?"

"College doesn't leave me much time for classes. I've got more important things to do. Excuse me, nature calls," Jason said, standing up to head for the washroom.

"Are you," Palance asked, "maintaining?"

"Live fast," he answered. "Die young. Leave a good-looking corpse."

"I need you around, man."

"Hey, you're a solo act. Remember?" Jason said, leaving him alone with Beth.

"I worry about him," he said to Beth.

"Do what you can," she said, "but be careful. He scares me, and I worry about you."

"About me?"

"Yeah, you," she said. Grabbing his shirt with both hands, she pulled him toward her. "You." She kissed him fiercely and wrapped her arms around him, as if she were afraid he would run away.

The musicians took a break and the L-train rumbled by. Palance and Beth sat quietly as the night washed over them. The waitress scratched her head with a pen, sauntered over, and asked if they needed anything else. Palance ordered one more espresso, and Beth asked for a glass of water.

"What about your friend?" the waitress asked.

"He'll be back soon," Beth told her. "Maybe you should check on him, Pal."

"Be right back," Palance said, and headed to the washroom. When he got there, the door swung open. Jason sat, fully clothed, on the single toilet, a lit joint in his hand.

"Just in time," Jason said, and reached out to hand Palance the joint.

Palance felt the sweet haze of being stoned. After all, Beth was the one who'd sent him back here, and he wasn't driving. But he didn't want to disappoint Beth. He had a song to play for her, and he needed it to be perfect.

"Nah, man," he told Jason. "You want more coffee or anything?"

"I've got everything I need right here."

"Sorry, man," Palance said wincing. "You might want to lock the door." He turned around and looked at Beth, sitting alone at their table. He looked at some of the other patrons, and saw the same look in their eyes he saw in Jason's.

"Jason doesn't need anything," Palance told Beth, leaning down to kiss her before taking his seat. The musicians reappeared on the stage, and Jason headed back from the washroom, wending his way through the tables. He looked lost. The man and woman sang an old English ballad, and Palance took Beth's hand.

"What?" she asked.

"Just you," he told her. The espresso machine *whooshed*. The music surrounded him. "So, old bean," Palance said, throwing the expression back at Jason, "thanks for bringing us here."

"No worries," he answered. "No worries at all."

Palance stared into his coffee cup. It unfolded like a fortune teller's crystal ball. In the thin layer of foam, he saw himself playing in this dark oasis to hone his skills, to write and perform his songs, hidden from sight, and then rising into a universe of bright lights, large speakers, and a darkened throng of fans cheering his every breath. He saw Beth standing nearby in the background, allowing him to be worshiped. He willed Jason and Kyle to be there with him, but they faded into the edge of his dream and disappeared like vapors. When he looked up, Beth was watching him, and Jason was nodding off.

Patrons were leaving. The waitress was bussing the tables and wiping them down. The L-trains ran less frequently, and the espresso machine was silent. Palance heard the music clearly. The din—which he had barely noticed—was gone, and the couple on stage announced their last song.

"It's getting late," Beth said.

Jason raised his head and pled for one more song.

"I didn't know you were listening, man," Palance said.

"I'm always listening," Jason told him.

"I'll be right back," Beth said, and headed toward the restroom.

Palance smiled at Jason and said, "Good find, man."

"You should have been a beatnik," Jason told him. "Hell, you are. Just fifty years too late."

"Yeah. You should have been one of those jazz bebop dudes. They played better the more stoned they got."

"Like, wow, man," Jason said.

"But take it easy, okay?"

"Live fast . . ."

"I know, man. But I want you around."

"I'll do my best," Jason said.

"You always do," Palance told him.

Beth came out of the washroom and walked back to the table. The music was over, and the waitress handed them their check. Jason reached into his pocket, but Palance stopped him and took out two twenties to cover their tab.

"Birthday money," he told him. "Your money's no good here."

"Hey, man, that's right. Happy damn birthday. What are you now, nine or ninety?"

"Nineteen tomorrow," Palance said, punching him on the arm. "Same age as you."

"I'm eighteen," Jason said. "I'll be eighteen until I die."

"Are you going to be okay at home tonight?" Beth asked Jason.

"Don't worry about me, *mon chéri*. The folks crash early, and tomorrow morning I am outta here, a free man."

"How're you getting back to school?" Palance asked.

"Who said anything about school?"

"Huh?" Beth said.

"We've got gigs lined up in bars from Carbondale to St. Louis. Far as I'm concerned, I'm fully educated."

"What's the name of the band?" Palance asked.

"Eve of Destruction," Jason answered. "Pretty righteous, huh?"

"Pretty appropriate," Beth told him.

"You live your life," he said, "I'll live mine."

The waitress removed the cups and spoons from their table, and they were alone in the café. Palance asked the waitress if he could sit on the stage for a minute, just to check it out. She shrugged and told him to go ahead.

"I'll just be a minute," he told Beth and walked up to the stage, looking out the window at the street and holding his breath before he placed one foot on the platform and pushed himself up onto the boards. They creaked under his weight, and he sat on the stool where the woman had been sitting. "Hey," he called to the waitress as she walked past, "Open mic on Monday?"

"Eight o'clock," she said.

Tonight, Palance had a song to sing to Beth, and this weekend he'd need to practice. For Monday he was hoping for a bigger audience. He walked back to the table.

"I guess we closed the place," Palance said to Beth.

"I guess we did," she replied, wrapping her arms around his waist and leaning against him as they walked toward the door.

"Later," the waitress said to them.

Palance looked back at her and then at the stage. "Later," he said. The night was cold and frosty. The wind off the lake sounded like the espresso machine. As they got into the car, an L-train roared by.

"How can I get in touch with you?" Palance asked Jason on the ride back.

"We're gonna be big," Jason said. "You'll know where I am."

"Until then?"

"Until then, I'm just dust in the wind."

"Dust in the wind?"

"Yeah."

They dropped Jason off in front of his house. Beth waited as he stumbled up the steps and managed to let himself in the front door.

"Quick stop at the park?" Palance asked.

"It's too cold for that," Beth said.

"Not that. Just five minutes. It has to be the park."

"Okay," she said.

They drove south to Morse, then west through the apartment buildings and old-world stores, the Korean restaurants, Jewish delicatessens, and shoe-repair shops, until the buildings scaled down into single-family bungalows, then north on Ridge, where the storefronts lined the street and the apartments squatted above them. Beth turned west on Touhy, where everything looked more modern, then north on Washtenaw. It was cold, and even with the heater on, she was shivering. He didn't want to ask her to get out of the car. He could manage this with her window open, but he wanted it to be here, where they first made love.

Palance asked Beth to stay where she was and to pop the trunk, and, when she saw him near the window, to crank it open a few inches, so she could stay warm. She nodded and said, "Okay." He walked to the back of the car, lifted the trunk, unlatched the guitar case, and took out the Seagull. His fingers were cold as he strapped on the guitar. He tuned it by ear, and saw Beth watching him in the rearview mirror.

His fingers formed a D-chord. It was too cold to finger-pick. He strummed gently and stood back a few inches from the window. Beth opened it wide. She had her jacket wrapped around her shoulders. Even before he started, the cold had invaded her eyes. They watered and sparkled. He played the opening chord progression, D to B-minor, then G to A, and softly—she was only inches away—he sang *Naked come into this world, cold and hungry, gasping air. With every cry a song unfurls and every breath a sacred prayer. Every day I rise to hear the parched and anguished cries.*

No words to speak, nowhere to go, a stranger place I'll never know. Jason and Kyle had deserted him. Beth and his music were all he had left. He wanted her to feel his gratitude, and his love. *I am held in loving arms, please keep me safe, and keep me warm.* He saw a single tear float under Beth's left eye and didn't know if it was the cold or the song.

Palance continued playing the A-seventh chord until her eyes met his, and then sang, *Precious child, young and wild, tended me with gentle hands.* Droplets ran down both sides of her face. *Gave me peace to reconcile, stranger in a stranger land, and every day I rise, to feel a love so deep and wide.* Palance stifled a tear of his own. *No words to speak, nowhere to go. A stranger place I'll never know. But I am held in loving arms, please keep me safe and keep me warm.*

There was a catch in Palance's throat. *And on that tender night, with nothing going right. Moon and stars and passing cars*—Palance closed his eyes—*shimmered as our souls took flight.*

Thought that I'd be cast away, left without a saving grace. Set aside and led astray, to disappear without a trace. Now every day I rise, and wonder how far I might fly.

Palance sang the chorus again, his voice remarkably soft and clear. The second time around, he sang only *No words to speak*; then skipped the next three lines, coming back on *I am held in loving arms*, and his final plea, *Keep me safe and keep me warm*. Palance kissed Beth through the window, her tears running down her face. He didn't care about the cold. This moment was perfect. He removed the strap, latched the guitar back in its case, shut the trunk, and climbed in next to her.

Palance wanted to hear Beth's words, but tears were streaming down her face. Her arms enveloped him. He felt her body pulse and held her, thankful for her and the warmth from the car heater. Beth released herself from Palance's arms and put her hands on the steering wheel. After a few seconds, she relinquished herself to him again, planting kisses on his head, though she did not meet his eyes. Two cars passed by, honked their horns, and a siren wailed in the distance. The windows fogged over, and Beth turned on the defroster, waited for the windows to clear, and put the car in drive.

It was only a short drive home. She, however, was headed in the wrong direction, east, back toward the lake.

"I can't," she said, and pulled over on Touhy before Ridge in front of the Mexican Restaurant. She bowed her head, her hands still at ten and two on the steering wheel, and turned to look at him. "I can't believe you wrote that for me. It's beautiful."

"Thank you," he said, thrilled and embarrassed by her reaction. Her tears overwhelmed him. He wanted to tell her that he loved her; he wanted to tell her everything that was in the song.

"You are so . . . creative . . . and so thoughtful. Sometimes," she added, her tears still flowing, "most of the time." After a moment, she calmed down and the tears stopped. Palance leaned over and kissed them from her face. "It's getting late," she said.

"You can come over for a while," he said. He didn't want to let her go yet. "I could make coffee."

"Coffee? More coffee? What kind of fiend are you?"

"I just . . ."

"I love you," Beth told him. "That was the most beautiful thing anyone's done for me. Ever."

"I love you, too."

"But no more coffee. Not tonight." A cruiser car came up from behind them with blue lights flashing, and Palance fought the urge to duck down in the car. It passed them, heading south on Ridge. Beth turned off the engine, unbuckled her seat belt, and turned toward him. She placed her hands on his face, holding him still. She released him as she belted herself back in and put her hands back on the steering wheel.

"I love you, Beth Howry," he said, and, with an air of recklessness. she floored the car into a U-turn, and headed west down Touhy.

"Uh, where are we going?" he asked as she sped past Kedzie and over the bridge.

"Anywhere," she said.

"Anywhere?"

"Anywhere I don't have to share you with Jason, or parents, or school. Anywhere else."

Beth looked determined and turned north onto the Edens Expressway, headed toward Wisconsin. He waited for her to slow down, but she didn't. She was driving seventy miles an hour in the left lane, passing slower cars on the right. He worried they were going to get pulled over, or worse.

"Beth," he shouted, exasperated.

She looked at him, straight at him, still going seventy, for several more seconds before facing forward, slowing down, and pulling into the middle lane and then the right lane. She took the Tower Road exit, which led them through the forest preserves, and pulled off on the shoulder, the moon directly ahead of them on the tree-lined road.

"What was that?"

"I want you, all the time," she said. "To myself."

"I want you, too. I love you."

"No. You don't get it. I've always been the good girl. I do what my parents say. I get good grades. I'm nice to your asshole friends." She looked at him apologetically. "Sorry, but it's true." Beth sniffled and blew her nose into a tissue from a box on the dashboard. "And you do something so wonderful for me, and then it's time to go home, and I don't want to go home."

"I don't want to go home, either," Palance said.

"We have to go home. I have to go home. I'll be late, and I'll get shit about it, but I have to go home." Beth looked at him, her cheeks still wet with tears. "I love you, Palance Heller. Thank you for the beautiful song."

Palance kissed her and said, "I love you, too."

"I'm taking the long way home," she said. "As long as I'm going to be late, I'm going to be damn late." She continued driving east. Palance was silent.

Beth headed down Tower to Sheridan Road, meandering south along the lakefront. Estates burgeoning with old money stood solemn amidst the trees. Occasionally they glimpsed the water or a mansion or exclusive shop. They held hands. On their right, the Bahai Temple emerged white and sparkling, like a beacon in the dark. It gleamed under spotlights, below the stars and beside the water.

"Hell of a thing," he said to Beth.

"Yeah," she said. Palance was amazed at how relaxed she was, considering she was half an hour past her curfew. He had thought he understood her perfectly.

They passed through Northwestern University's campus, the ancient stone buildings contrasting with modern glass and steel. Palance wished he had the money and grades to go there. He could see himself playing his guitar on the beach. Their music school was world-class. Past the campus, Sheridan thrust and parried through Evanston. Beth sighed and turned right on Oakton. Palance knew she was heading back to Rogers Park and home. He gripped her hand tighter. When the light turned red on Dodge, he leaned over and kissed her, and she extended the kiss, even after the light had changed.

"I want to do something special for you," she said. "But I don't know what."

"What about . . ."

"I want to decide," she said.

"Okay, you decide."

"I'll let you know tomorrow."

Soon they passed into their neighborhood. Beth was calm and Palance desperately dreaded their impending separation.

"Let's drive to Madison tomorrow," Beth said.

"Madison?"

"Yeah."

"Okay," he said.

"There's something I want to show you there," she told him, as if to answer his thoughts.

"What?"

"You'll see," she said.

"See what?" he asked.

"You'll see. That's all I'm saying," and she remained silent through a barrage of questions. His neighborhood felt unusually small and constrained. This was all he knew, all he had ever known, and it wasn't nearly enough.

When they got to his house, his mother's car was there. It was too late to invite Beth in. Her parents would be sitting up anxiously. He could hear them fretting to each other, and he knew those voices were in her head, too.

"Call me as soon as you're up," Palance said, embracing her, hesitant to let her go.

"I'll be up early."

"Call me early."

"Okay."

She leaned in to kiss him. They remained in the car a few minutes before she said, "I need to go." He pulled away from her and held the car door open to look at her again. Palance pulled his guitar out of the trunk and walked toward his house. He watched as she drove away, and then put the key in the lock and opened the front door.

The house was dark. He pulled a glass from the kitchen cabinet and poured himself some water. He drained the water, placed the glass in the dishwasher, and set off to bed.

There was a side of Beth more rebellious and wilder than he'd dreamed. He was proud of her for standing up to Jason. He needed to practice so he could play the open mic at the No Exit and win a gig there, and then, the sky was the limit.

Palance closed the door to his room before he flipped on the light and reached down to pull off his shirt. He spotted something on the bed, and his jaw fell open. His father's guitar case was sitting on his bed. He opened it. The Larriveé sat newly strung and freshly polished. There was a yellow post-it note stuck to the case with his mother's handwriting, small and ornate. *I'm sorry for having you remove the strings. I had to pay to get it fixed, but that was my fault, the neck warped. This is your father's gift to you. He would be proud. Happy Birthday.*

Palance stared down at the Larriveé in all its glory, and lightly flicked a finger across the strings. Music rose in waves, and forgotten memories came flooding back. He knelt in front of the guitar with a sense of awe and wonder.

"Tomorrow," he whispered to the guitar. Still on his knees, Palance closed and latched the case. There were no words to express how perfect his life was right then—how excellent the future appeared. He foolishly believed it would remain that way forever.

River of Arpeggios

Beth's Song

Naked come into this world,
Cold & hungry, gasping air,
With every cry a song unfurls
& every breath a sacred prayer.
& every day I rise,
To hear the parched and anguished cries.

No words to speak,
C *nowhere to go,*
H *A stranger place,*
O *I'll never know,*
R *But I am held*
U *in loving arms,*
S *Please keep me safe,*
  and keep me warm.

Precious child, young and wild,
Tended me with gentle hands,
Gave me peace to reconcile,
Stranger in a stranger land,
And every day I rise,
To feel a love so deep and wide.

Chorus

And on that tender night,

With nothing going right,

Moon and stars and passing cars,

Shimmered as our souls took flight.

Thought that I'd be cast away,

Left without a saving grace,

Set aside and led astray

To disappear without a trace.

Now every day I rise

And wonder how far I might fly.

Chorus

Icarus: Too Close to the Sun

*W*hen Beth left for school, she said, "It's only two hours away."

"Two and a half," he replied.

"They have coffeehouses you can play at. I'll be home lots of weekends. You can visit me." Then she said, "You can transfer there," as if that were possible. Afterward, she left, and he was alone.

Palance was working on a song for school when the phone rang. Beth told him about her classes, dormitory, and new friends. Palance listened and continued to work on his song.

"Tell me about it," she said.

"I asked my Mythology professor if I could write a song about Icarus, instead of an essay. He said okay."

"That's cool. Can you sing it to me?"

"I just started."

"I miss you," she said. He softened, but it was easier if he stayed angry.

"I miss you, too," he told her. "I've got a few lines. The chorus, anyway."

"Can you read me the words?"

Palance hesitated, but read the lyrics to her. *And as you rode the winds in wonder, thunder rumbling through the breeze, did you hear your father calling, falling and tumbling to the sea.*

"That's amazing," she told him.

"Do you know about Icarus?" he asked her.

"Sure. We had Greek mythology in English. Two years ago."

"Oh."

"Maybe they did something else when you took it," she said. Anyway, I wish I had your talent. You are incredible."

"Then how come you're the one with the scholarship?" he asked.

"I study."

"Oh," Palance said.

"Speaking of which," Beth told him.

Palance wished he had ended the conversation first. "I've got to go, too," he said.

"I love you," Beth added.

"Me, too," Palance replied.

The first verse was almost finished, but something wasn't right. He kept the first line, *They caught you flying too close to the sun*, but changed the second from *It felt like dying* to *It felt like drowning on the earth and numb*. The rest of the verse was, *I heard you crying before you learned to fly, I saw you dying, frail against the sky.*

Palance wanted to finish the song before the open mic tonight. He'd already played there three Mondays, but this would be his first time without Beth. He read the story of Icarus in his mythology textbook again, about his father, Daedolus, and the Minotaur. Palance's own life was a maze. Who would help *him* out of trouble the way Daedolus led the Minotaur from the labyrinth, pissing off King Minos? Palance had no trouble pissing people off. He put down a line. *Your father fashioned a vast and winding maze.*

There was something Palance was forgetting, something elemental. *His endless passion stirred the king's great rage.* Palance was irked at allowing Beth to piss him off. Like Icarus, Palance was ready to spread his wings and aim for the sun. *And like a sparrow, locked up in a cage, from wax and feathers grew wings to fly away.* He wanted to book a gig of his own.

Palance sang the chorus quietly in his room. He wondered why, after all the warnings, Icarus ignored his father and flew off into the sun. Was it a death wish? Was it too tempting not to try? *Were you lured into the sunset,* he wrote, *spurred on by the golden light, blinded by the tears that you wept, or running from the night?*

The rest simply appeared. *You were so restless, hard to satisfy, trying to impress, yearning to get high. You tried to possess sun and wind and sky, and for a moment you had wings to fly.* He wrote the words down and then took the Larriveé out of the case. He felt more graceful with it in his hands. He'd used the Seagull for open mics so far, but he'd use the Larriveé tonight. The weather would turn cold soon, and he wouldn't take it out during the winter. His hands automatically went from C to A-minor, then F, then C, and back to A-minor. The tag line at the end of the verse introduced the G-major chord and then returned to the root.

Palance added a bass run after the bridge to create motion. It was six-fifteen. The afternoon had disappeared. He scribbled the chords on the piece of paper with the lyrics and shoved them into his pocket. He had an hour to eat something and get to the coffeehouse. He'd record it for class tomorrow.

Palance stopped at Flukey's for a hot dog and fries. He loved the bright yellow and red décor, the smell of the food, and the redhead behind the counter was nice to look at. Tubs of condiments were set in stainless steel containers behind a glass counter: neon-green pickle relish, yellow mustard, sliced tomatoes, and translucent sauerkraut. He ordered a hot dog with everything, extra sport peppers, fries, and a large drink. "Oh, and can you throw some pickle spears on the side?" Palance was nervous apart from the Larriveé. He glanced back at the Honda on the street, and picked out a table where he'd be able to see his car.

"Hi, Palance," said the redhead behind the counter. "What're you up to?"

"Playing at the No Exit," he said, shrugging his shoulders. "Stop by if you get a chance. Open mic. It's only a two-buck cover."

"What's the No Exit?" she asked.

"Coffeehouse."

"I've got to work until eight-thirty."

"I'll sign up for nine," he told her.

He walked to the soda dispenser and filled his cup with ice and Green River. He loved the green color and the sweet, syrupy taste. Palance kept an eye on his car. Soon he planned to ask for a whole evening at the No Exit. He could make posters and put them up around school and in the neighbor-hood. Biting into his hot dog, he went through a list of friends and classmates who might come. What should he put on the posters? Most of the posters he'd seen had pictures of the performers on them. He wondered if Beth would come back from school on a weekday. Probably not. She told him she'd see him for Thanksgiving.

Palance watched traffic go by on Western Avenue as the light dimmed outside. He played his new song in his head, practicing it in his mind while he was chewing. It was one of the things he had learned in school: Score study. He heard the song in his head and imagined the chord changes as the words slid by. He was humming it to himself when the redhead came up to him.

"Just in case I can make it," she asked, "where is this place?"

"East on Lunt to Glenwood, then south on Glenwood. The No Exit. It looks like the dark ages."

"Who knows," she shrugged.

"This is embarrassing," Palance told her, "but I don't know your name."

"No, you don't," she said, and walked away.

Palance bit into a sport pepper that burned his tongue. He alternately ate his French fries and hot dog, occasionally glancing at the redhead. From the corner of his eye, he thought he saw her pointing him out and whispering with the girl who put the toppings on the hot dogs.

Palance glanced at his watch. It was almost seven-thirty. He knew if the sign-up sheet was full, he wouldn't play. He finished his last bites of food. On his way out he looked at the redhead, but she had her back to him, so he shoved his garbage into the trashcan, took his drink, and left. Leaves were blowing and the wind was chilly.

Palance started his car and turned on the heat. He made a U-turn on Western and turned left onto Pratt. The sun was going down. A siren wailed and a dog barked. He turned left onto Wayne, the cobblestone street. He imagined horses clip-clopping down these same avenues a hundred years ago and wondered if any of these trees were here then. Two-flats lined the streets. Great gray mansions stood back fifty feet from the sidewalk. *There must be stories inside them,* he thought. Wayne ended at Morse, and he jogged onto Glenwood, searching for parking, and found a space on Lunt.

It was seven forty-five when he walked into the coffeehouse, and the signup sheet was almost empty. Only a few people were sitting at the tables, most of them playing chess or Go. The L-train ran frequently. He signed up for the nine o'clock slot and hoped there would be an audience by then. An older man eyed the guitar case. Bare wood, looking as much like a coffin as anything else. Mandy was dressed in blue jeans with a pink button-down shirt and a necklace of bright-green beads.

"Espresso, Pal?" she asked.

"Sure, Mandy," he told her. "And date-nut bread with cream cheese. I'm hungry tonight."

"New guitar?"

"Kind of."

"New to you?"

"Yeah," he said.

Palance opened the case and took out his father's guitar. The Larriveé glimmered, light bouncing off the mother-of-pearl inlay. He laid his father's tuner on the table and tuned each string. Mandy came over with his mug of coffee and date-nut bread on a white ceramic dish. Palance listened to the *whoosh* of the espresso machine and rumble of the L-train, as if some sacred being were making its presence known.

The café and sign-up sheet began to fill. He recognized two women and one older man, Tim Einer, who had signed up to play before him. Tim was good, better than Palance by far. It was almost time for the music to begin. There were four acts ahead of him. The first was a new guy who looked younger than Palance. He was sitting in the corner, biting his fingernails. Onstage, he played folk songs from the sixties and seventies. He played badly, and the crowd applauded politely. Palance made certain to clap at the end of each song. He remembered his first time as a solo performer.

The next act was the two women. One had long blond hair and played a dulcimer. The other, a brunette, played a maple Guild guitar. They started with an original song about young love, and the drone of the dulcimer was mesmerizing.

Then came an old English ballad called "Maddy Groves." Usually each act played three songs, but Palance glanced at his watch, and they were near the end of their time, though he had no idea if or when this song was about to end. It sounded like one of the soap operas his mother watched, a woman married to one man, in love with another, a tale of lust, jealousy, and rage that ended in violent, bloody death.

While the women thanked the audience, collecting them-selves and their instruments, Palance took out his guitar and tuner, checking the strings again. Tim Einer took the stage and played a mixture of blues and originals. Palance envied his skills; fingerpicking in three or four different styles. Palance kept a notebook to try to write down the patterns, but he never quite got it right, and he didn't have the nerve to ask.

Tim played mostly instrumentals. When he did sing, his voice was a controlled growl. Palance loved the sound he evoked from the old Gibson, the way he used a slide, and gently nudged the strings with his left hand to pull them out of tune. That old Gibson sounded like an orchestra one moment, and a train whistle the next. Palance abandoned his notebook.

When Tim finished, Palance was surprised to hear his own name called. Instead of the smooth, professional entrance he had planned, Palance staggered his way onstage, bumping against the leg of the table, almost tripping as he caught his toe on the edge of the raised platform, finally managing to fall into the seat by the microphones. He adjusted them, and a howling noise filled the room. Everyone covered their ears until the man behind the counter fixed it.

Palance was set to play "Where Do We Go from Here?" when he glanced to his left and saw the redhead and her friend from Flukey's walk in. He played the run from F to C and launched into it. *My ships are torn and tattered, my cities are in flame.* When he got close to the end of the song and sang, *I know what's inside me, I'll brave the gale*, he saw the redhead nod to her friend.

Palance launched into Beth's song. He felt as close to her as ever, closer even, to this ideal love, while he kept eye contact with the redhead. He loved the chorus, *No words to speak, nowhere to go, a stranger place I'll never know. But I am held in loving arms, please keep me safe and keep me warm.* Palance looked away from the redhead only when he sang the bridge: *And on that tender night, with nothing going right, moon and stars and passing cars shimmered as our souls took flight.* He was able to look the redhead in her eyes and sing to her, *please keep me safe and keep me warm.* When he finished there was applause. She stood and looked straight at him until her friend found an empty table and waved her over.

Palance had the words and chords to "Icarus" in his pocket, but they were clear in his mind, and, while the applause died down, he thought of Jason.

"I'd like to dedicate this to my friend Jason," he said. *They caught you flying, too close to the sun.* The song was Jason's story as much as it was about Icarus. The room went silent. All he heard was his voice and guitar, and then there was only the song. *As you rode the winds in wonder, thunder rumbling in the breeze, did you hear your father calling, falling and tumbling to the sea?* The song and his set were over. He felt elated and disappointed. He wanted more. He stood up and walked off the stage toward his table.

The redhead intercepted him.

"You made it," he said.

"You were good," she said, her brown eyes sparkling. She was standing close to him, close enough to kiss. The Larriveé hung on his shoulder, between them.

"Thanks," he replied, and kissed her, a brief peck on the cheek, and told her not to move while he put his guitar back in the case.

"I'm with my friend, over there," she said, pointing at the small, dark-haired girl from Flukey's. "Sit with us?" Palance nodded, put the guitar case on his table, and carefully placed the Larriveé, strap, and tuner inside.

Mandy came over and asked, "Fan club?"

"Another espresso and whatever they want," he told her.

"Okay, Slick. But the coffee is strong tonight," she said with a sarcastic grin. "You'd better be careful."

Palance latched the guitar case and carried it with him to the redhead's table.

"This is my friend Angie," she said. "Angie thinks you're okay."

"Thanks, Angie," Palance said to her, smiling. "You know," he said to the redhead, "I still don't know your name."

"It's . . ." Angie started to say, but the redhead put her hand across Angie's mouth and shook her head.

"My name is on a need-to-know basis," the redhead said. "And you don't need to know. Not yet, anyway."

Angie looked at her and rolled her eyes. "My friend is very mysterious," she said. "I think she's a spy."

"Yes," the redhead said in an Eastern European accent. "I am here to uncover all of your deep, dark secrets."

"I don't have any secrets," Palance said, crossing his fingers.

"But oh, my friend," the redhead said. "I think you do."

"Ask me anything," Palance offered. "My life is an open book."

She turned to Angie. "Anything, he said. Okay, guitar boy, why did you invite me here?"

"I thought you might enjoy it," Palance replied. He was beginning to feel apprehensive.

"Where is your girlfriend?" she asked.

"Girlfriend," Palance stuttered. "No girlfriend." It wasn't really a lie. She wasn't there.

The redhead pursed her lips, looking at Palance with a glint in her eye. "I really liked your songs. Did you write them?"

"Uh-huh."

"Which is your favorite?"

"The one I'm going to write for you," he said. "Which is yours?"

"No one's ever written me a song," she said. "Has anyone ever written you a song, Angie?" she asked her friend.

"Never."

"How are you going to write me a song? You don't know anything about me."

"Maybe we can get to know each other better. Hang out."

"Are you asking me out?"

"Are you free this weekend?"

"I'll let you know after I see how tonight turns out."

"Uh, tonight is almost over for me," Angie said. "I've got an eight o'clock class."

"I can drive you home," Palance told the redhead.

The redhead whispered something in Angie's ear, and she whispered something back. "Angie says she can stay for a few more minutes," she told Palance.

He felt the tide turning in his favor.

"Do you want another cup of tea, Angie? I'm sure Palance will get you one and another coffee for me." She looked at him dismissively.

"I'd love one," Angie said.

"One cup of tea," Palance said to Mandy, who had walked up to them at that moment.

"Darjeeling," Angie said.

"And one coffee and an espresso."

"Two women," Mandy said. "You're doing well tonight."

Palance started to speak but was at a loss for words. He recovered enough to ask the redhead if she liked the place.

"Quaint," she said.

"Very quaint," Angie added, as if it were something significant. Then she whispered again into the redhead's ear. They smiled and nodded at one another.

"Where did you get the guitar?" the redhead asked. "It looks expensive."

"My father."

"Nice present."

"Not exactly a present," he said. "An inheritance."

"Lucky," Angie said.

"Not so lucky. I'd rather have my dad."

"What happened?" the redhead asked.

"It was a long time ago," Palance said. "I was eleven. Car accident."

"I'm sorry," Angie said.

Palance needed a minute to recover. He tried to put his father out of his mind, but when he looked at the guitar case, memories came flooding back. When Palance looked up again, the girls were eyeing him more sympathetically, their sarcasm less pronounced. Mandy brought their drinks and set them down. The redhead was quiet, and Angie sipped her tea. Palance started to talk, but the espresso machine and the L-train interrupted him. He asked Angie where she went to school.

"Loyola," she said, "with . . . so . . . so many people."

"So," Palance asked, "you both go to Loyola?" The red-head laughed and asked him what made him think she went there. "You are the mysterious one, aren't you?" he told her.

"And I'm the one with an eight o'clock," Angie said. "Statistics. First thing in the morning."

"Three more minutes," the redhead pled.

"Three minutes," Angie said, "and then I'm gone."

"So, Mr. Music, what are you going to do with your three minutes?" the redhead asked.

Palance leaned in and kissed her. She neither pulled away nor prolonged the kiss, but when he sat back, she smiled.

"You certainly are a curious fellow," she said.

"Curiouser and curiouser," Palance told her.

"My name is not Alice," she said.

"Maybe not," Angie said, "but I am late. Very, very late."

"One second," the redhead said to Palance and stood up to confer with Angie in the corner. She came back to the table and asked, "You'll drive me home?"

Palance nodded.

"You'll be a gentleman?"

"Yes, I will."

"Angie will call to check on me," she said.

"I'll have her home by midnight," Palance said to Angie. "She's in good hands."

"You're not going to sell me insurance, are you?" the red-head asked.

"I wouldn't know what name to put on the policy."

"Nice meeting you, Palance. I like your music," Angie told him. "See you tomorrow, O nameless one," she said to the redhead.

"According to the Egyptian Book of the Dead, knowing someone's name gives you great power over them, Palance," the redhead told him.

"And what are you going to do with the power you have over me?" he asked.

"What won't I do with it?" she said, leaning toward him with arched eyebrows and an impish smile.

"I'm glad you made it here tonight."

"How glad?"

"Your wish is my command."

"You must be desperate for some free hot dogs or something."

"Something," Palance said.

"I command you," she said, "to drive me home and play a private concert for me."

"Done."

"But first," she said, and hesitated with her index finger on her lower lip, "I want to know your deepest, darkest secret. Otherwise, I want you to drop me off, period. No concert."

"Is this a two-way street?"

"There are only one-way streets around here," she said.

Palance examined all the joys and horrors of his life, the love, lust, shame, and anguish of it, knowing that he would not reveal too much. He settled on one detail he was willing to disclose.

"I made out with two girls at the same party on the same night."

"Together?" she asked. Her eyes revealed neither admiration nor disgust.

"No," he said. "But they were cousins."

"Pretty proud of yourself."

"Not exactly."

"Exactly."

"Okay," he said.

"Never lie to me," the redhead told him. "Otherwise, you can tell me anything. So what do you do?"

"I'm going to school," he said. "Northeastern."

"Major," she commanded.

"Music. Plus some communications classes. Just in case."

"In case?"

"My mom thinks I should major in something else. Something practical. I don't want to be an accountant."

"You're not an accountant," the redhead said to him in earnest. "You're a poet."

"I don't know about that," he said to her. "But thanks."

He asked what she was majoring in, or if that was one of the deep, dark secrets she was keeping. She offered up "English," and he dared to ask her if she was, indeed, going to Loyola.

"I'll tell you this much," she said. "Yes, I am going to bloody Loyola, to make my parents happy. They think it'll make me a good Catholic," she whispered, "but between you and me, Palance, they haven't got a chance."

"Amen," he said.

She told him she'd rather he didn't use that word, even in jest.

"So, when and where would you like this private concert?" he asked her.

"Where the magnolia trees grow at the stroke of midnight."

"Where the magnolia trees grow at the stroke of midnight?"

"Are you going to repeat everything I say? It's disconcerting."

"Midnight is in fifty minutes," he said.

"Then we had better get going."

Palance looked around. The café was almost deserted. The music had ended and the espresso machine was quiet.

"Looks like you found a live one," Mandy told him as she handed him the check.

"I'll let you know."

"Red hair, beware," she warned and smiled as if she knew something he didn't.

"I can handle it," he told her.

"Famous last words."

Palance paid the bill and picked up his guitar. The redhead held onto his arm as they walked toward the door, and she rested her head against his shoulder. Palance leaned in to kiss her. She returned the kiss and flicked her tongue against his lips.

"So, where do the magnolia trees grow?" he asked her.

"All in good time," she answered. "Is your carriage nearby?"

"My carriage is in front of the Heartland Café."

She tightened her grip on his arm. The L-train roared by. They walked under the viaduct and passed a woman in a long coat walking two beagles. The redhead leaned down to pet the dogs.

"Hello, little fellows, hello," she said.

The moon was full and yellow. It loomed large in the eastern sky, just above the lake. The dogs yelped. The redhead stood and let them pass.

"So, tell me about this song you're going to write for me," she said.

"I have to get to know you," Palance told her.

The redhead laughed and spun away from him. "Maybe you will, and maybe you won't."

"Maybe I do, and maybe I don't," Palance replied. "Your eyes are mahogany, your hair gleams like fire, and your heart has a soul with a burning desire." He knew he was sporting a self-congratulatory grin. He wanted to prove to her that he was, indeed, a poet.

The redhead spun him off the sidewalk and onto the street. A few drops of rain fell. She didn't seem to notice. The street was deserted. They danced on the concrete, twirling in three-quarter time. When she stopped, he kissed her on the mouth. She wrapped her arms around him as the rain tumbled down. They were only a few feet from Palance's Honda, but he laid her against a Firebird, which set off the car alarm. Lights came on in the surrounding windows; he kissed her and hurried her into his car, sliding the guitar into the back seat. They escaped, bouncing over a speed bump, the car alarm fading in the distance.

"Okay," Palance asked. "Where do the magnolia trees grow?"

"They grow where you plant them."

"Okay. How do I get there?"

"Make a left up here."

"You'll guide me?"

"I will take excellent care of you."

"I'm counting on it."

"Don't count on anything."

The redhead guided him toward the lake and south. Her street, Magnolia, was mostly old apartment buildings with courtyards and stone archways. She directed him to park and took his hand. guiding him up the walk through one of the stone archways. There was a dry fountain in the courtyard with a young boy fruitlessly trying to spit water through his mouth. Ivy grew on the brown brick. She led him through a wood-and-glass door into an entryway lined with tarnished brass mailboxes.

The hallways held a musty odor of coriander and Lysol. She walked him up the stairs to the third door on the right and fumbled for her keys. Inside, the décor was a mix of elaborate antique and Goodwill chic. The heat overwhelmed him. The radiators hissed, and she opened a window, apologizing, "There's no thermostat." Palance set down his guitar and took her in his arms.

"I commanded you to serenade me," she said and indicated a couch where he could perform, while she took a seat in an overstuffed chair.

"It'll take me a minute to tune. The change in temperature."

"You want a beer?" she asked and brought him one without waiting for a reply.

Palance took his guitar out of the case, tuned it, and played a few chords. He looked around for some mail or something that might hold a clue to the redhead's name, but he couldn't find anything.

"What should I play?" he asked, taking a sip from the Corona bottle.

"Play something that reminds you of me," she said.

Palance played Van Morrison's "Brown Eyed Girl." She looked at him without blinking. He went straight into U2's

"Where the Streets Have No Name." She stood up, took her beer, and sat cross-legged in front of him on the floor. She asked him to sing the song about coming into the world naked.

"Okay," he said, feeling a small knot in his stomach. He thought about Beth in Madison and wondered what she was doing tonight. Stalling, he sipped from the beer bottle. What was that song his father used to sing? "Love the One You're With."

"You're somewhere else right now," the redhead said. "Aren't you?"

"There is nowhere in this world I would rather be," Palance said, and started playing. She leaned up and kissed him. He crooned to her, *Naked come into this world, cold and hungry, gasping air.* He watched her as he sang, how the song affected her, how it drew her like a magnet. She leaned closer; there were only inches between her and the guitar. Her eyes were fixed on his, her mouth was open, and she was still. *No words to speak, nowhere to go,* and he spoke to her heart, *keep me safe and keep me warm.* Love the one you're with.

"Icarus," she demanded, and when he sang, *As you rode the winds in wonder, thunder rumbling through the trees, did you hear your father calling, falling and tumbling to the sea,* he understood that it wasn't about Jason. It was his song. His father had fashioned a vast and winding maze, and he was wending his way through it. *For a moment, you had wings to fly.* He hoped to fare better than Icarus.

Palance played the final chorus, over and over, without words, letting the music wash over them and fade. When his fingers no longer touched the strings and the guitar was back in its case, she fell into his arms, her lips pressed against his, her breasts rising and falling against him. He muttered about the lights and she shook her head. She wanted to see him. She wanted him to see her. She was not gentle. She was ravenous and strong. He met her force with force and passion with passion. They rolled and tumbled against each other; sweated, slipped and slid, then grappled and released; exhausted.

Lying against each other on the floor, Palance took the last sip of beer from his bottle and scanned her body. Deep orange freckles adorned her and gilded her breasts. She was alluring in a thin layer of sweat. He kissed her lips, then down her sultry neck to her damp shoulder. He kissed her down to her sex, letting primal urges rule. He loved hearing her moan. He did not want this to end, but she pushed him off. He didn't want to leave. He didn't want to speak. He kissed her on the lips, as if to withdraw her name, and discovered it felt delicious not to know.

The redhead swung her legs over him so that she was sitting on his torso, and leaned her hands against his shoulders, pinning him down. "What will you give me for my name?" she asked.

"All I have are my songs," he said, wondering where that line came from.

"If I tell you my name, you have to write me a song."

"Okay."

She lowered herself down, lay against him, and whispered in his ear, "Sonara." Then she kissed him and told him she had class in the morning. "You know where to find me," she said.

"I do, Sonara." The name sounded appropriate and beautiful as it rolled off his tongue. Palance scurried for his clothes and looked back at Sonara, still naked on the floor, displaying herself to him. "Do you have a phone number?" he asked.

"You know where to find me," she repeated.

"Mysterious to the end," he said, dressing.

"Remember," she told him. "My song."

Palance took his guitar and walked toward the door. "I promise."

He took one look back at her before leaving her apartment. The night was crisp, and the wind was wicked. He stood still for a moment to cool off. He was grateful to the guitar for the luck it brought him, this wild and passionate night. He knew he should feel guilty. He loved Beth. But it wasn't that big a deal. It wasn't the first time he'd cheated on her.

River of Arpeggios

Icarus: Too Close to the Sun

*They caught you flying
too close to the sun,
It felt like drowning,
on the earth and numb,
I heard you crying
before you learned to fly,
I saw you dying,
frail against the sky.*

C

H   *And as you rode the winds in wonder,*

O   *Thunder rumbling through the breeze,*

R   *Did you hear your father calling,*

U   *Falling and tumbling to the sea?*

S

*Your father fashioned
a vast and winding maze,
His endless passion
stirred the king's great rage,
And like a sparrow
locked up in a cage,
From wax and feathers,
grew wings to fly away.*

Icarus: Too Close to the Sun

Chorus

Were you lured into the sunset,
Spurred on by the golden light,
Blinded by the tears that you wept,
Or running from the night?

You were so restless,
hard to satisfy,
Trying to impress,
yearning to get high,
You tried to possess
sun and wind and sky,
And for a moment,
you had wings to fly.

Chorus

I Am Awake

Years later, Palance debated if it had been a dream or a vision. In the twilight between sleep and waking, he looked into heaven where his father walked among the angels. Clouds floated above and below. His father and the angels appeared solid, while looking down at his own body, he saw himself as ethereal and translucent. In the background, he heard banshee wails.

"What was that?" he asked his father. "Why are they howling?"

"It's the angels," his father replied. They absorb the cries of mourners on Earth, and when they reach their limit, they let it out."

"Do they hear my cries?" Palance asked. "Do you?"

"I hear your cries. I hear your songs."

"What do you think of them?"

"I am proud. You have grown."

"Have I?"

"An artist is always becoming. Who you are now is not who you will become."

"What will I become?"

"Even the angels don't know. Always do your best. That's the finest advice I have. You have a gig soon."

"How do you know?"

"You will be surrounded by familiar faces. Take my guitar. It's yours now."

"I don't dare take it out in the cold."

"Take it. Both of you are stronger than you know."

Palance fell unconscious and woke the next moment. That was four nights ago. Tonight was his first solo gig. Even his dreams were unsettled. He could use an angel now.

Mandy actually got him the gig. As Palance left The No Exit one night, Mandy grabbed him by the wrist and pulled him over. She suggested it to the owner, and the deal was done. He had three weeks to make posters, distribute them, learn another two hours of material, rehearse it, memorize it, and put some kind of stage act together. Oh, yeah, and there was school. School could wait.

Palance jumped out of bed. It was the first full day of spring; the ground was frozen and snow was in the air. His mother had to work tonight. She wouldn't be there, and Beth wasn't going to come down from Madison on a Thursday night. Flukey's was out—he still hadn't even started a song for Sonara. He felt a twinge of guilt thinking about her, and desire, thinking about that night.

Palance threw on sweats, walked down the hall to the kitchen, and looked around for something to eat. He longed for ritual, something like Stonehenge, something sacred and meaningful. It was one thing to play in a band at a bunch of house parties; it was another to have an entire evening on stage—just him. Fifteen minutes was no problem. Three hours seemed like an eternity.

Palance brewed a pot of coffee, grabbed an Eggo waffle from the freezer, and, after the toaster popped, coated it in syrup. He had written a song for tonight, something abstract, based on the dream or vision, or whatever haunted him last Sunday night. It sounded mysterious, as if it were searching for meaning as well.

Palance had avoided the basement for a while. "Everything in its time and place," his father said. That voice called him down to the basement this morning. He placed his dishes in the dishwasher and went back to his room for the Larriveé. Hesitating at the top of the stairs, he carried the guitar down the steps with a set of new guitar strings in his pocket.

At the bottom of the stairs, Palance turned on the lights and was pleased to find everything in place. He set the guitar case on its shelf and took a pair of towels from the closet, laying one on the workbench, straightening the corners and lining up the edges. This had been his father's ritual. Now it was his.

Palance opened the guitar case, removed the guitar, carried it to the workbench and laid it on the towel. On the shelf against the furnace room was the empty box his father always used. He wrapped the other towel around the box and set it under the neck of the guitar for support. The furnace kicked on and graced him with its heat. He took the strings out of his pocket, removed them from the pack, and laid them out in two rows, the thicker bass strings in the bottom row, and the thin steel strings above them. He splurged for Elixers. They were fifteen dollars for the set.

Palance unwound the low E-string on the Larriveé. It groaned and wobbled, tapping against the body of the guitar. He removed the bridge pin and uncoiled the string from the tuning peg. He curled the old string into a loop, placing it on the workbench. Then he took the new string from its crisp paper packet, set the ball end into the hole, and pushed in the pin, tugging on the string to set it firmly in place. He slotted the open end through the machine head and wound it until it was in tune. Palance repeated this procedure for the bass strings, and then turned the guitar around to change the three higher strings.

The fluorescent lights in the basement bounced off the mother-of-pearl flourishes across the soundboard and neck, the sharp grain of the Sitka spruce, the black ebony fretboard, the deep, rich rosewood, and the silver tuning machines. The basement was quiet, the furnace momentarily dormant. Palance put the tools back in place. He strapped on the guitar and played scales to warm up his fingers and stretch the strings.

Palance felt too nervous to start practicing. He needed to dissipate some energy. He took off the strap, put the guitar back in the case, and left them on the shelf.

Outside there were three inches of snow on the ground. Palance put on his coat and gloves. The last thing he needed tonight was a cut or blister on his fingers. He grabbed the shovel from the garage and went to the sidewalk, where he lifted the snow onto the grass. The air was crisp. His face tingled. The shovel scraped against the sidewalk, and he worked rhythmically, hearing the crack of a tree branch, and feeling endless possibility. He worked diligently until the walk was clean and only a thin sheen of ice remained. The sun was shining, the ice already melting from the sidewalk, and a bright red cardinal flitted past.

Inside, Palance poured himself a cup of slightly burnt coffee, and began rehearsing. He set the old metal stool in the middle of the basement, faced the workbench, and sheepishly addressed an imagined audience, "Hello, ladies and gentlemen, I'm Palance Heller." He began with the first song his father ever taught him, a traditional tune, "Come All Ye Fair and Tender Maidens." The next was a Scottish song, "Wild Mountain Thyme." When he played it, girls perked up.

Palance picked up a few songs he'd heard at the No Exit, "The House of the Rising Sun," and some his father sang, Joni Mitchell's "Urge for Going," and Bob Dylan's "Tangled Up in Blue." Palance told the story about his Dad serenading a girl in college under her window. He had the wrong room, and, while the girl was impressed, her boyfriend, also in the room, was not. The girl was his mother. He felt his father's energy embrace him.

Palance played some songs from the Whispering Screams, the U2 songs, and Van Morrison's "Brown Eyed Girl," in case Sonara showed up. He didn't know what would happen after the gig, but at least, he wanted to find someone to go out to breakfast with him. Hopefully, the flyers he'd put up at school and around the neighborhood would do the trick. He didn't want to play to an empty room.

Palance played a couple of Beatles tunes. He pictured the audience holding up lighters at the end of the concert, requesting an encore. He played songs by Counting Crows. Tonight would be a make-or-break thing. School wasn't going well, and he didn't know how much longer he'd last there. He sang a few lines of "School's Out for Summer."

Palance thought he'd learn how to be more creative in school. Instead, he was stuck in Music History, Theory II, and Wind Instruments, where they learned just enough about every wind instrument in the orchestra to suck at all of them. He played Nick Lowe's "What's So Funny 'Bout Peace, Love, and Understanding?" feeling raucous, and wished Jason and Kyle were there, throwing up a wall of sound behind him.

Palance put most of his own songs in the second set. It was a weeknight, and he didn't know how long people would stay. He played "Beth's Song." She was gone. He played a few songs by local people, Michael Smith, John Prine, and Steve Goodman. Palance hoped he was good enough to pull off this gig. *I'd better keep practicing.*

Next on the set list was his song "Icarus," and it felt like a warning. He set the guitar back in the case and looked over the workbench: the wrenches and screwdrivers lined up neatly, the mahogany roll-top desk with old pens and yellowed pads of paper. There was a layer of dust. Apparently, his Mom hadn't been down here in a while, either. They had neglected his father and left him to languish beneath the dust. Soon, he promised himself, he would come back down, dust it off, examine the contents, and preserve the treasures.

Palance tore into the rest of the set list, a little Motown, a bluesy version of Blind Faith's "Can't Find My Way Home," and, for later in the night, some folk and blues, when the audience would dwindle to a smattering of diehards. He left a few open slots for requests, repeats of his songs if the audience turned over, and his last number, "Motherless Child, a Long Way from My Home."

Palance packed the guitar, tuner, and a spare set of strings back in the case. He placed the song sheets in a manila envelope. He broke down the music stand, and put it, along with the songs and guitar picks, in a cloth tote bag.

Palance walked over to his father's desk and opened the middle drawer. There were pencils, pens, a six-inch ruler, and faded yellow legal pads. In the corner, he found an ivory-colored feather, looking out of place, and a small, tarnished penknife, which he tucked into his front pocket, thinking it would make a good slide.

There was a picture on his father's desk: the four of them, at the beach on a cloudy day, he and Jilly wearing bathing suits covered with t-shirts, his parents wearing jeans and sweaters, a blanket laid out with a picnic basket on it. He remembered that day. His parents sent them out into the water even though it was chilly. His mother and father wanted to be alone. From the recesses of his mind, Palance recalled a knowing smile on the woman at the beach who took the picture for them, as if the three adults shared a secret. The image was burned in his memory, including the silver bracelet his mother wore, his father's oversized Bob Marley t-shirt, and Jilly's hair in pigtails. If he had a chance tonight, he'd play "Redemption Song." It was one of his dad's favorites.

Palance needed to leave by six-fifteen. He wanted to get a hot dog and fries, and be at the coffeehouse by seven-thirty.

The gig started at eight. He wondered where Jilly was. He hadn't seen her all day, and the girl with the gift of gab had not mentioned any plans.

He set the Larriveé and tote bag by the front door and went into his bedroom. He lit a candle and stared at the flame to clear his mind. He longed for some kind of revelation, something that would set him on the proper path—or at least let him know where the path lay and where it led. Attempting to meditate, he was distracted by his own thoughts and the sounds of the house, the hum of the refrigerator, and anxiety about his nebulous future. All he really had was this gig. Palance had never thought of himself as a solo act. He enjoyed being part of the Whispering Screams as much as he enjoyed the attention from the audience. The flame flickered and held its secrets.

Palance blew out the candle and took a shower. He went to his closet to look for something to set him up for success. Nothing stood out, but he found a pair of black jeans and a black t-shirt. He put one of his father's old guitar picks in his pocket. He still felt guilty about it.

At six-fifteen, Palance carried the tote bag out to the car. He wore his winter coat for warmth. He started the car and ran the heater so it would be warm for the guitar. He went back into the house for the Larriveé, laying it across the back seat. Palance headed east to California Avenue and south to Peterson, where he parked in Wolfy's lot next to the sign of a giant hot dog stabbed by a giant fork, where he and Jason used to meet when they discussed plans they didn't want their parents to know about. Kyle never liked it. "Too primitive," he said. Palance carried the guitar inside and went up to the counter.

"Two hot dogs with everything, fries, and a medium orange pop." There was an older man behind the counter, foreign, looking middle-eastern.

"You play?" he asked, strumming an imaginary guitar.

"I play," Palance said.

"Six thirty-five," the man told him, and Palance handed him a ten-dollar bill. The man assembled his order and returned with his change. "You any good?" he asked, handing him a paper bag with the food.

"Better than some, not as good as others," Palance replied.

"Maybe you be famous one day."

"Never know," Palance said.

There was a picture on the wall of the Mona Lisa eating a hot dog. Palance watched the traffic on Peterson. He smiled at the man behind the counter, who looked back at him and strummed his imaginary guitar. Palance thought about the night ahead, his place on the stage, and the years to come. He took a bite of the hot dog, a sip of soda, and dreamt of faraway places.

Two kids came into the restaurant, barely out of elementary school, one riding a skateboard and the other on a scooter. "Hey you," the man behind the counter chided. "Keep your wheels off my floor." The boys conspired in low snickers as if they were invisible. "Order something, or get out," the man said.

"French fries," the boy with the scooter sneered, slamming a dollar bill and some change on the counter.

Palance turned from the commotion and ran through the set list in his head. Tonight he was making twenty bucks. After dinner, gas, and new strings, he wouldn't break even, but this meant everything to him. Twenty minutes was one thing—a whole night was another. The boys took their fries and left. The traffic noises and a stiff breeze snuck through the door.

"Kids," the man said. It occurred to Palance that only moments ago, he was one of them.

It was after seven. Outside, flurries coated the cars and trees. He finished his food, crumpled the paper, and threw it in the garbage. "Gotta go play," he said to the man behind the counter, and imitated the guitar-playing motion back to him.

The man nodded, finished wiping down the counter, and got out a broom. "See you later," he said.

Palance picked up his guitar and carried it to the car. He started the engine, got out, and wiped the snow off the windows with his coat sleeve. Driving down Peterson, the snow was blowing toward him, and traffic slowed to a crawl. He turned off at Western and went east on Pratt, past Flukey's. He'd better write Sonara that song. Beth seemed distant, and he wanted to see Sonara again. Tonight, he was ready to play. It seemed like the key to everything.

Palance found a parking space on Glenwood, a few feet from the door. He gathered his guitar and stand, and pulled the door open. The room was empty and still. The cold had fogged the window. He set his guitar and stand on the stage, where there was a chair waiting for him. The microphone stands were naked, and the sound system was off. The L-train rumbled by. When it passed, the owner peeked out from the kitchen. "I'll be out to set up the microphones," he said, lethargically. Palance unpacked the guitar, and set it on the stand. "Put up any posters?" the owner asked.

"Yeah," Palance said, "a bunch."

"See what happens. Thursdays can be slow," he said, looking out the window, "especially when the weather sucks."

Mandy walked in, bundled up, and nodded to Palance. "Big night, huh?"

"Hope so," he said.

"Might be a short night," the owner told her.

Palance put it out of his mind, his mood dampened but still hopeful, and walked on stage to set up. He'd never played here long enough to settle in. He asked for a glass of water, and tuned his guitar. The owner came over with the water and set up the microphones.

"I'll adjust the sound once you start playing," he said.

A couple in their forties came in and sat down. A few minutes later, two men walked in and headed to one of the tables painted with a chessboard. They had their own pieces. Palance checked his watch. It was seven-fifty. Ten minutes to go.

He wanted to start off strong, hit the first few songs without pausing. He checked his hair and clothes in the restroom mirror. He wished he looked more mysterious. More something. Palance rinsed his face with cold water, dried it with a paper towel, and headed back to the stage. Two more groups came in, a young couple about his age, and three girls up in front. They looked familiar; he thought they must have been here before, or maybe they were in one of his classes. When he turned around, he realized it was Jillian and two of her friends. Jilly was smiling at him and had a tape recorder with a microphone pointed straight at him. Instead of launching into his first song, Palance stood there, dumbfounded.

"I can't believe you're here," he said to her.

"Where else would I be, guitar boy?" she said. "Play something, why don't you."

"Okay," he said, and fumbled for his guitar, his composure gone. His sister's friends, Cindy and Felice, had been fixtures around their house for years, practically members of the family.

"Yeah, Pal," Felice said. "Play something," and giggled into her drink.

Jilly elbowed Felice, and Palance launched into "Come All Ye Fair and Tender Maidens," which seemed appropriate. In the middle of the song, a group from his music-theory class walked in, seven of them. They pulled two tables together and sat down. Suddenly, Palance started paying more attention to his technique. These people knew what's what, and he didn't want to embarrass himself. His sister and her friends beamed at him. The owner looked less grumpy than usual. Palance played the U2 and Counting Crows songs, then hammed it up with "Tangled Up in Blue," strumming his guitar with a flourish and imitating Dylan's Minnesota drawl.

He played several of his father's old songs and told the story about an exhibitionist who was so cold he came up and described himself. Thanking the audience for coming in on a snowy night, he noticed the flurries had picked up. Palance played "Brown-Eyed Girl" and dedicated it to *a friend*. He looked around, and she wasn't there. Just like that, his first set was over and he announced a short break. He took a deep breath, put his guitar on the stand, and walked over to the people from school.

"Not bad," said a girl whose name he was blanking on, which was too bad. She looked cute. Not really his type. Too put together, but cute.

"Thanks for coming. I'm glad you're here."

"It's nice to see you outside of class. Someplace that isn't so . . . industrial," she said. "Rustic chic suits you."

"Thanks," he said. "I'll be back in a minute. I have to talk to my sister."

"No problem. Simply be prepared to discuss the various scales and harmonic modes for everything you played. Ten pages, double-spaced." His classmates broke up laughing. She looked frighteningly serious.

Palance walked over to Jilly's table just as Mandy got there. "Whatever they want," he told her. "It's on me."

"You're too big to talk to us anymore?" Cindy asked him.

"I remember Dad singing some of those songs, the first ones," Jilly said. Palance sat down, put his arm around her, and kissed her on the forehead.

"You're the best," he said.

"Just remember me when you get famous," she told him.

"What's your name again?" he asked her.

Mandy asked the girls if there was anything she could get them. Jilly and Cindy ordered hot chocolates, and Felice ordered an espresso, with marshmallows.

"We don't have marshmallows," Mandy told her. Cindy told Felice she was too weird, and Jilly's friends started giggling.

"Can you do me a favor?" Palance asked Jillian, handing her blank contact lists for anyone interested in his future gigs, hoping there would be some. "I need someone to pass these around."

"I can do that. We'll talk percentages later." Palance wasn't sure she was kidding. He walked over to the table from school and made small talk with them for a few minutes. He scanned the room. The crowd was small but attentive. He headed back to the stage and looked at the set list. He decided to play his new song first and dedicated it to Jillian, who looked at him as if he were a star.

I am awake, I am alone, the sun is high, the boy is grown, the end is far, the road is near, I take one step and disappear. Palance found himself mesmerized in a way the candle exercise never approached. It brought him deeper into himself.

I am alive, I am inspired, I will survive, the flame grows higher. The time is now, the place is here, I take one breath and disappear. He was alone, within himself, within the song.

And all the joy I know is real, waits in the wings for me to steal. behind the mystic veil, behind the mystic veil, behind the mystic veil the angels wail, he sang, and Palance knew his father was there with him.

As he continued, Palance heard other instruments in his head. Drums to frame the song and drive it. Bass to define the harmony. A second guitar to provide countermelody. A viola to cry, violins to shriek, and a cello for depth. The L-train punctuated the last line, *I am awake,* and the espresso machine roared.

The rest of the set was a blur. Palance was in a groove, the audience with him. He played the third set without taking a break. When he was done, a thin layer of sweat covered his face, and his hair was matted back. He turned and looked out the window. There were several inches of snow on the ground. Most of the crowd had left or was on their way out. The group from school came up to him and shook his hand, one by one. The girl, whose name he remembered was Elise, smiled at him.

"You weren't bad," she said, and the others nodded in agreement.

"Next week you teach the class," said a boy who always sat in the back row. "Be less boring."

Palance fell into the chair on stage, exhausted. His sister and her friends were all that was left of the audience. Felice and Cindy gave him a thumbs-up gesture. "Who knew?" Felice said, and Cindy kissed him on the cheek.

"We gotta go, school night," Cindy said, and she and Felice walked out.

"They were my ride," Jillian told him, "so I hope I can tag along with you."

"I'll buy you breakfast," Palance offered.

"I don't know," Jilly said. "It's a school night."

"Well, you're stranded, so what choice do you have?"

Jillian, for once, had no answer, and watched as Palance packed up his guitar and music. He walked over to the counter. The owner handed him a crumpled twenty-dollar bill.

"Thank you," Palance said. "It was great."

"Thanks for bringing an audience on a snowy Thursday. I'm Peter."

"'Night, Peter. Thank you."

Palance picked up his guitar, and Jilly carried the tote bag. He put his arm around her and kissed the top of her head.

"You're my favorite sister," he said.

"Whatever."

"I can't imagine a better one."

At that, Jilly turned around and looked at him, resting the back of her hand against his forehead. "Checking for fever," she said.

"Did you tape the whole thing?" he asked her.

"Every note. Plus the sheet of names and email addresses. I have pictures, too," she said, holding up a camera.

"I never saw the flash go off."

"You were out there, guitar boy. You were out there."

I Am Awake

I Am Awake

I am awake.

I am alone.

The sun is high.

The boy is grown.

The end is far.

The road is near.

I take one step

and disappear.

I am alive.

I am inspired.

I will survive.

The flame grows higher.

The time is now.

The place is here.

I take one breath

and disappear.

And all the joy I know is real,

waits in the wings for me to steal.

Behind the mystic veil,

behind the mystic veil,

behind the mystic veil

the angels wail.

I am unborn.

I am unknown.

I lie beneath
the unturned stone.
I have no doubt.
I have no fear.
I have no faith
to disappear.

And all the joy I know is real,
waits in the wings for me to steal.
Behind the mystic veil,
behind the mystic veil,
behind the mystic veil
the angels wail.
I am awake.

No Road Home

The last time Palance's mother called a family meeting was shortly after the death of their father, when she bought a new sedan with the insurance money, and needed help picking a color. Palance wanted black, but his mother and Jillian chose blue.

"Elaine wants what?" he asked Jilly as she peered into his room, shouting over the stereo.

"A family meeting."

"Why?"

"Just come downstairs."

"When?"

"Now."

"One sec."

"*Now!*" He heard his mother's voice from downstairs.

Palance's mother and Jilly took their usual seats at the kitchen table. Palance took his seat.

"I have an announcement, and it affects both of you," their mother began, straight-backed and stern. "I've kept us in this house all these years, while the taxes have gone up, and our savings . . . my savings have gone down." Jillian was perched on the edge of her seat, while Palance half listened, as he worked on a melody in his head. "So I'm selling the house and moving into a condominium," she told them. Jillian nodded, and the tune in Palance's brain became discordant.

"We're moving to a condo?" he asked.

"I'm getting to that," his mother said and paused to take a sip of her iced tea while the room turned silent. "You might want to get a drink," she said to Palance. "I'll wait."

Palance took her at her word and came back to the table with a glass of orange soda. "Okay," he said, and braced himself.

"It's a two-bedroom condo," she said, "in Evanston, on Hinman. Walking distance from St. Francis for work."

"Two bedrooms?" Palance asked.

"Yes. You're twenty years old," his mother said, "and the deal doesn't close until July 1st. Jillian will be in college in the fall. You'll be almost twenty-one, and you're not going to school . . ."

"But . . ." He took a sip of the orange soda. It tasted flat.

"You're not. It's time you figure out what to do with your life and do it. I'll do my best to help you out where I can, but it's time for you to grow up. Jillian will stay with me as long as she's in school."

"I'm hoping to get a scholarship to Northwestern," she said. She actually had the nerve to gloat about it.

Palance stood up and began pacing. "So, you're kicking me out," he said, much louder than intended.

"You haven't exactly included me in *your* life," his mother said. "How long have you been out of school?"

"How did you know?"

"It wasn't hard to figure out. No books, no homework, and your car sits in the same spot for days."

"I don't have to answer to you, since I don't really live here anymore," Palance said, stomping back to his room and slamming the door. The melodies had all left his head. He had no girlfriend, few friends, and now, no home. He paced his room in a four-four pattern; two steps forward, turn around, two steps back, and repeated it for several minutes. In a fit of rage, he grabbed his Seagull guitar, his car keys, and headed out, hoping to cause some commotion, but the living room was empty. His mother's car was gone.

Palance slipped the guitar onto the back seat and drove west on Touhy with no destination in mind. When he came to Central, he took it south to Devon. The gas tank was half full. He turned the radio up as loud as it would go and let his rage take over. The Rolling Stones were singing "Satisfaction." He pounded the steering wheel and turned left onto Nagle and then south onto the highway toward Rockford. He headed toward Madison, knowing full well he was on a fool's mission. Palance turned the radio down a notch and leaned back in his seat. He opened the console and found enough change for tolls.

There was no turning back. The city turned to suburbs and the suburbs to cornfields. He tried not to think about Beth, but saw her clearly in his mind's eye: her straight brown hair down her back, her freckled nose crinkled. Palance convinced himself this made sense. Beth had little time for him on the phone, complained about too much homework, and had no time to visit. Still, he willed her to be the young girl who looked starry-eyed at him at her sweet-sixteen party.

The gas gauge was down to a quarter of a tank. Palance wondered where Sonara had been. The last time he went to Flukey's, neither she nor her friend were there. Palance was alone with the ruminations of his mind. There was a sign for an oasis coming up, and though he was flooded with images of palm trees and crystal springs, he understood this was a place to get gas and maybe a sandwich. He didn't know how much money he had with him. He hadn't planned this.

He pulled into the gas station, a concrete bunker with a McDonald's and a convenience store. Checking his wallet, he found two twenties, a five, and a few singles. He might be sleeping in his car tonight. Maybe forever. A full tank of gas, a restroom visit, and a bag of chips later, Palance was down to twenty-eight dollars and change, returning to the cornfields with little idea of what he'd do when he got to Madison. The sane thing would have been to call Beth before he left. If there was a goal beyond Madison, he didn't know what it was. His mother's phrase played in his mind: *what to do with your life.*

Palance passed through Rockford. There were housing developments, factories, and shopping centers. He saw signs for a clock tower and zoomed by at seventy miles an hour. The Chicago radio stations had faded, and he was inundated with country twang and boring talk shows. Signs welcomed him to Wisconsin.

Farmhouses and small clusters of homes lined the highway. Roadside businesses at each exit catered to travelers; fast food, gas stations, and low-slung motels. Palance turned off the radio, mostly static, and opened the window. He heard his father's voice saying, "Keep your back to the wind," and, for a moment, he managed to forget where he was. When he came back to himself, the odometer let him know he had gone another thirty miles. He pulled off at Edgerton. Past the Wisconsin Cheese and Wine Chalet, there was a Culver's Frozen Custard, and he stopped for a coke.

Behind the counter at Culvers was a girl with red hair who reminded him of Sonara; she was young—younger than Jilly. For a split second, he thought of settling down here, working at one of the local tourist stops, and watching strangers pass by on the interstate. He wondered about this girl's life.

"Do you like it here?" he asked her.

"Huh?"

"Living here. Working at Culver's?"

"It's okay," she said, squinting her eyes. "Can I get you anything?"

"Just a Coke."

"What size?"

"Just a Coke," he said. She handed him a drink.

"Dollar twenty-seven," she told him, and he paid her. He took the drink, got back into his car and continued driving. The towns grew thicker and closer together. There were signs for the state capitol and the university. Each exit had a greater number of gas stations, motels, and fast food restaurants. The traffic increased, paling in comparison to the gridlock in the southbound lanes. The Coke tasted sour. He didn't know how to get to Beth's dorm. For all he knew, she was somewhere else. She could be anywhere. At Route 12, he left the highway and searched for a pay phone. If she didn't answer, he'd need a new plan. He had none.

Palance found a Marathon station and pulled in. He wished he had a cell phone. He plunked a quarter in the pay phone and dialed the number. She picked up after the third ring. He barely recognized her voice.

"Is Beth there?" he asked.

"It's me. Palance, is that you?"

"Yeah."

"You sound funny."

"How?"

"Far away. Where are you?"

"I'm close. Route 12 in Madison."

"What are you doing here?"

"I need to see you," Palance said, regretting his choice of words. "I want to see you."

"It's not a good time," she told him. "You just drove up here?"

"Meet me. Can I come see you?"

There was silence. Finally she said, "There's a coffeehouse on campus. Mother Fools—you'll like it. Ask directions. Anyone will know where it is."

"You'll meet me there?"

"Half an hour."

Palance cruised Madison, looking for the coffeehouse. After driving through campus town seven times, he spotted the building, brown brick with bright murals painted on the wall. A tile mosaic spelled out "Mother Fools Coffeehouse." The inside looked psyche-delic, with primary colors and mismatched furniture. The floor was blue, and the smattering of students had long hair and torn jeans. He walked up to the counter and asked for a double espresso and a lemon poppyseed muffin; then he found a table by the window.

Palance sipped his coffee and picked at the muffin. He pulled a pen from his pocket, and started doodling on a napkin until a line for a song hit him. *Setting out on Sunday morning, restless sleep still in my eyes, searching . . .* He didn't know what he was searching for. He put the napkin in his pocket and watched Beth walk up the street toward him. She looked different somehow, in a brown suede jacket. Her hair was longer. It had been a while since he'd seen her.

"Hi, Palance," she said and kissed him on the cheek, putting her hand on his shoulder. She sat down opposite him. "Didn't expect you."

"Didn't expect to be here," he said. "It just sort of happened. Can I get you coffee? Hot chocolate?"

"I can't stay long," she said. "I have a paper due tomorrow. It's almost finals. What are you doing here?"

"I was lost and ended up here. Is that so bad?"

"It's a great town. Good school. Palance, what's going on?"

"Does something have to be going on? Hell, Beth, I came up here to see you." Beth looked at him poignantly, as if he were a waif standing on a dock after his ship had sailed.

"Aren't you happy to see me?" he asked, regretting it immediately.

"Palance, I'm happy to see you, but I've got a paper to finish and finals to study for, and there's a lot you don't know."

"A lot I don't know about what?"

"You were my first boyfriend."

"I know that."

"I need a cup of coffee," Beth said.

"I'll get it," Palance told her.

"Two sugars and a drop of cream."

"When did you start drinking coffee?"

"There's a lot you don't know."

Palance got up and walked to the counter. He knew where this was going and was grateful to walk away for the moment. He pulled coins out of his pocket and gave Beth's order to a girl with long, wavy hair and an army jacket. He handed her two dollars in change. He added cream and sugar, stirred it for a while, and walked back to the table.

"I've been with someone else," he told her.

"Oh," she said. Her expression didn't change.

"How about you," he asked. "Dating anyone?"

"Sort of," she said, looking down at her coffee. She lifted the cup to her face and took a sip. "You weren't here."

"You weren't there," he told her, and for a minute the two sat in silence, drinking their coffee. "So, what's the paper about?"

"Modalities of learning," she said. "Some people learn better by doing, others by reading or listening."

"I think I learn best from my mistakes," Palance said, and both he and Beth laughed out loud, which quickly turned uncomfortable. "I make a lot of mistakes."

"It's a bitch, isn't it?" Beth said, and Palance felt a genuine smile cross his face. He saw the girl he fell in love with.

Palance told her what had been happening, dropping out of school, his gig at the No Exit, and his mom selling the house. He had three months to find somewhere to live and some way to support himself. He told her how Jilly was turning into a human being. The main thing he regretted about being kicked out of the house was that it would separate them. He didn't realize that until then.

Beth told him about the joy and terror of being away from home, having so many choices, and the pitfalls to avoid. The kids who partied too much, the kids who stayed for years without picking a major, and the kids who dropped out. Then she hesitated, looked at Palance and said, "I don't mean you. You have your music."

"Thanks," he told her. "I've been writing more."

"I'd love to hear some of it, but I can't stay too long. I really do have a pile of homework. Do you have your guitar?"

"It's in the car."

"Get it."

Palance stepped out to retrieve his guitar, and carried it inside. Beth was talking to the girl with the wavy hair, who was nodding. She disappeared for a moment, came back out to the stage with a couple of microphones, and fastened them to the stands.

"I come here a lot," Beth told him. "It reminds me of you."

Palance unpacked onstage, tuned the guitar, and wondered why the girl from behind the counter was adjusting the microphone stands for him. Beth was only four feet away.

"Pretend like it's an audition," Beth said.

The girl setting up the stage introduced herself as Dawn and told him he was on. The café lights dimmed. He played Beth's song to her, at first tentatively and then with conviction. She looked at him the way she used to, and he lost himself in the song. *I am held in loving arms, keep me safe and keep me warm.* Beth still held some magic for him—magic he needed badly. He played her his latest song, *I am awake, I am alone, the sun is high, the boy is grown.* His voice grew stronger. *And all the joy I know is real, waits in the wings for me to feel. Behind the mystic veil, the angels wail.*

He played "Icarus." In his mind, he saw his own image, with his father beside him. *Did you hear your father calling, falling and tumbling to the sea.* Finally, he played his first song, "Too Old to Be So Young." At the end of the chorus, he sang to Beth, *there is a fire on the shore to keep you warm.* He listened to a smattering of applause, the lights in the café brightened, and Palance felt calm and hopeful for the first time that day.

Dawn walked up to him and said, "We're booking June. It's slow and doesn't pay much, but I'll give you a Friday night."

"Huh," Palance said, looking over at Beth, who smiled back at him.

"Audition," Beth said, smirking.

"A real audition? I was just . . ."

"Do you want the gig or not?" Dawn asked. "June 14th. I think it's Flag Day. Fifty bucks or half the house, whichever is more."

"Yeah," Palance said. "I'll take it."

"Don't forget. Be here by seven. You're on at eight." Dawn winked at Beth. "Not bad," she said.

"At least the trip wasn't for nothing," Beth told him as Dawn walked away.

"It wouldn't have been for nothing anyway," Palance said to her.

"I have to hit the books."

"I know," Palance told her.

"I saw Jason," Beth said.

"When?"

"About a month ago. His band came through. They played at one of the bars."

"How did he look?"

"Not good. He barely recognized me. I had to tell him who I was."

"Wow."

"I'm sorry," Beth told him. "I've got to go."

"Thanks," he said. "For everything."

"You deserve the best," she said, hugging him. Palance watched as she walked away. He was a hundred fifty miles from Chicago with less than twenty bucks in his pocket. He started to leave but returned to thank Dawn for the gig and tell her he'd see her in June.

He put his guitar in the trunk, got back in the car, and headed for Sonara's street. It was three hours away. If he was lucky, he'd be there before eleven. It was Sunday. Nobody stayed up late on Sunday. He wound his way back to the highway. It was dark, and thoughts swirled in his head. The gas gauge showed two-thirds full. He could get there without filling up. He was tempted to turn around, head west, and start over. The only thing stopping him was the Larriveé guitar sitting in his bedroom.

Palance had another gig at the No Exit, and now one in Madison. There were blank dates to fill in—a lot of blanks in his life. No home, no girlfriend, no job, no money, but he had the gig in Madison.

Thoughts churned, and Palance was back in Illinois. Road construction took the highway down to one lane. Traffic bunched and slowed to a crawl. Lights shone from fast-food restaurants and department stores. He wondered about being on the road, a traveling musician. He had no other skills. If Sonara was home, if she took him in, perhaps his life would lie there. He thought this, knowing she was a one-night stand. He didn't even have an inkling of the song he promised her.

Another lane opened. Traffic thinned and sped up. The buildings faded, and the road cleared. Darkness removed the scenery. Mile markers were meaningless, and exit signs had no draw. He had to generate gigs. He needed a biography, pictures, CDs of his music, money, a job. He needed a home.

At Elgin, he was down past a quarter tank. Good enough, he hoped. The suburbs flew by thick and bright with office buildings, shopping centers, hotels, and restaurants. There were signs for Woodfield Mall and O'Hare airport; the streets became familiar. He'd left without warning, the same way his mother delivered the news. He'd lost his home. He'd lost his girlfriend, barely noticing until it was too late. He'd dropped out of college. He was adrift.

Palance pulled off the highway at Nagle, drove up to Devon, past Superdawg, and the sculpture of the hotdog couple dancing on the roof, their red eyes glowing menacingly. He was only minutes from Sonara. He passed the river and drove through the myriad of exotic stores with signs in Indian, Pakistani, and Hebrew. Rents here were cheap. He wondered if he could support himself with his music and a day job. He turned right onto Magnolia and looked for a place to park. He found a space half a block away and pulled in.

When he got out of the car, he was shaking. His legs were cramped, and his shoulders hunched. Though he tried to slow down, he was walking at breakneck speed toward her building, checking his watch. It was a little after eleven. *Not too late*, he thought. Palance knew which buzzer to push; he imagined himself in her apartment, in her arms. He could hear her telling him that it was all right—he could stay if he wanted to. They could share their lives together. He pressed the button.

Palance held the buzzer too long. He felt the fatigue in his back and legs from the drive. A sleepy female voice on the intercom mumbled something, and Palance imagined their triumphant reunion, the stories he could tell her, his dismissal from home, his triumph in Madison, their arms almost entwined, and said, "Sonara."

"*Sayonara?*" the voice came back, the sleepiness more pronounced. "Who is this?"

"Palance Heller," he said, unsure why he gave his whole name. "I'm looking for Sonara."

"Don't know a Sonara. I just moved in three weeks ago. Sorry."

"She used to live here," he said, but the intercom had gone dead. Palance didn't want to go home. It wasn't his home anymore. A siren down the street startled him. The only place open was the Golden Nugget Pancake House on Lawrence and Ravenswood. He had enough money for breakfast and enough gas to get himself there, just barely. Palance got back into the Honda.

The Golden Nugget was bright and seedy. Palance sat down. A middle-aged woman with heavy makeup brought him a glass of water, poured his coffee, and handed him a menu. He ordered two eggs, sunny-side up, hash browns, and pancakes. In the booths around him were a couple dressed in formalwear, slurring their words, and workmen in uniform getting ready for a third shift. Palance examined the packets of jelly on the table, stacking them into makeshift structures, breaking them down, and rearranging them.

Outside, traffic flowed on Lawrence. Palance thought about checking the bulletin boards at school. Then he remembered he didn't belong there, either. The waitress slid a plate of food toward him and refilled his coffee cup. She didn't say a word—just put down the food and walked away, last in a long line to abandon him. The coffee was hot and burned his mouth. He threw in an ice cube from his water glass to cool it off and took a long sip. He broke the yolk of an egg with his fork, watching the yellow liquid flow over the plate before wiping it with a chunk of hash brown and guiding it into his mouth. He was ravenous.

Two girls walked in, giggling, leaning on each other. He tried to get up the energy to throw out a line. The brunette was pretty, but he couldn't think of anything to say, and they didn't even glance his way. Palance slumped down in his seat, methodically chewing his food and sipping coffee. The girls sat down across from him. Their voices were annoying. The inevitability of returning to his mother's house washed over him. The waitress dropped off his check. He took one last look at the two girls as the tall one snorted and the brunette pounded her fist on the table. He found a couple of bucks in his pocket to leave for a tip. After paying at the register, he was down to seven dollars and change.

Palance walked to his car. Trucks rumbled by, not much else, and the night was still. He stood with the car door open, reluctant to get in. His legs were trembling, and his back was stiff. He sat inside and turned the key. Palance put it in gear, urging the machine down the street. He meandered in and out of familiar neighborhoods, Ravenswood Manor, and Lincoln Square, into Rogers Park, and then down Touhy, past the curve at Damen. When the engine started sputtering he turned down Washtenaw to get off the main drag. He put it in neutral and gunned it to try to get past whatever was causing the trouble. He looked at the gas gauge. Less than empty. The warning light was on, and the car died in front of Rogers Park, stranding him.

There was a gas station on Touhy and Western, half a mile away. His mother's house was further, and she was at work. He trudged down to Western and then up to the Marathon station. The clerk wanted a ten-dollar deposit for the gas can. Palance pled for mercy. The clerk shoved the gas can at him, took his seven bucks, and filled it with a gallon of gas.

"You'd better bring it back," he said.

"Yes, sir," Palance answered. "Back in a flash." The attendant scowled and went back behind the counter. Palance's arm strained under the weight of the gasoline. The road slipped by him, as it had all day. He had put 400 miles on the car, all to arrive back where he started, broke and aching. He put the gas in the car, turned the key, and was relieved when the engine ran smoothly. Palance drove back to the Marathon station, and dropped off the gas can.

"You got your money's worth," the attendant said. "I'm keeping the rest."

Palance didn't argue. He drove off, the man still glaring at him through the plate glass window. The sky lightened. He couldn't bear to go home, so he drove back to the park and pulled his guitar out of the trunk. The chilly air and faint signs of dawn were keeping him awake. Palance needed to write more songs. He began to put the thoughts that had been running through his head to music.

There was *no turning back*. He could use his bed for tonight, but his days were numbered. This was the first time he'd been in the park alone, just him. *Out here alone*. His heart was running in circles. *Heart like a wheel*. It was just him. *No road home*. When his father died, he hoped and prayed that somehow, his dad would return, knowing that was impossible. But the band breaking up, he and Beth, living at home, he thought he could go back to the way it was. *No road home*.

His father always told him, keep your *back to the wind*. So many obstacles. He needed to write songs, book gigs, and hit the road, literally. *Close to the dream*. He made it happen tonight. Beth helped, but he closed the deal. Fame and fortune or bust. *Heaven or hell, no in-between. No in-between.*

He found the napkin he had started in Madison, and used it for the chorus. *Setting out on Sunday morning, restless sleep still in my eyes, searching for some shelter underneath stormy skies.* The melody sounded familiar, and the chords rang out; this day, the endless driving, visiting old haunts in search of a new life. All the mistakes he had made, the love he took for granted, the opportunities passed over.

Reality was *sharp as a knife, cold as a stone*. Palance couldn't go back in time and fix his mistakes, go away to college with

Beth, pay attention in class. Water under the bridge, *past is the past, bare to the bone.* The night slipped away. *What I've lost is lost, so much more to find, just so hard to leave the past behind.* Leave *the past behind.*

Palance had enough time and gas, now, to stop at the lake and watch the sunrise. He jotted down the song, put the guitar back in the car, and headed out again. The car crawled eastward, no traffic, no hurry. When he arrived at Touhy Beach, he got his guitar out and started playing his song, over and over, like a mantra. The melody undulated as the waves lapped the shore, deeper with each verse and chorus. Then he just played. Not even a song, just notes and chords, bass lines and arpeggios, his mind and fingers following the waves. The sky filled in with blues and purples, and the music leaned on minor chords and discordant tones.

The birds sang louder as the sun rose. They swooped down looking for food, the seagulls gliding elegantly on outstretched wings, and the pigeons strutting nervously. Palance played in concert with the waves, strumming an A-major as the root every time they hit, modulating to B-minor, then C-major and resolving on E-major, and returning to the root. Always returning to the root.

The sky turned a vibrant pastel, the sun radiating through. He played an E-major chord, and let it growl in celebration for the dawning of the day, and the light flooded in yellow and full of promise. Palance played his song again. It sounded more hopeful. *Setting out on Sunday morning, restless sleep still in my eyes, searching for some shelter underneath stormy skies.* The sky was blue, and he felt a change. After some sleep, he would plan his future.

He sang the first verse one more time. *No turning back, out here alone, heart like a wheel, no road home.* It was his anthem. He packed up the guitar and got into the Honda. His body felt strong and powerful. He headed down Touhy. The sun warmed him, and he got to the house just as his mother was stepping out. He greeted her with a weary smile, surprised when she brushed past him without speaking.

"Morning," he said, without meeting her eyes.

"Morning," she replied, and though he waited for her disapproval, her questions, anything, she went to her car, turned and said to him. "I'm not happy about this, either. It's been a long time since I've been happy." She got into her car and pulled away. Palance went back for his guitar, the sun too bright for his eyes. All he wanted was to get to his bed, lie down, and let sleep overtake him. Inside, Jillian was sitting at the breakfast table, glaring at him.

"So, you're back," she said.

"Yeah, for now."

"You can be a selfish asshole," she sneered.

"Easy to say for someone who has a place to live."

"You want to live here forever? With mom?"

"What the hell do you care?"

"You think it's been easy for any of us?" she asked.

"It hasn't been easy for me," he told her, putting the guitar down on the floor, harder than he intended.

"I don't have a father, either," Jillian said, "and I don't get to fuck up all the time the way you do. I have to get good grades, stay off drugs, and not be out all damn night. Do something with your life, Heller. I have to go to school." She got up, rinsed her dish in the sink, picked up her books, went up to Palance, and kissed him on the cheek. "I love you, numbskull," she said, and walked out the door, closing it behind her.

Palance was lightheaded and weary but too riled to go to bed. He closed his eyes, and the road appeared before him; white lines streamed past. He went into his bedroom, put his guitar in the closet, tore off his clothes, turned off the light, and lay down. He struggled to imagine where he would get the knowledge and stamina he needed. Exhaustion overtook him, and his eyes burned. They had been open too long. When he closed them, the road appeared again, and he let it carry him away.

He dreamt he was on the road. He saw it fly by and observed the stops along the way. He envisioned performances he would give and watched as the people streamed by. He saw them for a bit and then bid them farewell. Along the road, there were old friends and new, seen once a season, and the years passed quickly. He felt joy and sorrow, heard songs constructed, emoted, and shared. He felt loneliness, and nights with women, coming and going like the tide.

The faces looked familiar. Some he had already met. He recognized the stages, the small rooms set aside to get ready, and audiences of every variety. He mingled with them between sets and after gigs. Posters and CD covers appeared. Some showed pictures of the guitar, others of him in a denim shirt with a red brick wall behind him. He looked older. Beth was there, and his mother and sister, and Jason appeared twice: once looking haggard and burnt out, and once smiling and well. Kyle showed up, looking preppy as usual, but not so stern. Palance accepted all of this as a set of instructions.

When he awoke, it was dark. Songs swirled in his head, and he wrote down the bits and pieces he could remember. He knew people from school with recording equipment who had invited him to record. He needed to call them. He had little time to waste. Sounds from the kitchen and living room shuffled and clattered. He set fear and resentment aside. There was work to do.

No Road Home

No Road Home

No turning back,
Out here alone,
Heart like a wheel,
No road home,
no road home.

Back to the wind,
Close to the dream,
Heaven or Hell,
No in-between,
no in-between.

C
H   Setting out on Sunday morning,
O   restless sleep still in my eyes,
R   searching for some shelter underneath
U   stormy skies.
S

Sharp as a knife,
Cold as a stone,
Past is the past,
Bare to the bone,
bare to the bone.

Chorus

What I've lost is lost,
So much more to find,
Just so hard to leave
The past behind
the past behind.

No turning back,
Out here alone,
Heart like a wheel,
No road home,
no road home,
no road home,
no road home.

Chapter Nine

When Morning Comes

Palance's mother handed him an empty cardboard box and walked him down to the basement. "I've taken the tools I need and a few things from your father's desk," she said. "Whatever else you want is yours."

She walked away before he had time to respond. They were moving in two days. The sparseness of the room startled him. He first checked for the guitar tools and removed them. The pictures from his father's desk were gone. Palance ran his hand over the desk where his father paid bills and wrote out song lyrics. He felt him slipping away, pissed he didn't have room for the desk. He was renting a room in an apartment near Northeastern with some of the students he knew. He had moved in this morning. He barely had space for his bed and dresser.

Palance turned to the tools that were left, taking the ones he remembered best: a screwdriver with a chipped yellow and blue handle, another his father used to work on bicycles, and a metal hammer with electrical tape wrapped around the grip. He also claimed a tape measure responsible for indicating his and Jillian's height on the furnace room doorframe. He found the green stub of a pencil and took that, too. For a minute, he went through a mad-grab phase, shoving things into the box at random to preserve his father's legacy. Gradually, he realized he was filling the box with trash, items he would never use, spare parts from appliances thrown away years ago. He put most of it back and added the diagonal cutters for trimming guitar strings, a Phillips screwdriver that matched the tuning machines on his guitars, and two pairs of pliers.

Palance sat at his father's desk, opening each of the drawers. There were several pens. Only two still wrote; the ink had dried up in the rest. A fountain pen looked old and stained. He wondered if it might have belonged to his grandfather and added it to his box. The other was a thin silver pen that twisted open, and he took that. He left the paper clips and thumbtacks but took a stapler, a box of staples, and a gold tie clasp he found in the lower drawer, wondering what it was doing there.

Palance swiveled in the desk chair. It was an old wooden office chair without padding or artifice. The lacquer had rubbed off, and the years had worn the chair smooth. He wanted it. Goodwill would come for the rest. They would remove his father's memory from this room.

At the top of the stairs, he peered into the kitchen at the two silhouettes, his mother and Jillian, their heads bent down, silent. Tears stained their faces. He poured a glass of water from the sink and set it on the table. Palance reached for his mother's hand.

"Hey, it won't be so bad," he said. "I'll come by once in a while. I can always use a home-cooked meal."

His mother barely looked up, an unconvincing smile creased her face. "That's nice, dear," she said.

"Come visit," Jillian said.

"You probably think this is too much to ask, Palance, but we need you to help us move," his mother said.

"Whatever I can do," he answered, gulped his water and headed back downstairs before they started crying again.

Palance looked at the pencil marks on the doorframe. They stopped before he ever had a growth spurt, before Jillian cracked the five-foot mark, before he had written his first song, before he had a girlfriend, before he was in a band. He found shoe polish and a brush that had belonged to his father. In one of the desk drawers were notebooks with coffee stains on the covers. The pages were yellow at the edges. In them, his father wrote out song lyrics and penciled in the chords. On the first page was "Get Together" by Jesse Colin Young. The chords were in the key of C-major and then transposed to G in blue pencil. He recalled his father singing the song with a rabble of his friends on the chorus. Other songs sounded familiar. Palance placed the notebook in his box.

In another drawer, he found loose cassette tapes, some prerecorded, and others that looked like mix tapes. Though he didn't have a cassette player, he took them. He grabbed a paperweight and dropped it into his carton, which he closed, one flap over the other, the way his father taught him. Upstairs, his mother and sister had not moved from the table, and Jillian had an arm around their mother, who was wiping a tear from her eye.

"If it's okay," Palance said to his mother, "I'm going to take Dad's desk chair from downstairs."

"Sure," she answered, not bothering to look up.

"Is there anything you have, something personal of his I could keep?" Palance asked. "A jacket or pin or something?"

"Let me look," she said, and went to her bedroom. Jillian glared at him.

"You're bringing up Dad? Now?"

"So what? Why is it your business?"

"That's all she needs."

"What about what I need?" Palance asked.

"What about me?" Jillian demanded. "I've been holding this family together for years."

"You?"

"Yeah, me!" she declared and then broke down, tears flowing into the napkin she was holding to her face.

He moved behind her, put his hands on her shoulders, and kissed the top of her head. "You've been a rock?" he asked her.

"Damn straight," she told him.

He knew she was right. "You have been a rock," he told her. "Are you ready to move?" he asked.

"You know me," she said. "I've been packed for days. I helped Mom pick the movers."

"That's not what I mean," he said. "Are you ready to move?"

She turned and looked at him, the tears dry on her face. "Yeah, I'm ready."

Their mother walked in carrying a faded brown fedora. The material reminded Palance of a puppy, and she placed it on his head. "This was your father's," she said. "Now it's yours."

Palance tipped the hat to her, smiling. "Thank you, m'lady." It felt right, something to complete his image on stage.

He sat down at the table. His mother told them there was a quart of peach ice cream left in the freezer. Palance got the bowls, and Jillian took out the spoons and chocolate syrup. "Finish it or move it," his mother said and found multicolored sprinkles and chopped nuts to add. It felt like a holiday. Jillian and his mom were wearing thin smiles.

Palance said chocolate syrup didn't go with peach ice cream, but that didn't stop Jilly. She told him chocolate syrup goes with everything, and the sooner he realized it, the better. His mother danced around the table as she ate her ice cream, slathered with chocolate syrup, and Palance, as usual, was in the minority.

"So where did Dad wear this?" he asked, holding the hat in his hand.

His mother stopped dancing and sat down, pushing her ice cream away. Jillian turned somber. "He wore it to the clubs," his mother said. "When he played."

Palance's mind flooded with questions he dared not ask. He nodded and placed the hat on top of his box from downstairs. Silently, they finished their ice cream.

"What time do you want me here on Tuesday?" he asked.

"Whenever," his mother said.

"Nine okay?" he asked.

"Fine."

Even with the tension, his curiosity was too much to bear. "Why does this freak you out so much?" he asked. Jillian stiffened.

"You were young," his mother told him. "He left us for a while. To go on the road. He wore that hat. He left me. Musicians leave. That's what they do."

"You kicked me out," Palance shouted, shocking himself. Jillian glared at him, and his mother stormed out of the room. He put his bowl in the sink, grabbed his box and hat, and headed to the door.

In the car, Palance felt tears well up inside him. Too agitated to drive, he went back into the house for the chair. He carried it up the stairs and out to his car. He stuffed it in the back seat, closed the door and left.

Feeling numb, he drove down Kedzie to Lincoln, then west on Balmoral to his new apartment. Palance placed the fedora on his head and walked in with the box. He walked up a single flight of stairs and opened the apartment door. No one else was home. He sat on the bed in his room. His instruments were in the closet, his stereo on top of the dresser, and his clothes in the drawers. Otherwise, the room was bare. His window faced east and allowed in meager light. He set the box down and threw the hat onto the dresser. It missed its mark and floated to the floor.

Palance rummaged through the box of miscellaneous tools, pictures, and office supplies, looking for anything useful. He threw the cassette tapes into his sock drawer. The tools went on the closet shelf. He picked the hat up from the floor and took it into the bathroom, where he put it on and stared at himself in the mirror, wondering what happened with his dad—why he left and why he came back. Palance felt guilty about leaving his mother crying.

Palance heard a key turn in the front door lock. When he walked into the living room, Ben was standing next to his bicycle, taking his helmet off.

"Nice lid, Sid. New image?"

"Maybe," Palance said. "And if things don't work out with the music, I can always join the FBI. Agent Heller, reporting for duty." He tipped the hat toward Ben.

"Don't go narcing around here," Ben told him. "We have our moments."

"Not a problem."

"Hey, Pal," Ben said, "I've got a project for school. Would you mind lending your dulcet tones to a recording?"

"Not at all, but it'll be weird going back to school."

"You don't have to. We can do it here," Ben said and opened his bedroom door to show him a new iMac sitting on the desk. "Copped a copy of Pro-Tools. Unlimited tracks just a click away."

Palance felt his eyes light up. "You can make recordings on that thing?"

"Recording, MIDI, the whole works. We can make an album right here."

"Do you mind showing me?"

Ben grabbed a microphone and cable out of his desk drawer, plugged it into a box next to the computer, and used a mouse to click on the Pro-Tools icon. He changed a few settings and told Palance to grab a chair. In an hour, Ben had taught him the basics: how to record, edit, and arrange music on the computer. He showed Palance how to change the pitch of guitars and voices, and add accompaniment like strings and horns by placing notes on a musical staff and assigning instruments to them. It seemed like magic.

"So, what's this vocal you want me to record?" Palance asked.

"I'll play what I've got so far, but I need to work on it a bit more before I'm ready for your part." Ben called up the song on the computer and played him a jazzy samba with a sitar on lead that transitioned into an orchestral arrangement with French horns and bassoons. "What are you doing Thursday?" he asked.

"I've gotta work in the morning, but I'm free after four," Palance told him.

"How 'bout if we do the vocal then and afterwards we can work on your stuff?"

"Excellent," Palance said.

"So, how's the move going, dude? Easy or queasy?"

"I'm done. Got a chair in the car, otherwise I'm all in."

"Traveling light."

Palance was grateful for all Ben was offering. "I think I'll get the chair," he told him.

"We're gonna jam soon," Ben said. "If you're interested."

Palance put the hat away in the closet before heading out to the car. Everything was in place—the apartment, everything he needed to produce and sell his music, these new friends. The chair seemed heavier than before, and he set it down on the sidewalk. He was wheeling it toward the apartment when he saw Elise walking toward him from the opposite direction, carrying a flute case.

"Heard you were moving in with Ben and Dennis," she said.

"It's a recording studio, it's an apartment," he told her. "It's two places in one. How could I refuse?"

"So, has Ben signed you to his label yet? Someone should have warned you about that."

"Label?"

"Resist the pod, Palance. Ben has dreams. Mogul-type dreams. He's got some good ideas. Just be careful. Don't sign your life away."

"He did show me his recording setup."

"Be your own man, Palance. I see you have your own chair."

"It was my Dad's."

"Be your own man."

"You going in?"

"Yes," she said, sitting down on the chair. "Wheel me in."

Palance opened the door, and Elise held it, still seated. At the stairway, she sighed loudly. Then she rose and grabbed one of the legs to help carry it up the steps. She chided him, though, not to treat her like a commoner. Once a princess, always a princess. When they reached the second floor, she sat herself back in the chair and again commanded him to wheel her in.

"So, what are you here for?" he asked.

"Jam session. Didn't they tell you?"

"Yeah," Palance said. "I might sit in."

"One of Ben's ideas. We perform for his highness. He records and edits it. If it's any good, he releases it on his label, if not—delete."

"I thought you warned me against getting involved."

"Sorry. I didn't tell you. I'm one of his minions. He can get a little bossy at times, but he's not a bad taskmaster. Just a bit fussy." Inside the apartment, Elise rose from Palance's chair with a curtsey and bowed before Ben. "At your service, my liege."

"Knock that off," Ben said. "What nonsense did she tell you?" he asked Palance.

"Something about starting your own label."

"Well, that's true," Ben said. "Someone's got to make money from music. Might as well be us."

"Us?" Elise asked, raising her eyebrows.

"Us," Ben replied. "So far I've raised an astounding two hundred forty-seven dollars."

"And I've seen none of it."

"I've spent more than seven hundred on microphones alone."

"Can we lose money?" Palance asked.

"Not a cent," Ben said. "Just your time."

"But you're bossy," Elise told him.

"And you, my dear, are a princess."

Elise curtsied to Ben, opened her case and put her flute together. Ben announced that Dennis would be arriving any minute. He invited Palance to join in, or at least be silent while they were recording. Any noise would show up in the mix. Palance took the Larriveé out of the closet and tuned it, while Ben brought out microphones and stands, adjusting one for Elise's flute and another for Palance's guitar. He pulled out his Korg keyboard and hooked it up to the computer. Palance sat next to Elise on the couch. Ben set out a series of hand drums in front of an overstuffed chair for Dennis.

"What should I play?" Palance asked.

"Whatever feels right," Ben told him. "Sing if you want to. Has to be original, though. No money for royalties."

"So, what's the name of the label?" Palance asked.

Ben told him it was *Music from Around the Bend*.

"Get it?" Elise said. "Ben DeMarco. Ben D. Bend." She blew a middle C into his ear. Palance couldn't tell if she liked him or had dismissed him. Nothing about her gave it away.

The door banged open, and Dennis burst in, gasping for air, a khaki green backpack slung over his shoulder. His hair was matted back, and sweat was pouring through his shirt. "I ran. I'm late," he said and collapsed into the chair behind the drums.

"Catch your breath, dude," Ben told him.

"A drummer should always be on time," Dennis declared, scolding himself.

"They are quite amusing," Elise explained to Palance. "We can't determine who's Frick and who's Frack."

Dennis began breathing more regularly and asked Ben, "Are they in the proper mood?"

Ben responded by bringing out a tray, which held a small bag of marijuana, a pipe, a beer, and a cup of hot tea. Ben handed the pipe and pot to Dennis, the tea to Elise, and picked up the beer, putting the tray down on the coffee table. "These delights and more can be yours for joining the circle," he told Palance. "What might be your pleasure?"

While Palance assessed the situation and contemplated his next move, Dennis loaded the pipe, took a hit, and passed it to Ben, who inhaled deeply and then waited for a response from Palance.

"Got any coffee?" Palance asked. He made too many mistakes when he was high, and he knew an audition when he saw one. At least this time.

"Instant, French press, or Mr. Coffee?" Ben asked. "Take your pick."

"French press," Palance answered. "But I can get it."

"Not tonight," Ben said. "Tonight you serve the muse, and I serve you. While I am away," he began—ducking into his room before heading into the kitchen—"play, children, play."

Dennis took another toke on the pipe, picked a *djembe* from the floor and played a slow African beat. His long, brown hair swayed with the rhythm, and Palance followed his hair like a metronome. Elise joined in with her flute, short gusts of wind to dance around Dennis' drums. Palance joined in with a minor seventh chord. They looked toward him, and he played the ninth, to add color. Dennis drove the rhythm, Elise played a smooth harmonic minor scale, and Palance replied on guitar. Elise began the scale again and extended it, adding elevenths and thirteenths. Palance stayed with her.

Ben came back holding a cup of coffee and nodding as the music wove itself around him. Elise played a lilting melody, interspersed with short percussive bursts. Palance played soft chords behind her melody. Dennis slowed the rhythm, matching the beat to Elise, and Palance timed his chords to Dennis' accents. Out of the corner of his eye, Palance saw Ben place the coffee in front of him, silently; and then walk to his keyboard. Elise slowed down. Dennis and Palance followed, until she ended on the tonic, trilling and holding the note for several measures. When they were done, Ben opened his eyes. Before Palance could say anything, Ben played a riff on the keyboard, Dennis picked up a tabla, and they were off again.

The rhythm was fast and pointed. Palance played chords behind Ben, while Elise wove a countermelody. The beat was infectious. Dennis continued on tabla with his left hand; picking up a wood and ball-bearing cabasa with his right, adding a metallic scraping sound to the mix. Palance felt the rhythm and played rapid seven-note riffs followed by two quick downbeats on the chord to drive the melody. They were in a hypnotic groove.

Palance wailed in the groove until he noticed the volume fading in the room and looked at Ben, who choreographed the ending with a conductor's hand, the volume dropping to a whisper and then rising for one last crescendo.

Palance didn't know how long the break would last, so he reached for his coffee and took a quick gulp before realizing that everyone else was putting down their instruments. Dennis was sweating and raised his empty water glass, which Ben picked up.

"Anyone else need anything?" he asked, apparently taking this serving thing seriously.

"Hey, you got chops," Dennis told Palance. "Not bad for a college dropout."

Elise put her hand on Palance's arm. "You keep up pretty well," she said. "So far."

"Hey," Ben said, walking back into the room with Dennis' water, toking on the pipe. "That sounds like a challenge to me."

Palance gulped down the rest of his coffee and asked Ben for another. He noticed Elise out of the corner of his eye, enough to know that she was looking straight at him.

"It was a challenge," she told him.

"Coffee first," he said. "Then I'll be ready."

"Brave man," Dennis told him. "You've never heard her pour it on." He gestured with the pipe toward Palance, and, when he refused, said, "You don't know the penalties involved."

"Penalties?"

Elise held up her hand to stop Dennis. "Don't give too much away," she said.

"Drink up," Ben said, handing the cup of coffee to Palance. "You'll need it." After he took a sip, Ben looked at Dennis and said, "Count the time, Mr. Stein."

Dennis picked up a pair of claves and slapped out a beat, "One, two, three, four, one, two, three," and clapped them together rapidly.

Elise played a series of triplets. He duplicated them on guitar. She repeated the sequence two times, until he felt comfortable; then she switched keys and played a series of descending triplets down to the lowest range of her register. Again, Palance was able to duplicate them, but at the very edge of his abilities. Elise seemed unnaturally relaxed. Once more, she repeated the previous lines. He was lulled into complacency, until she began to trill a series of notes that flowed from one key and scale to another in brisk fashion. Palance's fingers tangled in the strings, and he hung his head in shame.

"So, what's the penalty?" Palance asked Ben. He didn't dare face Elise.

"Ask her," Ben told him.

Dennis and Ben were smiling broadly. Palance looked at Elise with trepidation. She appeared to enjoy his discomfort and didn't offer any relief. It forced him to ask her.

"You will address me as Mistress for the rest of the night." Palance breathed easier, having tortured himself with thoughts of embarrassing rituals that might have been required. "However," she continued, "you will first kneel in front of me and admit defeat."

Dennis and Ben cracked up laughing. "Is this standard?" Palance asked Ben.

"Hey," Ben said, "you're getting off easy. She made me kiss her feet."

"He kept up better than you did?" she told Ben.

"She's a ringer," Dennis said. "And dangerous, too."

"Kneel down," Elise told Palance.

Palance knelt in front of her. If he had to do this, he would do it with style. "Mistress Elise, I have been bested by your skills and beauty, and I readily admit defeat."

"Very well, plebeian, rise then," she said to him, holding out her hand to be kissed, and Palance complied.

Ben started the playback of the session. Elise leaned over and kissed Palance on the lips, and then withdrew.

"Just testing the cut of your jib," she told him.

Palance looked at Ben, listening to the recording with his eyes closed, and at Dennis, gently snoring, the pipe still in his hand. Elise winked conspiratorially at Palance and then pushed her foot against his leg.

"Mistress," Palance asked, approaching a British accent. "Would you care to attend supper with me?"

"A bit out of your class, aren't you?"

"Yes, Mistress."

"After the playback," she told him. "Benjamin can't abide anyone leaving during the playback."

"But Dennis . . ."

"Dennis hasn't left, has he?"

Quietly, Elise disassembled her flute and packed it into the case. Palance put his guitar down too loudly, and Ben opened his eyes and glared at him.

At the end of the first piece, Ben said, "Not bad," to no one in particular.

When the second piece began, Ben retreated to his silent reverie, eyes closed and head bowed. The only sound in the room was the music. When it was over, he said, "Good job," and then told Palance and Elise they could go to dinner.

"He hears everything," Elise said.

Palance put his guitar away. When he came out, Elise had her flute case in hand. "Ready to go?" he asked her.

"Hmmph," she said and stared at him severely.

"Ready to go, *Mistress*?" he corrected himself. She took his arm. Ben had disappeared, and Dennis was asleep in the chair.

"Leona's?" he asked, as they descended the stairs and walked out into the cool evening air.

"I believe that would be acceptable. Do you have a chariot nearby?"

"Blue Honda. Right over there," he said, pointing.

"It's not polite to point," she told him.

Palance opened the passenger door. Elise sat primly with the flute case in her lap. She peppered him with questions. *Why did you quit school and move in with Ben and Dennis? What are your future plans? What is your relationship status?* Palance revealed an intention to book gigs and hit the road, as well as his lack of a romantic situation, at which the corners of her mouth turned up ever so slightly, and only for an instant.

At Leona's, the hostess sat them at a small table near the bar. Elise asked for a Mojito. Palance ordered a Margarita, which they brought without carding him. Looking over the menu, Elise commented on the myriad of choices.

"Too many options," she said, and then, "Ah-hah, Caesar avocado wrap."

He chose the hamburger with blue cheese and mushrooms.

"So, Palance, tell me, is it your goal to become rich and famous?"

Palance winced at the question. "I don't know about famous. Make a living. Play my music. I guess I'd like to be known, and famous wouldn't be bad. Rich would be spectacular, but I'm not counting on it."

"Sensible attitude," she said. The waitress came over and took their order. "Caesar avocado wrap, easy on the dressing, no tomato, no onions, and a cup of minestrone soup."

Palance asked for his burger with minestrone soup, and a side order of French fries.

"We have wedge fries," the waitress told him, and Palance nodded.

Palance asked Elise if she wanted to be famous, and she asked him how many famous flautists he knew. He could identify only two—James Galway and Jean-Pierre Rampal—and she said *Exactly, how sensible would that be?* Besides, she was attending Northeastern, not Juilliard; she had dreams but was neither foolish nor flighty.

"So, what are your dreams?" he asked.

"What are my dreams?—*Mistress*," she commanded.

"Yes," he said, "Mistress."

"Make music. Probably teach. I'd like a family someday, but not soon. Not sure I'm qualified."

"Qualified?"

"I am an acquired taste, rather difficult to deal with at times. Speaking of which, you neglected to use my title," she told him—"*again*"—arching her eyebrows.

"Yes, Mistress," Palance said. "Difficult, but intriguing."

"I'm glad you feel that way, plebeian. There may be hope for you yet."

Palance was relieved to see the waitress with their soup. He felt a bit uncomfortable around Elise and wondered if it stemmed from her formality or her level of comfort with her own quirkiness. He decided to let her take the lead for now, a role for which she seemed amazingly well suited. She told him she had considered his compositions, repertoire, and stage show, and had ideas for furthering his career. "You need recordings, and a CD to sell from the stage. Of course, Ben will set that up for you, but if you require a flautist, I would be happy to oblige."

"Mistress," Palance said, "I would be more than pleased if you would lend your flute to my humble compositions."

"I am also a fair graphic artist. I can put together a brochure or a CD cover"—she paused, taking a spoonful of soup—"if you'd like."

"Why are you doing this for me?" he asked and then began to add the obligatory title, but she interrupted.

"I may be a pain in the ass," she said, "but I am also," and again, she hesitated, "a woman."

"A woman?"

"In case you hadn't noticed," Elise said, and continued with her soup.

The waitress brought their entrees. Elise explained that she saw him as the poetic singer-songwriter type. He needed a tagline, something to stand out. She threw a shower of adjectives at him: young, wistful, innocent (he winced at this), lyrical, sensitive, sentimental, sensuous (his eyes grew wide), and . . .

silly, at which he flicked a wedge fry at her. She ducked and used the thin straw from her drink to shower water on him.

"Do not mess with me, plebeian," she said. "I take no guff."

Palance was lightheaded and intoxicated. The waitress offered them each another drink, and Elise accepted, so Palance nodded his head, and wondered how he'd be able to drive home. This seemed like a night to take chances.

"I'd love your help, Mistress."

"And what might you do for me?" she asked.

"What might you like . . . Mistress?" Elise seemed to have gained the upper hand, through every fault of his own.

"I might like dessert," she said. "They have something called Decadent Chocolate Cake, and I am a decadent girl. Anything else," she added, "we can discuss when you call me."

"But I don't have your phone number."

"No, you don't. Nor did you refer to me as 'Mistress.'" She looked at him with widening, angry eyes.

"I see this is going to be a challenging relationship. Mistress."

"Oh, now we're in a relationship. You're a brash young man, pleleian,"

"Mistress," he said, "would it be possible to obtain your phone number?"

"Anything is possible," she said, rolling her eyes at him.

"May I have your phone number?"

"Do you have a pen? Or paper? Of course not," she answered for him. She took paper and pen from her purse, wrote down her number, and handed it to him. "Must I be responsible for everything?"

"Mistress," he answered, "I thank you for your indulgence."

"Speaking of indulgences," she said as the waitress came over. "Your Decadent Chocolate Cake, please."

"I'll have the cheesecake," Palance said. "And coffee. Lots of coffee."

"Have things gone to your head tonight?" Elise asked.

"Yes, Mistress. They have."

"That's the trouble with men," Elise told the waitress. "Everything goes into their heads, yet so little comes out. I'll have coffee, too, please."

The waitress looked at Palance. "Something tells me you're in trouble," she said.

"You have no idea," he told her.

"So, when do you plan to get started on these recordings?" Elise asked him.

"Thursday. It'd be great to have you there."

"So now you want me as your groupie?"

"Consultant," he said, and when she didn't react, he added, "advisor . . . producer?"

"*Producer* sounds excellent. They get credit. I will get credit, won't I?"

"Extra credit, Mistress," he said, careful not to slur his words.

"Any other plans?" she asked, and Palance leaned across the table and kissed her. She pulled away. "I was referring to your career," she said in a stern tone.

The waitress brought coffee and dessert. Palance burned his tongue with the first sip of coffee, and knew he needed three or four cups and at least half an hour before he'd be able to drive home safely. He tried to think of his music, his career—anything other than the way Elise looked and smelled.

"Tell me about your family," she said, and it sobered him quickly.

"My family," he said and instantly remembered his obligations on Tuesday, and the scene before he left. "They don't like me being a musician. They don't like me going on the road, and they weren't too thrilled about me dropping out of college."

"Both of your parents?" she asked.

"My father died years ago. I was eleven."

"Sorry. My mom died two years ago, but my dad's still around. They were older when they had me."

"You get what you get," he said. "How does your mom feel about you playing music?"

"She's okay as long as I have backup plans—teaching and graphic design."

"So, if you just did whatever the hell you wanted to, what would that look like?" he asked her, taking a forkful of cheesecake.

Elise picked at her cake and took a sip of coffee. "You don't want to know."

Palance smiled, finally feeling like he had the upper hand. "Yes, Mistress, I do."

He watched the muscles around her eyes relax. The waitress refilled their coffee cups. "I've always liked musicals," she said. "I love to dress up in costume, be on stage, and belt them out. Broadway . . . or burlesque even."

"Why don't you?" Palance asked.

"Community Theater," she said.

"That's not an answer."

"It's as close as I have any chance of getting."

"You don't know if . . ."

"What makes you think I haven't tried? Just some silly idea left over from my youth."

Palance gazed at her without talking, feeling as if he had discovered an amazing toy in a box of cereal. "You really are something," he told her.

"You really are something . . . *Mistress*," she chided him. "Try to remember that, plebeian. How swacked are you? I can drive home."

"I'll be okay."

"You're not twenty-one yet, are you?"

"How did you know?"

"Feminine wiles. Besides, your face is red as a beet, and your eyes are spinning in opposite directions."

"I'll be fine."

"Hand me the keys."

"I can drive."

"Do you know the penalty for driving while intoxicated under the age of twenty-one?"

Palance handed her the keys. The waitress asked if they wanted anything else. Palance shook his head "No," and Elise asked for the check.

"I'll get it," Palance said.

"Oh, is this a date?" she asked.

"Yes, Mistress. I believe it is."

"Thank you, kind sir. The evening has been my pleasure."

"The pleasure is all mine," Palance said. He pulled out his wallet and sighed in relief as he found enough money to cover the check and a tip.

"Normally," she told him on the way out of the restaurant, "I would have you walk several paces behind me, plebeian. However, I am in a generous mood. You may take my hand and walk me to your chariot. There are vandals about, and I may require your services."

"And what services might those be, Mistress?"

"We'll discuss that on our second date," she told him, leaning against his arm. The moon was full above the lake. "It's almost midnight. You are relieved from referring to me by title."

Palance heard a screech of tires and boisterous laughter nearby. "To what do I owe this favor?"

"I do not allow my subjects to kiss me."

Palance had difficulty processing this riddle. When he did, they were by his car, and she was opening the passenger door for him. He cupped her face between his hands, pressing his lips against hers.

"You're a slow study, Heller, but you kiss well," Elise said. He kissed her again, and when their lips were millimeters apart, waited until she leaned into him.

"I can drive home," he told her.

"Get in the car, Heller," she commanded.

"Yes, Mistress," he told her with an impertinent smile. On the way home, he said, "Well, you turned out to be a pretty spectacular pain in the ass."

She gave him a stern look, and he shrugged. "Your words, not mine."

"And you're not bad for an underage college dropout who can't hold his liquor."

They turned onto his street, and Palance asked Elise if she wanted to come up.

"Put it on hold, Romeo. You got everything you're going to get on a first date. You didn't even ask me out again, did you?"

"I . . . I . . . ," Palance stuttered.

"That's okay," she said. "You will. Help me look for a parking space."

"Up on the left." he said.

"Call me," she told him, expertly parking in a tight fit.

"Hey, where do you live, anyway?"

"See that building down the block? Good night, Heller. Thank you for dinner." Palance leaned over to kiss her, but she put her index finger up to his lips and shook her head "No." "Good night," she said, and walked staunchly from the car, handing him the keys.

Too late, Palance wondered if he should have walked her home. She was already down the block and entering her building. This was his first night in his new apartment. He walked up the stairs, quietly put the key in the lock, and turned it, the way he did at home when he would come in late. Ben was still awake watching television, and Dennis was asleep in his chair. The drums were gone.

Palance felt buzzed but not tired. He thought about the cassette tapes stashed in his sock drawer, and asked Ben if he had a player. Ben walked into his room and returned with an ancient portable unit someone left ages ago. Palance took the machine into his room. He plugged in some earbuds, but only the right earpiece had sound. He pulled the tapes out of the drawer and listened to each for a few minutes, separating them into piles to keep or toss. He found one with no label and put it into the machine.

At first, there was no sound; then the tapping of someone testing a microphone. He heard breathing, and then a guitar. It sounded familiar. When the singing began, it was deep and resonant. The song was on the tip of his tongue. He couldn't recall it, but knew each next line before it came. *I've stood upon the river's edge and watched the water as it rolled.* He had a memory of a man beside him. He was a young boy, and the man was his father.

Listened to the ebb and flow in summer's heat and winter's cold. This song had always been in the back of his mind, just out of reach. It was a lullaby his father wrote and sang to him. It had been a decade since he'd heard it, maybe more. When the chorus played, his breath halted. *When morning comes the earth turns still, 'til sunlight finds the windowsill, and pours its light into my soul, in summer's heat and winter's cold.* It was a memory, not in words, but in images and sounds. He saw the light pour through the kitchen window, his father writing in a notebook, pausing to play his guitar, then back to the notebook. Palance felt the sun on his face, and his father telling him about the seasons, and later that night singing him the song.

Palance paused the tape and went to the kitchen for a glass of water. He tiptoed, to avoid waking Dennis. Ben's light was out, and Palance gently closed the door to his room behind him. He put the earbuds back on and pressed "Play." *Down the road, around the bend, past the concrete sidewalk's end.* Palance quietly sang along, *past the Earth, the moon and Mars, where wishes ride on shooting stars.* He listened to the chorus again, less for the words and melody than his father's voice, the way it made him feel, and the memories it evoked. They were sounds as familiar as the sound of his own breath.

Before the third verse began, it played in Palance's head. *Each beginning has an end, begin and end, begin again.* He felt something drip on his hands and wondered if there was a leak in the ceiling. He looked up only to realize they were his own tears. He felt them increase and allowed them to flow.

When he was able, Palance rewound the tape and listened again. One line overwhelmed him: *even though we all pretend, you will not pass this way again.* Did his father know what was going to happen? Palance shuddered under the weight of his questions and turned the tape back on. The first verse repeated at the end, then simply, *summer's hot and winter's cold.* Too final. The worst things about death were the unanswered questions.

Palance listened to the last few chords. The song finished, and then, before the click that ended the recording, he heard his father say, "Goodnight, Pal, sleep tight." He played those words repeatedly—he didn't know how many times—until the words lost their meaning. Then he rewound the tape and listened to the song again, letting it wash over him. He took out the Larriveé and played along with his father, doing what he was never able to before; play a duet with the man whose guitar was in his hands.

Palance put the guitar away, lay down on his bed, and listened to the silence. His father's hat was in clear sight on the dresser. He heard the occasional siren in the background, a truck rumbling down the street, and the sound of his father's voice, "Goodnight, Pal, sleep tight." Suddenly he was fast asleep, dreaming of a cobblestone road speckled with shimmering light. He took a step toward it, and the road opened before him.

When Morning Comes

I've stood upon the river's edge
And watched the water as it rolled,
And listened to the ebb and flow
In summer's heat and winter's cold

C
H   *When morning comes the earth turns still,*
O   *'til sunlight finds the windowsill,*
R   *and pours its light into my soul*
U   *in summer's heat and winter's cold.*
S

Down the road, around the bend,
Past the concrete sidewalk's end,
Past the Earth, the Moon and Mars
Where wishes ride on shooting stars.

Chorus

Each beginning has an end,
Begin and end, begin again.
And even though we all pretend,
You will not pass this way again.

Chorus

I've stood upon the river's edge
And watched the water as it rolled,
And listened to the ebb and flow
In summer's heat and winter's cold
Summer's hot, and winter's cold.

Going on the Road

The box of CDs were in the trunk, along with a suitcase, duffle bag, and a set of blank notebooks. Palance was heading out for two months, playing coffeehouses and bars: the Ginkgo in St. Paul, Minnesota, then out to New England, New York, and back across the country to California. Ben had made a few phone calls, Elise had worked miracles, and things started happening. Palance was going on the road.

Elise came up behind him and wrapped herself around his waist. "Last night in town," she said, pressing her head against his back.

Palance turned around and took her in his arms. "Seven weeks," he said. "I'll be on the road when I turn twenty-one."

"I keep forgetting I've robbed the cradle."

"It's only a year and a half. Not like you're some old hag or something." Elise released herself and glared at him. "I didn't mean that," he said, but she was still glowering. "You are beautiful," he told her.

"Don't forget that when you're on the road. Or how jealous I get. I will know if you stray, Mr. Heller. I will know."

Palance pointed to the new cell phone on the dining-room table and told her he'd be in touch. "Besides," he said, "who could measure up to you?"

Palance wasn't thinking about her. He wondered how he was going to make it. He'd saved a few hundred bucks from his job at Target. The gigs wouldn't pay enough for restaurants and hotel rooms. He'd still owe Ben rent. He had a list of names and phone numbers, places he could crash and maybe get a meal—but not everywhere—and there was gas money. Palance didn't know if he was prepared for any of it. Elise took his hand and led him toward her bedroom.

"I'm going to miss you," she said, unbuttoning his shirt and helping him off with his pants, promising to have everything washed and hung when he returned. Palance removed her nightgown and pulled her close. Her eyes were watery and bright. She rested her hands on the small of his back and rose to meet his lips. She was strong and deliberate. They held each other without speaking, slipping into bed, where she grasped him from behind, her breasts tight against his back. Her heart beat against his and her hair fell between his shoulder blades. He flipped toward her, and they moved through the night, her breasts massaging his chest, her limbs enveloping him. They explored and tasted each other's skin and sweat. Her legs grasped and held him inside her, clasping him to her. Their bodies moved together as they climaxed and released, collapsing in unison.

They whispered about the days and weeks to come, his itinerary, her practice schedule, and the sessions with Ben and Dennis he would miss. She packed him stationery, envelopes, stamps, and the car charger for the cell phone. Palance let her know he would miss her. He didn't admit how afraid he was of ending up stranded on the road somewhere, no money for gas or food, sleeping in his car. How lonely he felt, even in her arms, knowing he would be alone.

"You'd better be faithful," she told him, punching him in the arm, and then lying down and snuggling against him.

Palance wanted to tell her he loved her, but the words wouldn't leave his throat. He held her until her breath slowed and her body became limp. He turned on his side and faced her, resting on his shoulder to watch the shallow rise and fall of her breasts. When she was deep in slumber, he leaned over and told her he loved her, in a whisper, so she wouldn't wake and hear him. He was afraid his words would come back to haunt him.

Palance lay awake and motionless. When the sky lightened, he fell into a shallow dream: he was walking down the center of the highway, one leg on each of the two yellow lines, careful not to step off and fall into oblivion. His feet froze as vistas of oceans, mountains, and vast plains of wheat rose up and disappeared. Birds in colorful pastel plumage flew by, singing arias in Italian, and he understood these were prayers. When he woke, there was a swallow sitting on a tree branch outside the window. He smelled coffee brewing and bacon frying.

Elise was standing by the stove in her robe and slippers, pulling hash browns from the oven. "At least you'll get a good breakfast." The table was set. "Sit down. I don't want it to get cold." Elise said nothing about the fact that he was in his underwear, something she never tolerated at the table. She placed a plate of bacon, eggs, and potatoes and a hot cup of coffee in front of him, and sat by his side.

"Aren't you going to eat anything?" he asked.

"Later," she said, watching him closely. He felt her memorize his features. Palance dipped a forkful of potato into the egg yolk, and it dripped onto his chin. Elise reached over to wipe it off.

"Are you going to clip my gloves to my coat and sew my name in my underwear?"

"Have you checked your underwear?"

"Get something to eat, please."

Elise walked back to the stove and fixed herself a plate. She brought it to the table and moved the food around with a fork, like a puzzle she was attempting to solve. "When do you have to be in St. Paul?"

"If I leave by ten, I'll be there by five, six if I stop for lunch. I don't go on until eight." Palance finished his breakfast and headed for the shower. He savored the hot water and comfort of knowing where the shampoo was without looking. He dressed and picked up the Larriveé. Elise waited in the hallway, holding a small box wrapped in silver paper.

"I thought you were going to take both guitars," she said.

"Less stuff, less hassle."

She handed him the box. "Don't open it until you get somewhere."

"I am somewhere," he said.

"Shut up, plebeian. Kiss me goodbye, and get the hell out of here."

Palance set the guitar and package down, took her in his arms, and studied her face: the firm jaw and wide eyes, her small nose, and delicate ears. He kissed her gently, letting his tongue brush against hers before retreating. "I'll miss you," he said.

"Drive safely. Call."

"I'll call you tonight," he told her, picked up the guitar and package, and was out the door and down the stairs.

For the first half hour in the car, he replayed the morning in his head and everything leading up to it: the first time Elise took her clothes off for him, her music, and her guidance. Palance saw Elise in all her forms: the sardonic aristocrat, the artist with her flute, the strategist who would carve out empires, and the lover who enchanted him. He passed Rockford, nearing the Wisconsin border. He would pass Madison. He had a gig there later in the month.

Palance entered Wisconsin, and his thoughts left Illinois and Elise. He focused on what lay ahead. He wondered about the gigs, the women, and if he could remain faithful to Elise. The further from Chicago, the weaker her pull. Back home, it was barely autumn. Here, the leaves had already begun to change color—yellow and pale orange at first—and then his first glimpse of red. The forest around him ignited, and the passion was contagious.

He played his CD, the one he put together with Ben and Elise, just his voice and guitar. He was ashamed and thrilled at the shivers it gave him. Palance wondered if he could elicit that reaction in a group of strangers. He imagined his music on the radio. In a few hours, he would perform in an unfamiliar city at a new venue for an unknown audience.

Palance streamed through the countryside until he saw the turnoff for Culver's. There was a young girl with blond hair at the window. She took his money and handed him a paper bag and a coke.

Palance ate in the car, watching the traffic, mostly semi-trucks. He had a long way to go. He put the car in drive and let the sound of the road and music wear him into a groove. When the CD ended, it repeated. The land became voluptuous; the trees thickened and burst into bright oranges and rust, and when openings appeared in the trees, there were rivers that crisscrossed the highway and lakes dotting the landscape. Palance opened a window and let the cool air in. He heard birds sing and leaves rustle. The cows lined up along fences, and the horses grazed leisurely. Then suddenly, like the fox he saw off in the distance, he felt immobile, his eyes glazed over, and his skin moistened with sweat.

There were tricks Ben used in the recordings: reverb, pitch correction, and other enhancements. Palance felt his body stiffen until he noticed his knuckles were white. He feared he was a myth, the CD a fable Ben had created, and which he had no chance approaching. Palance pulled the car over to the side of the road and sat immobilized as a woodpecker tapped in the distance. A red Ford truck whizzed by him, blaring country music.

Palance got out of the car and walked alongside the inter-state, following the sound of the woodpecker, heading into the woods, where he heard the tapping clearly. He stopped dead in his tracks; a large buck deer four feet in front of him was standing frozen, close enough for Palance to see portions of his fur worn away and smell the musky odor. The two of them stared motionless into each other's eyes. In syncopated steps, they each turned away from the other, the buck galloping into the forest. Palance returned to his car and continued his journey. The highway was empty and straight, as if there was only one available path. St. Paul was an hour down the road. He turned on the radio and left it on the first station he found: a classical music station out of Minneapolis, playing Schubert's Unfinished Symphony, and showing up at the Ginkgo Coffee House almost three hours early.

They fed Palance lasagna and vegetable soup. Afterward, a tall man with bright orange dreadlocks and wire frame glasses guided him and his guitar into a small room in back where he tuned his guitar and waited. Palance asked what the crowd was like. "You never know," the man said. Palace looked at the set list he'd prepared. He'd adjust if needed. Start with some popular stuff and then his own songs. He had a couple hundred CDs to unload during this circuit. If he wanted to keep eating he would need to sell a few in each location.

Palance promised Elise he'd call when he arrived, so he took out the cell phone and dialed. It rang four times before she answered, sounding breathless. She told him she missed him, and he said it back. After they'd hung up, he practiced. He heard his name announced over the PA system.

The audience appeared disinterested as he walked on stage. He heard a few laughs, the rattle of cups and plates, and a smattering of conversations that rang against the tile floor. Rather than the short introduction he'd planned, he dove into his first song: Bob Dylan's "Knocking on Heaven's Door," singing with a vehemence that stunned them to silence. Instead of his usual gentle fingerpicking, he banged out chords and growled through the lyrics. When the song was over, they applauded. He took a moment to scan the crowd, about thirty of them. The place was more than half-full, and a small group entered.

Palance introduced his song "Icarus" and talked about his friend Jason. He no longer talked about his father onstage or anywhere else, not even to Elise, and teared up when he sang, *Did you hear your father calling, falling and tumbling to the sea?* He played "Beth's Song." *Naked come into this world, cold and hungry, gasping air. No words to speak*, he whispered, *nowhere to go*, and watched as faces softened and eyes grew wide. He tried to imagine Beth, but, in his mind, he saw Elise.

Palance mixed his songs with covers by Steve Earle, Bruce Springsteen, and Van Morrison. The audience tracked his movements. He felt their energy flow into him and back out in a loop. When he sang "Brown-Eyed Girl," they sang along on the chorus. When he sang a gentle ballad, they sat silently, as if he were preaching. At the end of the first set, he finished with James Taylor's "Fire and Rain," and announced he had CDs for sale

The waitress asked him if he'd like anything to drink. He nodded and said, "black coffee." People came up to buy his CD and asked him to sign it. A woman in her late thirties told Palance she was touched by his music, and he blushed. A girl about his own age watched carefully as he signed her CD, *To Angie, love Palance*, and hugged him after she read the inscription. Men shook his hand, and an older woman kissed him on the cheek. By the time his coffee came, he had sold fourteen CDs, and his next set was about to start. He took an email signup sheet out of his guitar case and passed it around.

The rest of the night went well; his anxiety evaporated. On his second break, he sat with a group of students from the university, occasionally interrupted long enough to sign a CD and collect money. He swelled with each compliment, though it ebbed when one of the girls asked him if he thought he might go to school there. He glanced at his watch, and told her his break was over.

Back on stage, he played through his early stuff, "Too Old to Be So Young," and "Where Do We Go From Here?" He sang "No Road Home," and "I Am Awake." He played several covers and ended with The Beatles' "Here Comes the Sun." He thanked them for coming out, and waited to see who would come up to him, dismayed at the number of people filing out, surprised at himself for expecting them all to flock to him, but expecting it nonetheless.

A few people stayed; two girls, an awkward brunette and a willowy redhead with a boyfriend hovering next to her. The staff at the coffeehouse were wiping tables, stacking chairs and sweeping the floors. The brunette had a high, small voice and asked him about writing songs. She wrote poetry, she told him, and would love to set her poems to music, only she didn't play an instrument. He asked if she had any with her. She shook her head solemnly. Out of the corner of his eye, Palance saw the redhead's boyfriend roll his eyes. The redhead asked where he was from and if he thought he'd be famous any time soon. He told her he was from Chicago. A woman from the coffeehouse called him over, thanked him, and handed him an envelope. She told him it was ninety-four dollars, and they'd love to have him back. He signed up for a Friday in the spring. Palance gathered his guitar, music, and CDs, and walked out. The brunette was standing on the sidewalk, alone. She told him her name was Lisa and asked where he was staying.

Palance stammered. He wanted to do the right thing, but it was late, he was tired, and she wasn't bad looking. He told her, "I really don't have anywhere to stay for tonight. Got a car I can crash in."

Lisa held his arms in her hands, her eyes lowered as she offered, "You can stay with me. If you want."

"Thank you," he said, "that would be great." She grasped his arm tightly as they walked to his car. "I can look at your poems if you'd like."

"Oh, God," she said, admiration dripping from her eyes, "I'd love that," and Palance felt pity for her and revulsion toward himself. "Maybe just a few," she said, giggling.

Her apartment was a third-floor walk-up studio with a myriad of Indian print fabrics draped across the couch and hung from the walls as decoration. A curtain of beads separated the kitchen from the main room. It reminded him of pictures his parents took during their college days. She lit candles and turned off the lights.

"Make yourself comfortable," she said. "I'll go get my poems."

Palance wondered where she was going. The couch unfolded to a bed, and the only door was partially open and led to the bathroom. She rattled through the curtain of beads into the kitchen and emerged with two glasses of wine and a notebook poised on her head.

"I wanted to be a model when I was a little girl, but I never got tall enough." Lisa giggled, sounding exactly like the little girl she was, setting the wine glasses down on the faded wooden end table and sitting cross-legged in front of the couch where Palance was seated. "Don't you want to take out your guitar?"

"I'll just read them first," he told her.

"Can I read them to you?" she asked.

Palance nodded and waited for the onslaught, as he pushed away a mental image of Elise scolding him. If she called, he'd say his cell phone died. Lisa read one of her poems, something about a bird, and he was thinking this would go more quickly if he took out his guitar and played some chords behind her. She had switched to a poem about death, so he played in E-minor. She turned her notebook toward him. He made up a simple melody and fit most of the words to it. She kissed him on the lips and blew out two of the candles, leaving one to sputter in the dark. He put away his guitar and entered a different kind of misery with her, their naked bodies searching for a flicker of hope.

In the morning, Palance left before Lisa woke, not bothering to leave a note. He heard her murmur in her sleep as he gently closed the door behind him, without showering or eating. He'd figure that out on the road. He didn't have to perform again until tomorrow, and he waited until he was twenty miles out of town before calling Elise on the cell phone. He told her he'd spent the night in the car, crossing the fingers of his right hand, and how well the concert had gone, and how many CDs he'd sold. She said she could have another couple hundred made and shipped to him with a week's notice. When she hung up, he felt guilty and looked for somewhere to take a shower.

Driving through Owatonna, he saw a sign for Rice Lake State Park. They advertised camping. Palance veered off the highway into the park. He bought a bar of Ivory soap from the park store, unpacked a towel and toiletries from his suitcase, and went into the washroom to shower and shave, to wash away the smell of Lisa and her apartment. He bought a small package of donuts for breakfast, unpacked his guitar, walked to an open meadow, lay on his back, and played until the sun rose above him and glared into his eyes.

When he got back to the car, he put the guitar in the trunk and saw the silver package from Elise. He unwrapped it, noticing the perfect edges she'd created, and discovered six pictures in a small acrylic cube. There was a picture of Elise, one of him, Ben, and Dennis in his apartment, playing their instruments, and a third of him at the No Exit. The fourth picture was the band with Jason and Kyle, a fifth of him and Elise, and a sixth of his father, performing with the Larriveé at a party at their old house. She must have got it from his mom. Palance was a toddler, sitting at his father's feet.

Palance held the cube delicately, as if it might break, and when he lifted it to take a closer look, he found a note.

Palance,

Take us with you where you go, keep us in the guitar case, your memories and memories to come, the bitter, sweet, sacred, and profane. Explore the world, only take us with you, and come back home to me.

Love,
Elise.

Palance placed the cube in front of him as he reread the note. When his eyes were dry, he tucked the note behind the picture of Elise and walked back to the car. The day was free. Palance took his guitar out of the trunk and walked over to the meadow near the small lake.

He sat in the grass and played, listening to the sound of his guitar ringing off the lake and the trees. He tried to make the sounds fit the environment, the rippling of the water, the murmur of voices, and the rustling wind. He saw a young family walk nearby and let their pace set the rhythm. A small child appeared in front of him, a boy about four years old. Palance sat up and looked into the boy's eyes. A slightly older girl joined them and asked Palance if he knew "Michael Row the Boat Ashore." She told him her brother's name was Michael.

Palance sang to her. *Michael row the boat ashore, Hallelujah, Michael row the boat ashore, Halle-lu-u-jah.* The girl sang along as the boy stepped behind her and held onto her shirt. Palance played a fast rhythm, and they danced. Palance switched to a waltz, and the girl took her brother in her arms, and they twirled. A man and woman walked toward him, hand in hand, looking like older versions of the children, waltzing toward them.

"Hey, we didn't know there was entertainment," the man said, holding a quartet of fishing rods. The boy and girl stopped dead in their tracks. Palance kept playing.

"You're very good," the woman said meekly.

"Thank you," Palance told her. "Should we do 'Michael Row the Boat,'?" he asked the children, who nodded, looking at their father for final approval.

"Let's have a show then," the man ordered.

Palance played the whole song through, prompting them for each line, and filling in when their voices failed. The children and their mother clapped and laughed, and then packed up the fishing rods and drove off in their SUV. Palance started playing again, loudly, hoping to attract an audience. A small group of teenagers stopped by, threw two nickels into his guitar case, and walked off. He played until dusk, and then, alone in the meadow, packed up and headed for Iowa.

Palance thought about the parties his parents used to throw, the ones where their cadre of friends would sing and laugh, the joy that surrounded his father and abandoned his mother. Palance was alone on the road. No other cars in sight, just a few trucks. The landscape rolled in gentle hills and alternated between farm fields and trees. Ahead of him, he saw something cross the road. He slowed down and stopped. A herd of elk crossed the highway, ethereal in his headlights as they bounded before him.

Palance hadn't called Elise to thank her for the cube. He picked up the phone, but it was dead, and he had to get the cord out of the glove compartment and let it charge before he could make the call. When she answered, there was sleep in her voice. He pictured her in her flannel nightgown, her hair pressed flat from the pillow, and apologized for calling so late.

"That's okay," she said. "I like hearing from you."

"I had a free day, so I spent some time in a state park here, and now I'm driving to Iowa City. All the glamorous places."

Elise hesitated and he imagined she was trying to wake up, yawning the way she did on one side of her mouth. "Where you gonna stay?" she asked.

"Honda motel, most likely. Did well in St. Paul, but I need to save bucks if I can."

"That's nice," she said, and he could hear her yawn again.

"I'll let you get back to sleep, but I wanted to thank you for the photo cube."

"You're welcome."

"I love it. It's in my guitar case. And the note. Especially the note."

"Don't forget me," she said.

He told her he missed her. He knew she was lying back down, almost asleep, so he hit the button to end the call but heard, "You, too," and resolved to spend the rest of his nights alone. He thought about the kids in the park and wondered if there were children in their future. Back on the road, his stomach growled. A hundred miles from Iowa City, he exited the highway into Charles City and passed a sign that said, "America's Home Town." He spotted "Dave's Restaurant." It looked like a barn. All the other vehicles were semi-trucks. The waitress was an older woman.

"What can I get ya', hon?" she asked.

Palance ordered black coffee and a steak sandwich with home fries. The waitress told him it came with split pea soup, and he nodded. When she returned with coffee, he asked about her day. She told him it was the same day she'd had for years, and he asked about before that.

"I'll be back with your soup."

When she came back, he asked her how she ended up here. She gawked at him.

"Honey, eat your soup, and live your life. You come back here when you're about forty years older and have gray hairs, and we'll talk. For now, you just enjoy what you got. What you asking so many questions for?"

"I write songs."

"Good for you, hon. I'll bring your dinner soon. You can write about that. I got work."

Palance ate his soup. Outside, it was quiet and dark. Across from him sat a man and woman, not talking, dressed in jeans and t-shirts. Palance finished his meal, thanked the waitress, and left her a tip. He paid at the counter and walked to his car, feeling like a character in a western movie. A few minutes out of Iowa City, he saw a sign for a hotel, thirty-nine dollars. He pulled up, walked into the office, and rang the bell. The manager came out from a room behind the desk, yawned. and scratched a day's growth of beard. Palance signed the register and paid him in cash; then he drove around to door number seven and brought in his guitar and suitcase.

Checkout time wasn't until noon, and the gig was close by. He clicked the TV on, lay in bed, and scanned the room. This was the most alone he'd even been. He watched reruns of old sitcoms and drifted to sleep. In the morning, he stood under the shower for fifteen minutes, until the hot water began to wane; then he shaved and dressed, feeling oddly extravagant. He checked out and headed to Iowa City. Famished and long-ing to be onstage again, he turned on the radio to hear the DJ howling and announcing tonight would be a full moon. He searched the radio for something to energize him, Led Zeppelin screamed "Whole Lotta Love."

Ben and Dennis told him to check out The Mill in Iowa City. They said it wasn't bad, and prices were reasonable. He pulled in a little after one in the afternoon. They seated him quickly. He ordered the Bleu Burger, with blue cheese and bacon. His mouth was already watering when the waitress, who, he quickly discovered, was a political-science major, brought him a Coke.

"You in school?" she asked him.

"Dropout," he said, as if it were an achievement. "On a break, really," though this was the first time he'd thought of it that way.

"What was your major?"

"Music. I'm a musician."

"Oh," she said, smirking as she walked away.

He sat staring ahead, trying to get the road out of his eyes. Every time he closed them, he saw white lines. With them open, he felt the vibration and had trouble looking anywhere but straight ahead. He read the paper placemat; it had a map of Iowa on it with tourist traps highlighted. The waitress returned with his burger and asked what he was doing in town.

He told her about his gig at The Java House, pulled a CD out of his jacket pocket, and handed it to her. "Check it out."

"Blues," she said, "is the people's music. Do you play the blues?"

"Sometimes," he told her. He held up the plate of food, and said, "Blue cheese, blue tunes." She walked away without comment, and Palance dug into the burger and fries. The juice from the hamburger ran down his chin. He wiped it away with a napkin, and occasionally traded barbs with the poly-sci waitress. "Delicious," he told her when she asked how the food was. "No reason to sing the blues."

"No reason not to, Preppy," she replied.

"Preppy?"

"If the shoe fits," she said and walked away. She reminded him of his sister, and he wondered how Jilly was doing. They rarely talked anymore; the last time was almost a month ago.

"Hey," he asked the waitress the next time she appeared, "were you a precocious little kid?"

"Why do you want to know?"

"Just curious—you remind me of someone."

"I was precocious as hell. Still am."

"Keep it up."

"I've got plans tonight, Preppy. And a boyfriend."

"Good for you."

He wondered if she'd be there tonight, but, right now, he was more interested in his food than he was in her. He needed a way to figure out how he was going to play these next seven weeks—so much time on the road with so little to do between gigs except drive. When he finished his food, he sighed and looked at his watch. It was only two-thirty, and he had the afternoon to kill. The waitress handed him the check.

"You'll play the blues sooner or later, Preppy," she said, and walked away as if she knew a secret he didn't.

Palance drove to The Java House to check it out. It was as clean and shiny as the No Exit was dark and dank. The staff was friendly, and by the way, the college radio station was broadcasting the show.

"Cool," Palance said, biting his lip. "Any place to warm up?"

The guy behind the counter said there was an alley behind the club and went back to making lattes. Palance wondered how he'd do on the radio. They used multiple takes on the recordings he made with Ben. This was one and done, and out over the airwaves. He ordered a double espresso to jolt him into action and headed out to find someplace to practice. He asked for directions to the university and their music department, where he found an empty rehearsal room.

Palance tried to come up with something using the piano in the practice room, but it eluded him. He took out his guitar and attempted some chords he'd barely used, and it came to him in one solid lump: *Going on the road, going on the road, looking for a story never been told, going on the road.* He could use that for a chorus—it sounded simple and fresh, and he had an idea for an introduction with minor seventh and ninth chords. He worked it out: *All my life, close to home, but now it's time to hit the road.* He wanted to finish the song, but he looked at the clock in the rehearsal room and needed to get back to the club. Maybe he could finish it when he got there.

At The Java House, they'd moved the tables to reveal a stage. There was a crew from the college radio station and a young girl, barely out of high school, who had been sent to interview him. She pointed a microphone at his mouth and asked him to tell the audience about himself. He hadn't even put down his guitar.

"Uh, Palance Heller, from Chicago. Singer-songwriter on the road."

"So, what kind of music do you write and sing?"

"The kind I like," Palance said. Her questions poked and prodded him, but it was his first interview, and he didn't want to piss her off. When she finally asked him what he was looking forward to most, he told her, "Playing here tonight." When they finished, it was seven forty-five, the show started at eight, and they needed a sound check now.

"Give me a minute to tune," he told the crew setting up microphones.

Palance took his time. He'd rather get it right than rush to meet their deadlines, and when he was done, he stepped in front of the microphones and played "No Road Home." The man by the mixing board nodded and said, "We've got it." Palance had nine minutes before the show. He headed for the bathroom, did his business, and noticed the door to the alley was open. He stepped out for a breath of fresh air. He had six minutes and the poly-sci waitress from the restaurant was out there, smoking a joint. She passed it to him. Without thinking, he took a hit and handed it back to her.

"You coming in?" he asked.

"I'll check it out from here," she told him. "See if you're worth it."

Palance took one more hit off the joint and stepped back inside. He was on, playing *Too Old to Be So Young*. He looked at the audience: all the chairs were full. The radio crew was standing in back near the mixing board, and the woman who interviewed him was wearing headphones. They clapped when he finished the song, and he welcomed in the radio audience the way he'd heard it done, addressing the "folks at home listening to me on the radio." Then he turned his attention to the faces in front of him and played *No Road Home*. Halfway through, the pot kicked in, and he felt adrift. He played Van Morrison's "Brown-Eyed Girl," always a favorite. The man behind the mixing board looked apathetic. He played an acoustic version of "Breakaway" and felt the audience lose focus. He heard bits of conversation in the room.

Though there was applause, he felt an overwhelming pressure to do better. Palance started playing the song he wrote this afternoon, not knowing what he'd do after he ran out of the intro and before the refrain, but as soon as he got to where the verse should be, he kept playing the chorus and changed the words a bit. *Going on the road, going on the road, going where it's hot, going where it's cold. I'm going on the road, going on the road*, and he was right back to the chorus, *looking for a story never been told. Going on the road.* The audience began clapping along, and he played a couple of measures while he thought up another verse and then spewed it out. *Up to Minnesota, got ten thousand lakes, out to California where the whole earth quakes*, and then repeated the chorus. This time, a few people were singing along, and he felt that, if he could just get through it, he'd be okay. He sang *Headin' out to Philly, ring the Liberty Bell where I'm gonna wind up ain't no way to tell*, and then back to the chorus—and he was telling the truth: he had no idea where he or the song would end up. *Goin' to New York City and the Poconos, down to Kentucky where the bluegrass grows.*

He was giving them his itinerary, making it rhyme, and everyone was singing along on the chorus. He made up the next verse, *Going on the road, gonna meet my fate, gotta get movin' it's getting late*, and he knew to end the song where it began. They sang along on the chorus and he followed up with *Goin' on the road, goin' on the road, goin' on the road, I'm going on the road*, and one final rousing chorus, and then he repeated the line: *looking for a story never been told. Going on the road*, and the audience cheered. He thought, *Hopefully, I can get a copy of the tape, because I'm too stoned to remember it all.*

The poly-sci waitress was inside now, standing up in back. Sweat was pouring off him. He sang her "The St. James Infirmary Blues." The room became quiet and attentive. *On my left stood Big Joe McKennedy, his eyes were bloodshot red, as he turned to the gang around him, these were the very words he said.* The poly-sci waitress smiled, she knew the song was for her. *Now that you've heard my story, I'll take another shot of booze, and if anyone should happen to ask you, tell 'em I got those St. James Infirmary Blues.* He played "Beth's Song" and "Icarus," and then, from the corner of his eye, he saw the manager giving him the sign, *one more song.*

He played "Where Do We Go From Here?" *My ships are torn and tattered, my cities are in flame, the sky is dark and shattered and turned to rain.* He played the chorus one last time and knew he'd done okay. He left to loud applause; the man behind the mixing board was lowering his hand. Palance grabbed the box of CDs and headed for an empty table.

Everyone at the table asked if the song he'd just written was on there. He shook his head while the people from the radio station let them know they'd air the concert again tomorrow at nine, and they could tape it off the radio. Half an hour later, the room was empty and he'd only sold two CDs. The woman with the headphones walked over to him and handed him a copy of the concert on a blank CD.

"Not bad," she told him. By the time he'd packed up his guitar, their truck was loaded and gone. He looked for the poly-sci waitress, but she was gone, too. They were cleaning up the coffeehouse for the night, and he asked a girl his age if she knew a place to crash for the night.

"They'll let you stay on the couch at one of the dorms. Try Maple Hall. They're pretty cool there."

Palance snuck off, feeling abandoned. At least he had the recording, and he'd been on the radio. When he found Maple Hall, he avoided anyone who looked like they were in charge and asked a student if he could crash on a couch. The student shrugged and walked away. Palance lounged on the couch, tucking his toiletries and a small backpack underneath. He watched the TV in the corner. David Letterman was reading a top ten list about President Clinton and Monica Lewinsky. Students filed past him, with textbooks and backpacks, wearing headphones. Finally, alone in the lounge, Palance turned off the TV and shut his eyes.

In the morning, he headed for the washroom to shave, shower, and start his day. It was after ten, and he had to be in Omaha by dinnertime. The students jostled against each other on their way to class. Amid the camaraderie and chaos, he was anonymous—and then back on the road. It finally hit him just how much of his time on the road was exactly that—alone in his car, on the road.

River of Arpeggios

Going on the Road

All my life, close to home,
but now it's time to hit the road.

Going on the road, going on the road,
going where it's hot, going where it's cold,
I'm going on the road, going on the road,
looking for a story never been told,
going on the road.

Up to Minnesota got ten thousand lakes,
out to California where the whole earth quakes,
I'm going on the road, going on the road,
looking for a story never been told,
going on the road.

Headin' east to Philly ring the Liberty Bell,
where I'm gonna wind up ain't no way to tell,
I'm going on the road, going on the road,
looking for a story never been told,
going on the road.

Goin' to New York City and the Poconos,
down to Kentucky where the bluegrass grows,
I'm going on the road, going on the road,
looking for a story never been told,
going on the road.

Goin' on the road gonna meet my fate,
gotta get movin' it's getting late,
I'm going on the road, going on the road,
looking for a story never been told,
going on the road.

Goin' on the road, goin' on the road,
Goin' on the road, I'm going on the road,
I'm going on the road, going on the road,
looking for a story never been told,
going on the road.

Looking for a story never been told,
going on the road.

Long Grind

n the third row at McGraw Hall in Ithaca, there was a blonde girl with glasses Palance had his eye on, but his attention shifted to a man in the shadows behind her who looked strangely familiar. Palance was tired. He'd played thirty-nine dates in forty-two days and been on the road most of the last two years. After tonight, he was scheduled to go home, if you could call it that. Most of his stuff was in the car, and he didn't know where he stood with Elise. A few more songs, and, with a head start, he could be back in Chicago tomorrow afternoon. Elise wanted to talk. *That couldn't be good.* When the show was over, Palance set up a table with the twenty CDs he had left. If he sold ten, he could take Elise out for dinner and buy her some flowers. He sold twelve and then looked up at the next guy in line, the guy from the shadows.

"Hey," the man said, "weren't you the lead singer for the Whispering Screams?"

"I," Palance began, looking up past the goatee of the familiar face. "Kyle, is that you?"

"I hope so. I was going to leave yesterday; then I saw your poster and figured I'd hang around long enough to say hello."

"What are you doing here?"

"I've been here five years now. I just finished my master's degree in regional planning. Got a job in Minneapolis. I start in two weeks."

A woman behind Kyle tapped him on the shoulder and asked him if he'd let her buy a CD.

"Never one to stand in the way of commerce," he said, and stepped to the side.

"Can you stay a while?" Palance asked, turning away to take the woman's money and ask how she wanted it signed.

"To Barbie," she said, "like the doll," and Palance gave her his signature smile and wrote, *To Barbie, more beautiful than the doll.* She kissed him on the cheek, giggled, and sauntered away.

"You're pretty slick in your old age," Kyle said, chortling the same way he did in high school. "I can stay all night. Tomorrow morning, I get on the train and head back to Chicago to do time with the folks before heading up north."

"Bought your ticket yet?" Palance asked.

"Nah. I'll just pick it up when I get there."

"I'm driving back tonight and tomorrow. I was gonna grab a cheap motel on the way. You interested?"

"You got room for a suitcase and a laptop?"

"I'll make room. You've been holed up here five years?"

"Hey, it's the best thing that ever happened to me. Seven hundred miles from Norm and Shirley, enough freedom to figure out what I want to do, no one breathing down my neck."

"Yeah, man. The chin hair got me."

"Yeah, it surprised Shirley, too, but there's not a damn thing she can do about it."

"Hey, you're a rebel."

"I'm my own man," Kyle said. "And you—I can hardly believe the difference."

"Difference?"

"We had to push you to the front of the stage. You wanted to stay in back and let Jason take over. Now you're the man."

"You ever hear from Jason?" Palance asked.

"Me, nah. You?"

"Saw him about a year and a half ago. He looked burnt."

"How burnt?"

"Crispy critter."

"Too bad. A year and a half, though. A lot can happen. You still a player?"

"Me?" Palance asked. "I was never a player."

"You were always a player," Kyle told him. "How many girls this road trip?"

"Not a lot," Palance said defensively, extending the fingers on one hand as he counted the names to himself.

"I've been with one girl since the end of sophomore year. She's trying to get a job in Minneapolis so we can be together. We're going to get married."

"Married?" Palance said. "Why regional planning?" he asked.

"Make a difference. Try to straighten out this fucked-up world."

"Man, you have changed," Palance told him. He listened to Kyle, wondering why he hadn't mentioned Elise when asked if he was still a player. He hadn't been entirely faithful to her, but he'd tried. "What's her name?" he asked.

"Who?"

"This girl you're gonna marry."

"Shellie, Shellie Winnoway. You about ready to go? I've just got to swing by my apartment and pick up what's left of my stuff. I had the rest shipped to Chicago."

"Grab a CD, and we can go."

"No kiss for me?"

"Don't tempt me."

Kyle gave Palance directions reminiscent of their old days—no ambiguity, very specific, watch your speed.

Kyle ran in and was out fifteen minutes later. He had their route to Chicago planned, including a stop in Erie, Pennsylvania, for the night, and, by the way, Perkins was the best place to grab breakfast on the road—reasonable, good food, and quick. Palance asked why Erie, and Kyle held up one finger, asking him to wait, and dialed his cell phone.

"Hey, Fernando, you staying up late tonight? One or two. We just need a couple of couches to crash on—is that okay? *Hasta luego mi amigo.*" Kyle turned to Palance. "That's why. Friend from school."

"Erie it is, then. What've you been doing?"

"Studying my ass off and spending time with Shellie. She's been busy, too. Double major, anthropology and business. One for love and one for money."

"Where do you fit in?" Palance asked, grinning.

"You're out gigging, running free and easy. How's that?"

"I may be easy, but I'm not exactly free," Palance told him. "There's this girl . . . Elise, at home. We're kind of shacked up together, but like you said, I may be easy."

"You're a dog."

"Hey, I'm good when I'm home. I'm out here for a couple or three months at a time, and in-between gigs there's a lot of time in the car, cheap motels, and sometimes it's nice to spend the night with someone. Saves money, too."

"Tell me about Elise."

"You wouldn't believe I'm with her, man. Straight shooter. Colors between the lines. Hard to figure what she sees in me. Got her degree, plays with a local symphony, and teaches music to high school kids at Sullivan. Keeps me in line when I'm home."

"What about marriage?"

"What about it?"

"You ever talk about it?"

"She's got a don't-ask, don't-tell policy that's fine with me."

"You ever think of going back to school?"

"Huh?"

"Back to school?"

It started to drizzle, and Palance turned on the windshield wipers. "It's not my thing," he told Kyle.

"Your thing? You were hell on wheels in class when you wanted to be. Don't give me that crap. What really happened?"

"Dazzled by fortune and fame."

"How's that working out for you?"

"I do okay."

"What about down the road?"

"I've been up the road, down it, and back."

"Where do you see yourself ten years from now?"

"Does it matter?"

"Do you have health insurance, a pension plan, IRA, anything?"

"You sound like my mom. Hell, you sound like your mom." Kyle grinned, like he'd won the damned argument. "I just want to play my music."

"Hey, I'm the last one to stop you," Kyle said.

"Where are your drums?"

"I'm not you. It was fun in high school, but I don't have it in me the way you do. You scare me a little. Not as bad as Jason, but you do."

Palance's plans didn't extend beyond these nickel-and-dime tours, and after two years of it, he was tired. "Got any ideas?" he asked.

"You'll figure it out," Kyle said, with the same annoying grin he had in high school. "Like I said, you're hell on wheels."

"So, tell me about Fernando," Palance asked, knowing Kyle would spit out trivia for the next thirty miles and he could space out. He wondered about his future. His life seemed like one long grind. A lot of time alone. There was a crack of thunder, and Kyle stopped talking. Rain spilled on the windshield, and Palance slowed down, wondering how far they were from Erie. "Hey, Kyle. You feel like driving for a bit?"

There was a gas station up ahead. Palance filled the tank and then crisscrossed Kyle in front of the car. They looked at each other, yelled *"Fire Drill!"* and laughed at their past, when they were cool because they were in a band. The laughter was bittersweet.

"You were pretty weird when you left for college," Palance told Kyle.

"Lot of pressure from the folks. You weren't their favorite person, and they couldn't stand Jason."

"Family," Palance said. As the word left his lips, he had a sudden longing for his own. He thought about Elise and felt guilty about cheating on her.

"Next exit," Kyle said.

"Huh?"

"Fernando. Next exit."

"How long have you been driving?"

"About an hour and a half. You seem pretty spaced."

"Think Fernando would mind if I just crashed when we got there?"

"He'll be asleep. He said he'd leave the door open. I told you that already. There are two couches in the living room. Pick one, and it's yours." Kyle wound his way around the city streets, zipping down one after another.

"You've been here before," Palance said.

"Once or twice. I'd spend holidays here sometimes."

"Can't believe how much you've loosened up."

"Me. How about you? No plans, just day to day. Can't get much looser than that."

"That's J-bird," Palance said.

"Glad I hung around an extra day. We're here."

They walked in on tiptoes. A lamp was on, and there were cookies on the coffee table. Palance stuffed a cookie into his mouth and laid down on the nearest couch. The next thing he knew, sunlight was streaming through the window and Kyle was shaking his shoulder.

"Morning," Kyle said, already showered and dressed.

"What time is it?" Palance asked, opening his eyes.

"Eight-thirty. You wanted to be home in time for dinner. You've got time for a shower if you make it quick."

Palance walked in circles until Kyle directed him to the shower. "Fernando?" he asked.

"Gone to work."

Palance showered and was ready to go in ten minutes. They drove off, Kyle behind the wheel. Palance heard himself on the car speakers.

"CD you gave me," Kyle said.

"Heard it before."

Palance felt strange about Kyle listening to his CD. He tried to maintain an air of mystery, even with Elise, but Kyle had known him forever. Palance closed his eyes, occasionally opening the left one a slit while Kyle listened and drove.

Palance heard every string buzz on his guitar and every catch in his voice. The songs sounded tinny and weak to him. He hoped that Kyle's ear for detail wasn't picking up the flaws. He had six weeks at home; maybe he could record some new tracks. Kyle might be a pain in the ass, but he was always perfect, whatever he did.

When "Beth's Song" started playing, Palance felt the pain of her loss. Kyle brought back those days. *Every day I rise, to hear the parched and anguished sighs.* "Icarus" played next. Kyle leaned over and said, "Jason, right?" and Palance nodded.

"What do you think?" Palance asked when the CD was over.

Usually, Kyle's words flowed quickly, as if he were afraid he couldn't get them out in time, but this time he hesitated. "I underestimated you," he said.

"Huh?"

"I thought you hadn't grown up. I was wrong. You act like you just want to get high and laid, but there's a lot of depth in your songs."

"I haven't been high in a year and a half," Palance said.

"What happened?"

"I gave it up before I went on the road; then I tried it once, got creative. Second time I got goofy. Third time I forgot the lyrics and almost fell off the stage."

"I'm proud of you," Kyle said.

"For falling off the stage?"

"For giving it up. It means something."

"It does?"

"Yeah, man. It does."

"Really, because I feel like I'm drifting."

"What are your plans?"

"Plans?"

"Yeah. Are you going to keep playing clubs? Promote yourself more? What if the gigs start drying up? Do you have a backup plan?"

"Not really. I guess I could use one. I know I could use one. I feel like I'm chasing my tail all over the country, and I'm barely breaking even. Palance looked out the window; the clouds were puffy white, just a glint of blue sky pouring through. "Maybe you can help me come up with a plan."

"That's what I do. I'm a planner. We've got a few hours. Let's see what we can cook up."

"I'm not a city."

"So, what do you love?"

"I love music," Palance said. "Playing my guitar and writing songs. I like hanging with friends when I get a chance. I wouldn't mind settling down for a while. Spend some time at home with Elise."

"Are you willing to go back to school?"

"Maybe, if the classes make sense. I don't think I could stand any more music theory."

Kyle asked thirty other questions. He wanted to know if Palance wanted to work nine to five or on his own schedule, alone or with others. Palance asked if he'd learned this stuff in urban planning. Kyle mentioned a minor in psychology. He said he needed to figure out some stuff, about himself, his family, and where he fit in. Outside of Toledo, there was a Panera Bread Restaurant, and they pulled over for a sandwich and coffee. Kyle tossed him the car keys.

"A teacher?" Palance asked, after they'd ordered and found a booth. "You're nuts." Palance took a sip of coffee and realized how long he'd been on a steady caffeine buzz and how desperately he needed to crash.

"There's a couple ways to do it," Kyle told him. "You can teach through a school, and you'll have benefits and a steady income. You can teach privately, like at the Old Town School, or on your own, out of your apartment. Play mostly in the city on the weekends, short trips for gigs out of town."

Palance saw himself coming home to Elise at night and wondered how that would work. The women willing to take him in on the road seemed less appealing at each stop. It'd been fun, but he wanted to try something new. Palance took a small bite of his sandwich and chewed slowly. He needed some clarity—before he got to Chicago.

"Or," Kyle said, "You could do almost anything."

"Like what?"

"What do you love—besides music?"

"Women," Palance said.

"Seriously."

"Performing."

"One-man musical," Kyle said off the top of his head.

"Like *Oklahoma*?" Palance laughed.

"There was a guy in Chicago who came out on stage looking like Mark Twain and played music. Riverboat songs. You could do something like that. Even write it yourself."

"Yeah, right," Palance said.

"You bet your ass you could," Kyle told him.

"I could give guitar lessons."

"Songwriting classes, too."

"Tell me about Shellie," Palance asked.

"What do you want to know?"

"Anything."

"She wants to work in a museum. She has an interview in two weeks at the Bell Museum in Minneapolis. Loves kids. I got her down to three. She wanted seven; she was going to name them after the days of the week. She likes ice skating, theater, and ballet. Doesn't mind if I listen to rock 'n roll, but it's not her thing. She's into classical."

"Elise is into classical, too." Palance imagined himself beside her in a concert hall, her hand resting on his arm. "How did you know?"

"Know what?"

"You were ready to get married."

"We like the same things and have the same goals. She's fun. We fit."

"And you're not looking around?"

"No reason to."

Palance took a bite of his sandwich and ate a few potato chips. Kyle seemed to be rubbing off on him. "You've got the future, but I've got the present," Palance said.

Kyle looked puzzled. "Hey, we're both starting out."

Palance refilled his coffee. He'd been a one-man band too long. He thought back to that day Jason came over—they got stoned, played music together, and it was magic. They added Kyle's drums, and it rocked.

Palance put a hand on Kyle's shoulder. "I've got a lot of growing up to do," he said.

Kyle smiled at him. "You're a little hard on yourself."

Palance took a deep breath. "I miss him," he told Kyle.

"Jason?"

"Yeah," he said. "And my dad."

"You never talk about your dad."

"Too many questions. Too few answers."

They finished their sandwiches and went back to the car. Palance got into the driver's seat. He found a U2 CD he knew Kyle liked, and they sang along, thick as bandmates.

Soon, they were in northern Indiana, straddling the Michigan border, three hours from home, and he wasn't ready to end this journey. He turned to Kyle and asked if he'd mind taking a break. Kyle nodded, and Palance called Elise on the cell phone, leaving a message that he'd be delayed, but in time for a late dinner, maybe seven or seven-thirty at the latest.

"What's up?" Kyle asked.

"I just need some more time."

"Time for what?"

"I don't know what to say," Palance told him.

"To who?"

"To Elise."

"What do you want to say?"

"I want to be with her. But I don't know if she can take me full time."

"Why do you have to know now?" Kyle asked.

"Because I feel lost," Palance said and realized he was, in fact, lost. He pulled off the highway and started driving down roads he didn't know, and had no idea where he was. "How's your sense of direction?" he asked Kyle.

"Good. Why?"

"Where's the highway?"

Kyle told him to pull over. "I think you need a break," he said.

Palance pulled over and got out of the car, stretching. They traded seats, and Kyle drove until they came through a grove of trees and stopped by a lake. Kyle parked the car and asked Palance where his guitar was. Moments later, Palance was sitting by the lake, and Kyle handed him his guitar.

"Play," Kyle told him.

Palance began in the key of A; it sounded lonesome and weary, tottering between hope and desperation, and he looked out over the lake while he played. Dissonant sounds swirled through his head. Palance threw in an F-sharp minor chord and resolved on E-major. Words came to him, and he sang, *It's a long grind from childhood to where I am.* The sun was setting, and he stood up. He handed Kyle the guitar.

"How long?" he asked.

"You've been playing for about an hour."

"Let's go," Palance said and insisted on driving.

"So, what happened to you?" Kyle asked.

"I think it's like when you're diving and come up too fast. I couldn't breathe."

"Like a panic attack?"

"Maybe. I'm okay now. I've got a new song," Palance said. "Lay me down a beat. "Ba-pa-pa-pa, Ba-pa-pa-pa," he sang. Kyle played the beat on the dashboard with his fingers. Palance sang, *It's a long grind from childhood to where I am. I'm walking tall, but there are times.* Kyle continued to drum on the glove compartment, and the road hummed by. *All the strides I've made just slip away, and I watch the years unwind.*

It's a long grind from Chicago to where I am, I've seen the stars in other skies. He pictured the night sky, the constellations Elise always pointed out to him—the first thing she looked for at night outside. *And though they rise and fall above us all, they do not feel as kind.* The chorus came at once, *I don't know where I'm going to, though my path is writ' in stone. Am I grinding out or grinding home? I spend the long grind alone.* He looked over at Kyle scribbling in a notebook.

"You're writing this down?" he asked.

"I remember the melodies were always solid," he said, "but the words could get lost."

Traffic bunched and slowed near the Illinois border. Palance paid attention to the rhythm and melody in his head. He thought about growing up, when they were kids.

It's a long grind from family to on your own, town to town and day by day. And though I've gained more than I've ever lost, I live my life out on a stage. Kyle sang the chorus with him, and they harmonized, *I don't know where I'm going to, though my path is writ' in stone. Am I grinding out or grinding home? I spend the long grind alone.*

Traffic came to a halt. Kyle stopped drumming, showing Palance the notebook. The song was almost complete, and traffic was heavy with semi-trucks and families on vacation. Things were about to change again. Palance didn't know how, and it scared him.

There was an accident on the left, pulled onto the shoulder. The orange construction markers and yellow lights blinked a warning. *I know that there will come a time,* Palance sang, *when my path will turn away. And if I'm rising up or slipping down, there will be joy along the way.* Kyle kept writing.

"It's done," Palance said.

"What about the harmony?" Kyle asked.

"Just have to match up the chords with the ones in my head. Play with it a little."

"So, when is this new time when your path turns away?"

"It's here," Palance said, and grew quiet, turning off at the Lincoln Oasis in South Holland. "Can you drive? I'm beat."

"I'm gonna run in and use the washroom. Can I get you anything?"

"A Coke, please."

Palance moved to the passenger seat, rested his head against the doorframe, and closed his eyes. He startled when Kyle came back and handed him his drink. "Must have dozed off."

"Get some rest," Kyle told him. "It sounds like you have a busy night ahead."

"I should call Elise," Palance said, pulling out his cell phone and dialing. Kyle drove back onto the highway. Elise answered, and Palance asked what she was doing.

"Getting ready to go to practice. I shouldn't be out later than nine."

"I'm an hour, hour and a half away, depending on traffic," he told her. "I miss you."

"You must be leaving again soon," she said.

"See you when you get back." He felt disconnected. He loved her, but it was different in his head. "What are you doing tonight?" he asked Kyle.

"Dinner with the folks. They still don't know," he told Palance. "About Shellie."

"How are you gonna spring it?" he asked, wondering what he would say to his mother if he decided to marry Elise.

"Just tell them. She's coming up on Thursday. I told her not to smile too much. They don't trust anyone who smiles," Kyle said and laughed. "They never trusted you."

"I'll take that as a compliment," Palance said. Traffic on the Dan Ryan opened up after 95th Street, and they sailed north through the loop and onto the Edens. "Same house?" Palance asked Kyle.

"They don't like change."

"I wish my family hadn't changed," Palance said, looking out the window at the city passing by.

"I guess I shouldn't complain."

Palance didn't have the words to tell Kyle how much this trip meant to him. Kyle exited the highway at Touhy. As they passed over the bridge, Palance half-expected him to stop and pick up Jason. At Washtenaw, he looked left toward the park, and then they were in front of Kyle's house.

"You still have the number?" Kyle asked him as they pulled up. Palance nodded, and Kyle handed him the paper with his lyrics written on them. They got Kyle's bags out of the trunk and embraced. "Be here for two weeks," Kyle said. "Give me a call."

Palance drove away, and his thoughts turned to Elise. He had so much to say to her. She wouldn't be home for an hour. He found a parking space in front of the building and carried in his guitar and a duffle bag filled with dirty laundry. Trudging up the stairs, he tucked the guitar in the closet and the duffle in a corner of the bedroom. He went to lie down for a few minutes, closed his eyes, and dreamt back to his childhood.

His father was there. They were in the backyard. There was a fence that never existed in real life. He was a child. Kyle, Jason, and Beth stood there as adults, looking at him and shaking their heads. Palance's father came over and picked him up so that he was the same height they were. They smiled and waved, and he waved back. Then they all disappeared, and he felt a hand on his shoulder. He turned toward the hand and opened his eyes. Elise was there in her nightgown, and kissed him on the forehead.

"What time?" he asked.

"One-fifteen," she told him, stroking his hair. "You've been asleep for hours. I didn't want to wake you."

"Too late for dinner."

"Tomorrow," she said.

Palance tried to talk to her, but she kissed him lightly on the lips and wished him sweet dreams. Her words were soothing. She curled up against him, and he was fast asleep again.

In the morning, he heard the shower running, and his eyes opened slowly. He wanted to make a commitment, but he entered the bathroom as Elise was exiting, and he needed a shower worse. She said, "Welcome back," as they brushed past each other; the smell of soap on her clean skin moved his lips onto hers.

"Shower first, then breakfast, then we'll see," she told him.

Palance stepped into the tub and ran the water. His razor was still in the duffle bag. It was a good excuse not to shave. He dried himself with a towel and smelled bacon and eggs. He knew what he needed to do. He wished he had a ring, but it had to be now. He found clean clothes in the dresser and put them on. Breakfast was on the table.

There was bacon on the plate, crisp, the way he liked it. He took a bite along with the scrambled eggs and swallowed some orange juice.

"I have something to ask you," he told her.

"Okay."

"I'm not sure I should just come out and say it."

"Whenever you're ready," she told him, and got up for more coffee.

Palance kept eating, beginning to feel uneasy. When she set the coffee in front of him, he leaned forward in his chair and got down on one knee. Palance placed his hand on her leg and asked, "Will you marry me?"

"Very funny. Eat your breakfast."

"I'm serious," Palance said, still on one knee, his eggs growing cold on the plate.

Elise reached out, placing her fingers on his arm, arching her eyebrows. "Are you having trouble getting laid on the road?" she asked.

"What?" Palance asked, too loudly, rising up and banging his knee on the edge of the table, hopping around the room. Elise's laughter exacerbated the pain shooting through his leg. "I," he started to say, but was at a loss for words.

"When you've been faithful to me for a year," Elise told him, "you ask me again, and I might consider it." She took a sip of coffee and went back to her breakfast.

Palance returned to the table. His orange juice tasted bitter.

"I do love you," Palance told her, after cleaning his plate and rinsing it in the sink.

"I know you do," Elise said, patting him on the head like a child.

"How would you feel if I were around more?"

"What do you mean?"

"Like if I got off the road and went back to school?"

"Interesting idea."

They talked for more than an hour, and then Elise went to work. Palance told her about the ride home with Kyle. She said she'd be home by four, and he offered to take her out wherever she'd like.

"Top of the Hancock." she said.

"If that's where you'd like to go," he told her.

"You are changing, aren't you?"

"I love you," he said.

"How about Leona's?" she asked.

"Why?"

"Return to the scene of the crime. What are you going to do while I'm gone?"

"Laundry. And I have a song to finish."

"You're doing your own laundry?"

"Time for a change," he said.

Elise kissed him on the lips and said, "We'll see."

"You will," he promised.

Palance walked her out and brought in a load from the car. He seethed at his clumsy proposal. He had gigs booked through most of the summer, starting in two weeks, but nothing after that, and thought about everything Kyle had suggested. He was grateful Elise had a washer and dryer in her apartment and wondered what it would be like to live there full-time, to wake up next to her each morning. Palance dumped the duffle bag full of dirty laundry on the kitchen floor, next to the washer, and sorted the clothes. Teaching guitar wouldn't be bad. He'd be close to home, and he censored thoughts of naïve young women coming to him for lessons. He started a load and unpacked.

In between loads, he took out his guitar to finish the song he'd written in the car.

"I'll prove myself," he said out loud and wondered if he really meant it.

Long Grind

It's a long grind from childhood to where I am,
I'm walking tall, but there are times,
All the strides I've made just slip away,
And I watch the years unwind.

It's a long grind from Chicago to where I am,
I've seen the stars in other skies,
And though they rise and fall above us all,
They do not seem as kind.

C
H *I don't know where I'm going to,*
O *Though my path is writ' in stone,*
R *Am I grinding out or grinding home,*
U *I spend the long grind alone.*
S

It's a long grind from family to on my own,
Town to town and day by day,
And though I've gained more than I've ever lost,
I live my life out on a stage.

Chorus
I know that there will come a time,
When my path will turn away,
And if I'm rising up or slipping down,
There will be joy along the way.

Chorus
I spend the long grind alone.

Family Ties

I t wasn't easy giving up life on the road. Palance played out the gigs he had scheduled for summer and early fall, and then enrolled back at Northeastern in the Music Education Department. He'd been faithful to Elise ever since.

Palance had a gig tonight at Bill's Blues, a dive bar in Evanston, and all three of the women in his life would be there: his mother, Elise, and Jilly. His mother had never seen him perform outside their home. Palance was nervous. He'd started a song, but it wasn't finished yet. *There were always three, there may be more, but in my mind there were always four. There was always love. I was never lost. Even when I could not pay the cost.*

Palance had read something, years ago, about how much progress someone's father made from the time the son was fourteen and felt his father was an idiot, until the time he turned twenty-one, and his father appeared newly wise. Palance was never able to have that experience with his Dad, but lately, his Mom was making more sense than she used to. Palance's image of her, set in stone after his father's death, was grief stricken and helpless. She wasn't helpless, though. He'd always viewed his father's death as a tragedy for himself and Jilly, only recently considering what it meant for his mother. For years, the only connection that really mattered to him was with his father. The guitar. The music. *You were always there, standing by my side, though I was a boy on the day you died. Each and every chord, every song I sing, I sing for you like you sang for me.*

Palance had bickered with his mother for so long that it was hard to see anything else in their relationship. This gig made him nervous. Clearly, she mattered to him. The squabbling, the rejections, the anger, the conflict, all of it mattered. It bound them together. *The heart of the family lies in the sticks and stones of the family ties.*

Palance went to the kitchen to make a pot of coffee, and thought about the song while he waited for it to brew. *I mourned your loss; I turned and tossed, till I was cold as the winter's frost.* He really had been an asshole to his mom, and to Jilly, too.

Palance drank coffee and pulled out a pad of paper to make set lists for tonight. He wrote down, "Too Old to Be So Young." He played it for her the night he wrote it. He could play his songs in the order he wrote them and start with his father's song, "When Morning Comes." He wanted tonight to be special. Elise was going to play the flute on "Icarus."

The coffee was strong, and his hands were shaking. He didn't know if it was nerves or caffeine. Either way, he needed to do something. Palance put on a pair of sandals and, leaving his jacket behind, ran down the stairs to the street. He headed toward Loyola, to the lake, walked past the L-stop and then started running, breaking out in full stride.

At the beach, he took off his sandals and carried them. The cold sand stung his feet. A few people were on the beach, more on the bike path. Palance dipped a toe in the lake and walked out a few feet until the water was up to his ankles; his pant legs were wet, and he began shivering. Palance sat on a bench to warm up, watching people go by on the bike path, walking, jogging, and bicycling. He saw a family laughing, a young mother with three toddlers, two boys and a girl. The woman turned toward him and smiled. The children laughed and skipped.

Palance searched for similar memories from his childhood, and discovered him and Jilly on a boat ride at Kiddieland, taking turns steering. He was wearing a pair of blue jeans and an orange t-shirt. Jilly was dressed in a peach-colored sundress with a ribbon in her hair. She was four years old. His mother was sitting on a bench, watching, eating an ice cream cone. Palance recalled the look on her face: An effusive smile, not a care in the world. He hadn't seen that expression in years. His father stood behind her, strong and peaceful, his hands on her shoulders.

Palance put his sandals back on and walked along the bike path, joining the parade of pedestrians and bicyclists, feeling the contrast between the cool breeze and the warm sun. He thought about Elise.

"You never talk about your feelings," she told him.

"They're in my songs. In my music."

"Can't you talk to me?"

He didn't know how to express his feelings of abandonment and loss. He gave her a line from his song, "I don't know where I'm going to." She shook her head and went back to what she was doing. His father's death broke more than the family. It broke him as well. Even now, a parade was going on, and he could only watch.

A bicycle whizzed past him on the left, and he sidestepped to get out of its way. He passed a couple holding hands on his right. Then there was a series of bicycles on either side, and he stepped off the path, tripping and turning his ankle.

"Are you okay?" a female jogger asked him as he lay on the ground.

Palance tested the ankle. It was sore, but he stood up and could hobble with a small amount of pain. "I'll be okay."

"Sure?" she asked.

"I'm okay."

"Traffic here is worse than the Kennedy," she told him, jogging away.

Palance staggered back toward his apartment. He passed a hot dog stand. He was hungry but didn't have his wallet. He took one painful step after another. Two blocks later, the pain began to subside. He remembered the song he wrote and sang it to himself, *There were always three, there may be more.* The pain diminished and faded. At the apartment building, Jilly was sitting on the front steps.

"Hey, Jilly Bean."

"Why are you limping?"

"Jogging injury."

"Since when do you jog?"

"Since now."

"Mom is psyched about tonight. She's fretting about what to wear and calling all her friends. She acts like you're starring on Broadway."

"I'm not?"

"You said tonight was going to be special. One for the books."

"I did. When have I ever let you down?"

"You want a list?"

"I'll be good. Best behavior, I promise."

Jilly followed Palance up the stairs. Inside, he drained the rest of the burnt coffee into his cup.

"You shouldn't leave the coffee pot on when you're gone."

"I was just out for a little while."

"What's so special about tonight? And why are your pant legs wet?"

"I went jogging by the lake. I have something to show you."

Palance went into the bedroom and came back with a small jewelry box. He opened it for Jilly and showed her the ring.

"Why, darling," she said in a southern accent, "I'm flattered, but I really don't think it would work out. I don't feel the same way about you." Jilly wrapped her arms around him. "It's about time you grew up."

"I need your advice," he told her.

"Really," she said. "You never ask my advice, and when I give it to you, you do the opposite. Do you remember why I'm here?" she asked.

"Because you love me?" he said.

"We're supposed to go to lunch."

"Good idea. I could use the company. Where do you want to go?"

"Hamburger Mary's. You promised."

"Don't you ever forget anything?"

"Why would I do that?"

"Do you want to drive?" he asked her.

"Of course. You don't think I'm foolish enough to trust *you* behind the wheel."

At the restaurant, Palance told Jillian, "I'm almost ready to ask, but I don't know how to be a husband. I barely know how to be a boyfriend."

"That's true. You're not the greatest boyfriend in the world. You're a decent brother, but with serious deficits."

"I'm not sure she'll say 'Yes,'" he told Jilly.

"Of course, she will," Jilly said. "She stuck with you this long."

"She said 'No' before."

"You were an ass, then."

"And now?"

"Less of an ass."

"Hey, how do you know?"

"Know what?"

"About the last time."

"Who said I knew?"

"You did. You implied . . . anyway, how did you know?"

The waitress asked their order.

"I'll have the Bird of Paradise on a brioche bun with rosemary mashed potatoes," Jilly replied.

"Anything to drink?" she asked.

"Diet Coke."

"And you, sir?"

"I'll have the Black and Bleu Boy with fries, and a Miller."

"So predictable," Jilly told him.

"So, as I recall, you had something to tell me," Palance said.

"I thought you forgot," Jillian told him.

"I don't forget as much as you think I do."

"Thank God. I thought you were losing your mind."

"So, are you going to tell me or not?" Palance asked her.

"Here's your beer," the waitress said. "Lover's quarrel? And your diet Coke."

"Hardly," Jilly told her. "He's my brother."

"Oh," she said. "Sibling rivalry."

Palance and Jilly burst out laughing, and the waitress walked away before they recovered.

"It's serious," Jilly said when she regained her composure.

"What is?"

"Me and Jared."

"How serious?"

"I caught him at the jewelry counter at Target. He was looking at rings."

"For my kid sister. He's going to have to ask for my blessing."

"Why you?"

"Stand in. For Dad."

"We'll see. He'll be there tonight. Don't say anything to him."

"Anything?"

"About the ring."

"So how do I do it?" Palance asked her.

"Do what?"

"Be a better boyfriend. Maybe even be a husband."

"First, you need to listen. You're so lost in your own world that you don't pay attention to anyone else. Learn to appreciate the women in your life. Me, obviously. And Mom, too."

"Mom?"

"Look, Doofus, I know you're still mad at Mom for kicking you out of the house, but where would you be if she hadn't? You'd still be in your bedroom, alone with your guitar, playing for no one and obsessing over Beth. Share a feeling once in a while."

"That's what Elise says. Why do I feel like there's a conspiracy?"

The waitress brought their food. Palance didn't know whether to be angry or grateful to Jilly for telling him the truth. The corners of her mouth were uncharacteristically pointed up, and her eyes sparkled.

"How soon?" Palance asked her.

"How soon what?" Jilly said.

"How soon are you thinking about getting married?"

"Not until I'm done with college—and that includes a master's degree. But it's nice to be asked."

Palance was amazed at how alike Jillian and Elise were. "I'll buy lunch," Palance told her.

"Yes, you will," she said. After they finished and Palance had paid the check, they walked to Jilly's car. "You're not planning to wear that outfit tonight, are you?"

"What's wrong with it?"

"Wear something nice."

Back at the apartment, Palance reached for a pen and his notebook. He thought about his mother. Suddenly she was a single mom—the love of her life removed in an instant—with two young kids. One income where there were two. All the decisions dumped in her lap. Jilly had been taking care of herself since she was seven years old. She never needed much parenting. Maybe it was time for him to be there for his mother. He was still figuring out how to be there for someone else.

Through the kitchen window Palance saw rain falling as sun streamed in. He wrote, *but the ice is gone, the dragon's slain, and I feel the warmth of the summer rain.* For the first time in a long while, he felt gratitude. *Still we are one, we are still young, though you are gone like the setting sun, your memory lights the path you've shown, we're blossoms from the seeds you've sown.*

Palance thought about the ring and Elise onstage with him. He saw it in his mind, all planned out. After showering and dressing, Palance drove to the gig. He shoved his hand into his right pants pocket. When his fingers grasped the ring box, he exhaled in relief. Then he took it out to be certain the ring was still in there.

Bill's Blues was empty, apart from the waitress, bartender, and manager, who came up behind him and asked how he was doing. Would he like a drink while he was getting ready?

"Just some water, please."

"How many microphones do you need?"

"Three. Vocal, guitar, and a flute part, just for one song. I need three. Microphones. Three microphones." Palance was stammering.

"No sweat, buddy. Three it is."

Palance sat onstage and tuned his guitar. He played a few chords and then practiced whipping out the ring. *Is this really the way to do it?* he wondered. Too many chances for a misfire in front of everyone. In front of people he didn't even know. The bartender looked at him oddly, and Jillian walked in with Jared.

"Hi, sis," he said, kissing her on the cheek. He extended his hand to Jared.

"I'm looking forward to hearing you tonight," Jared said. "Jilly played me your CD."

"It'll be an interesting night," Palance replied, fearing the worst as someone behind him covered his eyes with her hands.

"Guess who?"

"Hi, Mom."

"People come here to hear you play?" she asked, and Palance's confidence dipped.

"Hope so," he said. "You never know who's going to show up."

"I want a seat in front. I want to watch everything you do. Hear everything," his mother said.

"Maybe we can sit back a little. It gets loud in front," Jilly recommended.

"Nonsense," Elaine said. "You don't have those boys who played with you in high school pounding on the drums and bass, do you?"

"No," Palance replied. "Jason and Kyle aren't here. Just me."

"Don't say 'just me,'" his mother chided. "Say *It's me.* With pride."

"Let's sit down," Jilly said to her. Jared stood obediently silent. He followed Elaine to the front table. Jilly shrugged her shoulders at Palance and said, "I guess we'll sit here." Jared pulled out Jilly's chair, and, after she was seated, sat down next to her.

"Good choice," Palance said with resignation. Everything needed to be perfect, but all his instincts were gone.

Elise walked in with her flute case in one hand and a small black-and-white checkered purse in the other. Palance felt his breath become more regular. His shoulders relaxed as Elise hugged him. Jilly got up from the table, kissed Elise on the cheek, and whispered in her ear. Elise apologized for being late—*traffic on Clark Street*. She asked Palance if he was nervous.

"Why would I be nervous?"

"You seem on edge. I'm looking forward to being onstage with you."

"Me, too," Palance told her, imagining himself kneeling down before her.

"Shouldn't you be getting ready?" Jilly asked him, looking at her watch.

"Yes, Boss," he said, stepping up on stage. "Do we need a sound check?" he asked Elise.

"I'll blend with you," she said to him. "I have experience."

Palance tuned his guitar and watched the three women in his life. The audience was sparse, only nine or ten people in the room. It would be awkward to do this in front of a packed house.

"I'd like to start with a song my father wrote," Palance said. He took a breath and played the opening chords. *I stood upon the river's edge and watched the water as it flowed, and listened to the ebb and flow, in summer's heat and winter's cold.* When he started the chorus, he saw his mother smile. *When morning comes the earth turns still, 'til sunlight finds the windowsill . . .*

There was a smattering of applause. Palance looked at his mother and saw a glimpse of approval. "This song is dedicated to my mother," he said to her. "It's not easy raising a musician. It wasn't easy raising me." *Too old to be so young, too young to be so wise, too wise to be a child, you are as ageless as the tides.* He watched their faces, the four of them at the front table, Elise quietly unpacking her flute, Jared holding Jilly's hand, and Mom staring without blinking.

A half dozen more people came in, filling two tables, and there was a couple at the door. He didn't know anyone outside his family, though he recognized some from other gigs. He looked at Elise and began "Where Do We Go from Here?" He focused on Elise assembling her flute. The audience applauded, his mother the loudest of all.

Palance invited Elise up onto the stage and wiped the sweat from his hands onto his pants, feeling the bulge of the ring in his pocket. He took her hand to help her up and kissed her cheek as she stood beside him. He introduced Elise to the audience and began playing "Icarus" on his guitar. While he sang, he looked straight into her eyes, never allowing his gaze to wander. Her flute wove the threads of his voice and guitar together.

On the chorus, his father's image appeared before him: *As you rode the winds in wonder, thunder rumbling through the breeze, did you hear your father calling, falling and tumbling to the sea.* Seamlessly, the applause began, the ring box materialized in Palance's hand, and he knelt before Elise. Her eyes were fixed to his. Time moved in slow motion. Her eyes widened, her mouth opened into an oval of surprise, and he, like a storybook knight, opened the box toward her.

"Elise," he said, his voice quivering, "You are the love and light of my life. You are the melody to my harmony, the timbre of my heart, and the heart of my soul. Will you do me the honor of marrying me?" Elise placed the flute on the chair and knelt before him until they were inches apart. She ignored the ring, cradled his face in her hands, and kissed him. He watched her eyes dance while her lips remained still. Elise stood up and extended her hand down to him, guiding him upward until they were again face-to-face.

"Palance Heller, I will not bow down to you. I never want you to bow down to me. I would be honored to marry you," she told him and kissed him passionately. An eruption of whoops and applause reached out to them. Palance remembered where he was, turned, and looked to see every table full. The entire audience was standing and applauding.

Palance announced a short break, remaining onstage until the applause died down. He took Elise's hand and sat next to her at the front table. His mother and sister crowded and hugged them, welcoming her into the family and letting him know *it's about time*.

"No," Elise told them. "It's the right time. The exact right time."

Elaine talked incessantly. "It's a night of surprises. He never warned me," she said to Elise. "Frankly, he never tells me anything."

"He doesn't tell me much, either," Elise said to her. "I need to keep a close eye on this one."

"It's nice that he's in town more often. I once went a year without seeing him."

"It was only eight months," Palance said.

"Eight months is a long time when you're a mother."

"You're the one who kicked me out," he retaliated.

"He'll always hold that against me," she told Elise, not even looking at him.

"No, I won't. You'll see. It's time."

"Time for what?"

"Time for my next set."

"What are you going to play?" his mother asked.

"You'll see."

"Elise will tell me."

"She doesn't know."

"So, what am I supposed to do?" his mother asked.

"Live and learn," he said, stepping up onto the stage.

Palance played a cover of "Fire and Rain." He looked at his mother, his sister, and at Elise, who resembled Jilly in some ways, and at Jared, who reminded him of someone he couldn't quite place. He played them his song, not knowing how anyone would react. *There were always three, there may be more, but in my mind, there were always four.*

Palance realized his mother probably didn't know he wrote it, and he saw Elise nudge her arm and whisper in her ear; he knew that Elise would know it was his song, even though she hadn't heard it before. *There was always love, I was never lost, even when I could not pay the cost.* Now his mother was looking into his eyes, her mouth set, her posture stiff—she knew. *And the heart of the family lies in the sticks and stones of the family ties.* Her mouth turned up at the corners, something he'd waited a long time to see.

He continued, *and I mourned your loss, I turned and tossed, 'til I was cold as the winter's frost.* This was what he wanted, to take his family on the path he had traveled. *But the ice is gone, the dragon's slain, and I feel the warmth of the summer rain. And the heart of the family lies in the sticks and stones of the family ties.* His mother looked at him differently, no longer the wayward child, the way he'd always seen himself. He wasn't sure how she saw him, but it was different.

Palance closed his eyes. *We are still one, songs to be sung, though you are gone like the setting sun, your memory lights the path you've shown, we're blossoms from the seeds you've sown. And the heart of the family lies in the sticks and stones of the family ties. Yes, the heart of the family lies in the sticks and stones of the family ties.*

Palance was spent, but there was one more song he had to sing before he could leave the stage. Tonight he had lost track of the audience. He was there for his family. He pulled an empty chair onto the stage and invited Elise back.

"I'm not sure I can stand any more surprises," she whispered.

He looked into her eyes, not playing chords but just a series of notes and sang: *Deep in the still of night, you know the time is right, I see the northern lights in your eyes. We live a fleeting life, quick as a switchblade knife; I get the northern lights when you smile.*

Everything besides Elise faded as he sang, adding the low E bass string to the melody. *I see the northern lights, I see the northern lights, I see the northern lights in your eyes. I get the northern lights, I get the northern lights, I get the northern lights when you smile.*

Palance let the harmonics ring between verses and felt himself carried away as he switched the bass to the open A string: *Freedom is faith in flight, love living in your sight, I see the northern lights in your eyes. Your eyes are sparkling bright, even in darkest night, I get the northern lights when you smile.* Once more he played the melody alone on the high E string, and let it ring. He heard applause from the audience while he and Elise kissed.

Palance wanted to take her home and make love to her until they fell asleep in each other's arms. Elise told him his mother was taking them out to dinner and had made reservations at Dave's Italian Kitchen. Palance collected himself and told them he'd be a few minutes—he had to make a stop.

"Where do you have to stop?" Elise asked him after the two were alone in the car together.

"I have to stop for this," he told her, pulled her to him, and kissed her passionately. "And I have to tell you how much I love you."

"It'd better be a lot," she said.

"It is."

"How much?"

"More than Anthony loved Cleopatra. More than Romeo loved Juliet."

"Oh, and those worked out well."

"More than I love music," Palance told her.

"Really?"

"Really."

"Okay, I'll marry you," she said.

"You already said you'd marry me."

"That was for them. This is for us. Start the car. We'll be late."

"I don't care."

"I do," she said. "You'd better drive now, before I have my way with you."

Dave's Italian Kitchen was only a few blocks away. He knew his mother and Elise would start planning the wedding.

"Let's elope," he told Elise.

"You shouldn't have told your mother if you were planning to elope. Besides, I don't want to elope. I want to wear a white dress and walk down the aisle."

"There are aisles in Vegas."

"There are hookers there, too, but I'm not one of them. Somewhere pretty would be nice. Somewhere by the lake."

"Where?"

"Up north, there's a Bahai Temple."

"What's Bahai?"

"Somewhere between New Age and New Testament."

"And you want to join?"

"Be joined."

"Is that what you want?" he asked her.

"Yes."

"Then that's what I want, too." Palance put the car into gear and slowly navigated the streets; they were deserted and solemn. "Do you like the ring?" he asked.

"I love the promise."

"But do you like the ring?"

"I do like the ring," she told him. "I *love* the promise. And you."

They found parking a few spaces down from the restaurant. The streetlights illuminated Elise's face, and he parted his lips to mesh with hers as they headed down the stairs. "You have to be nice and pay attention to her," Elise told him.

"To who?"

"Your mother."

"I wrote her the song."

"You wrote the song for your father. Be nice to your mother. She's still alive."

"Okay," he said. At the bottom of the stairs, he kissed his mother on the cheek.

"Your father would be proud of you," she told him.

Jilly and Jared walked in. Jilly took Elise's hand and examined the ring. "Not bad for the Bro," she said. "He's done worse," she let Elise know.

Jared shook hands with Palance, congratulating him. They followed the hostess to their table.

"Like a wedding procession," Elaine said.

"Not yet," Palance told her.

"Then, when?" she asked.

"We don't know when," he told her. "But we know where."

"My baby," she said, looking him in the eyes.

"I thought I was your baby," Jillian protested.

"You're both my babies."

"Sorry," Palance said. "All grown up."

"Hardly," Elise remarked. "Just a little boy in a grown-up body."

The women surrounded Palance. Jared broke a smile as they traded barbs.

"So, Jared," Palance asked him. "Are you ready to accept the shackles and chains that go along with being part of this family?" Jillian glared at Palance.

"Shackles and chains?" he asked. "She is the joy of my life."

"Tell the truth," Palance said. "I've lived with her."

"Then you know her true beauty," Jared replied. Jillian's face glowed with satisfaction.

"Touché," Palance said. "But don't let her know."

"Enough already," Elaine announced. "Study your menus, and let's order. Hardly grown."

The waitress took their orders and came back with a bottle of Champagne and five glasses, pouring one for each of them. Palance was surprised when everyone looked at him; then he realized they expected him to deliver a toast.

"To Elise," he said, "the love of my life, and to my family, for all the love they've given me . . . and all they've put up with from me."

The waitress brought their soup, and the conversation flowed. Jared was animated. He wanted to know how the two of them met. His mother and Jilly leaned in. He told them the story of his first night at his apartment, leaving out the pot that Ben and Dennis smoked, but not the music, and Jared remarked how beautifully they played together. Elise reminded him they met in class, and at the No Exit, and let them know more about the first night he was at the apartment, how vulnerable he seemed.

Elise talked about Palance's transformation, his growth as a musician, the new maturity in his songs and his lyrics, the slow and often unsteady path to manhood he was approaching. Elaine smiled and hugged Elise, telling her she was grateful to have her in their lives. Jilly came over, too. As a unit, they marched over to Palance and placed their hands on him.

Jared raised his Champagne glass and pronounced words that left Palance speechless. He hoped that one day he and Jillian would be as happy, as successful, and as accomplished as

Palance and Elise. Palance was certain he was being sarcastic, and scanned his face for telltale signs.

"That's sweet," Elise told Jared. Palance studied her face, shocked at the sincerity.

"Thank you," Palance told him, his eyes narrowing.

The night unfolded, and Palance watched. His mother sat at the head of the table and scanned her children and their partners. Jillian guarded Jared in the same way, and Elise alone seemed herself. She ate and conversed without a care in the world.

The waitress brought their salads. Jared recounted his education: business and engineering, his plans for the future; a career in the corporate world, saving up for his own company, his passion for alternative energy. Jilly beamed. Elise clapped her hands and applauded. Palance sipped his soup and marveled at his family.

"So, what are your plans?" Jared asked Palance, who wasn't sure if Jared was asking about the wedding or career plans. He was glad when Elise took over.

"Palance is almost a teacher. I can hardly believe it."

"Neither would any of his teachers," Jilly chimed in.

"My family didn't believe I was going to college for business," Jared said. "They thought I was going to try to make a living playing video games."

The entrees arrived, and everyone marveled at the portions and aroma. Elaine commented about *enough to feed an army*, and Jillian proclaimed she would be lucky to eat half. Jared talked about the meals he grew up with, the food so plentiful it barely fit on the table. His grandmother begged him to eat. He was too skinny. Jillian cackled, elbowing Palance and commenting at the familiarity. Elise said her relatives were all overweight. They watched the children like hawks, worried they should eat too much.

"And so, I grew huge as a kid, grabbing any morsel of ice cream or cake that I could find. It was such a treat. Once I ate half a birthday cake at a party and was sent home early."

"How did you lose the weight?" Elaine asked.

"My first year at college, I ate everything in sight. After that, even the thought of too much made me ill, and I went for long walks along the lake and cut back to normal portions."

"Should we avoid dessert tonight?" Elaine asked.

"Not on your life," Elise told her. "Tonight, we celebrate." She looked at Palance. "Tonight, I am engaged to the love of my life."

Jillian grinned. "I knew you were the sister I always wanted."

"You have the most harmonious family," Jared remarked, and they all burst out laughing.

"You've got to be kidding," Palance said.

"You're not serious," Jilly told him.

"I am. My family was one constant argument."

"At least you got it out," Elaine said. "We brood."

"In my family," Jared said, "if you give a compliment, someone takes offense."

"We never give compliments," Jilly replied.

"I tell you both how proud I am of you," Elaine told her children.

"Was that on a Tuesday or a Wednesday?" Palance asked Jillian.

"Ninety-eight or ninety-nine?" Jillian inquired. "I can't remember."

"Very funny," their mother scolded. "Is that the kind of argument in your family, Jared?"

"Oh, no," he said, "in our family, the fights last hours, and often, at the end of the evening, no one is speaking to anyone."

"Sounds peaceful," Palance said. Elise elbowed him in the side.

"You'd think a performer would be more gregarious at home," Elise remarked.

"He was the brooder of the brood," Elaine told her. "Once, he didn't talk for a week."

"I remember that week," Jillian said. "It was peaceful."

"Nothing you'd ever try," he argued back, "not that I didn't beg you."

"Maybe I'm better off if he doesn't talk," Elise said.

"He can be a real pain in the ass," Jilly explained. "It's better you find out now."

"Oh, I know," Elise told her. "Believe me, I know."

"Hey, what is this?" Palance asked. "Maybe you all want to divorce me."

"Can't divorce you," Elise said. "Not even married yet."

"This is like my family," Jared said. "By the end of the evening you'll have gotten it all out."

"And you get off scot-free?" Jillian said, "I don't think so."

"What did I do?" he asked.

"You started this whole thing," Palance said. "We were peaceful . . ."

"Brooding," Elaine said.

"Stuffy," Elise told them.

"Stuffy?" Elaine and Jillian asked together.

The waitress came over, letting them know the dessert choices and offering them take-home containers for the leftovers. The five of them were laughing too hard to respond. Palance looked at Elise, put his hands on her shoulders, and pulled her to him. He kissed her and told her he couldn't believe how lucky he was to be with her.

Elaine came behind Palance and Elise, placing one hand on each of their shoulders. "Palance," she said, "this is what I always wanted for you. A future, and Elise."

Jillian smirked. Palance glanced at Jilly, amused at her expression, as if she resented being upstaged by her brother.

"You're not jealous, Jilly Bean, are you?" he asked.

"I'm too old to be called that."

"Still haven't answered the question."

"It's a stupid question."

"Why?"

"Because I've always been jealous of *you*," she told him.

"Why?"

"You really have to ask?" she said.

"Yes," he told her. "I've always been jealous of you."

"Why?" she said.

"You're the perfect child."

"You're the star," Jilly told him. "Always in the limelight. I have to try twice as hard as you for everything. You have it all handed to you on a plate."

"Handed to me on a plate. What are you smoking?"

"Not as much as you did. And you never studied."

"You got better grades," Palance told her.

"You got B's and C's without even cracking a book. Do you know how hard I studied to get my grades? And you were the popular one."

"Popular. I hung out with the outcasts."

"At least you had a gang."

"Children," Elaine yelled. "What are you fighting about?"

"It's not fair," they cried in unison.

"Jared," Elaine said, "They are acting like your family, the way you described them—loud and argumentative and frankly obnoxious. Why?"

"Because they can," he told her.

"What do you mean?"

"They'll argue tonight, but tomorrow, they'll still be family. They'll still love each other."

"Exactly," Elise agreed.

Family Ties

We were always three, we may be more,
But in my mind we were always four.
There was always love, I was never lost,
Even when I could not pay the cost.

C

H   *And the heart of the family lies*

O   *in the sticks and stones*

R   *of the family ties*

U

S

You were always there, standing by my side,
Though I was a boy on the day you died.
Each and every chord, every song I sing,
I sing for you, like you sang for me.

Chorus

And I mourned your loss, I turned and tossed,
'Til I was cold as the winter's frost,
But the ice is gone, the dragon's slain,
And I feel the warmth of the summer rain.

Chorus

We are still one, songs to be sung,
Though you are gone like the setting sun,
Your memory lights the path you've shown,
We're blossoms from the seeds you've sown.

Chorus

Northern Lights

Deep in the still of night,
you know the time is right,
I see the northern lights
in your eyes.

We live a fleeting life,
Quick as a switchblade knife,
I get the northern lights
when you smile.

I see the northern lights,
I see the northern lights,
I see the northern lights
in your eyes.

I get the northern lights,
I get the northern lights,
I get the northern lights
when you smile.

Freedom is faith in flight,
Love living in your sight,
I see the northern lights
in your eyes.

Your eyes are sparkling bright,
Even in darkest night,
I get the northern lights
when you smile.

Chapter Thirteen
Entwined

Palance *was always nervous* before a gig, but not like this. He wanted to spend the night with Elise in their apartment, but she said "No." He was staying at his mother's condo and felt like an interloper. His mother fawned over him as if he were a little boy.

Palance had no idea where she kept the coffeepot. It wasn't on the kitchen counter, and he had to look through the cabinets twice before he found it in the pantry next to the refrigerator. As he poured in the water and started brewing the coffee, his mother entered the kitchen and kissed him on the forehead. "I never trusted that one boy. He was always up to no good."

"He'll be fine. We'll see you in a couple hours."

"You can get in a lot of trouble in a couple of hours."

Palance sighed. "We'll be good," he told her.

"Don't listen to them," his mother said. "Especially Jason. Don't ever listen to him."

"Who should I listen to?" he asked.

"Me, of course," she said, laughing.

Palance poured himself a cup of coffee and stared out the window. He thought about getting into his car and driving, west to California, or north to Canada, maybe Winnipeg. *I've never played Canada*, he thought. Palance imagined the road changing from concrete to asphalt to gravel, and mistook the knock on the door for tires crunching over stones. Kyle, of course, was early.

"Big day," Kyle said.

"Glad you're here. I need a rhythm section."

"Jason's going to be late. He'll meet us at the gig."

"Whatever."

"I told you not to count on him," Elaine yelled from the other room.

"He'll be there," Kyle said.

"Okay," Elaine conceded.

"Big day, Mrs. Heller," Kyle told her.

"You're old enough," she told Kyle. "Call me Elaine."

"I'll try," he said.

"Now can we relax a little?" Palance asked him.

"Are you kidding? We need to get dressed and get everything ready." Kyle pulled out three lists, one for what to wear, one for what they needed to do for the next two hours, and one for what to bring. Kyle was three minutes into his speech when he mentioned they would take his car—he had the trunk and back seat mapped out. Palance snorted coffee from his nose and laughed.

"I knew you were the right choice," he said.

"Let me see the program," Kyle demanded, without breaking a smile, and Palance handed it over. "I don't think this is right."

"Too late to change it now."

"We'll just have to do the best we can. You finish your coffee. I have to make some notes, and then we need to go."

Palance knew Kyle would take care of all the details. It's what Palance disliked most about being on the road by himself. He was the one taking care of the details.

"You lucked out," Kyle said. "The weather is perfect." Are you ready for this?"

"I haven't been ready for anything since the fifth grade," Palance told him. "But somehow, things work out."

Kyle smiled for the first time that morning. "So, that's your secret?" he said.

"I don't have any secrets."

"You have secrets."

"What are you talking about?"

"You've got more secrets than the CIA. You always play it close to the vest."

"That's what Elise says. She wants me to share more."

"What do you want?"

"I've always wanted something," Palance said. "But I never knew what it was."

"Do you know what you want now?"

"I want Elise. I want to be married. I want to teach, and I want to keep performing."

"Why?"

"It keeps my dad close to me."

Kyle put his hands on Palance's shoulders, and the two friends looked at each other. "I think we're ready," Kyle said.

"A few more minutes?" Palance asked and waited for Kyle's nod before he walked around the apartment looking at the pictures. He stopped in front of a picture taken when he was only ten, his parents, he and Jillian, posed formally. Palance placed his fingers on the image of his father and held them there, before turning to go. "Ready," he said, and the two walked out the door. Palance carried his father's guitar.

"I've got a place carved out for the guitar in back," Kyle told him.

"I'll hold it."

"There's not enough room."

"I'll hold it."

Palance barely fit in the front seat with the wooden case. They turned east and drove along the lakefront, past downtown Evanston and the Northwestern campus, buildings of ancient stone and brick rising up from the lake. They slipped past modern houses and strip malls. The Bahai Temple came into sight, and Palance asked Kyle to pull over into the park.

"Gilson Park?" he asked.

"Yes."

"It's your day, man. You're not freaking out, are you?"

Palance smiled at him and Kyle pulled into the parking lot behind the amphitheater. Sunbathers lay in rows on the beach, and sailboats dotted the lake. Kyle followed Palance up the grassy hill, down the steps toward the concrete amphitheater, and onto the stage below.

Palance walked to the edge of the stage, sat down, and opened the guitar case. No one was paying attention, and for once, he was grateful.

"I've never played you this song," Palance told Kyle. "Never played it for anyone—yet." Palance strummed a chord and sang, *I don't remember the first time I loved you, I can't imagine the last, I don't remember the moment the die was cast.* A small family looked up from the seats, and Palance suddenly felt shy.

"I don't want an audience yet," Palance told him.

"Too late," Kyle said, pointing to an approaching pack of teenagers.

"Then let's do something else." Palance moved the guitar case toward Kyle and instructed him to play it like a conga drum.

"What should we play?" Kyle asked.

"Just make it up," Palance told him and launched into a series of power chords followed by a delicate set of cascading arpeggios imitating the waves and wind, blending in with them. Kyle punctuated the melody with a calypso beat, and the teenagers danced. The sun was warm overhead, and Palance felt as free as the vast expanse of water before him.

"Gotta go, man," Kyle said.

"That's right. We've got a wedding to go to, don't we?"

"Yeah, and we're going to have to get cleaned up now."

"Don't worry. Someone will take care of that. Let's walk," Palance said.

"Can't. Too much stuff," Kyle told him, pointing to the car.

Palance got into the car, once again clutching the guitar case. Kyle scowled at Palance's feet, covered with sand, and took care to brush off his own shoes before sitting down. Kyle drove across Sheridan, where the Bahai Temple was festive: white tents billowed in the wind; colored streamers and balloons flew from tent poles; violets and chrysanthemums filled vases.

Chairs sat in a dozen rows, with a single aisle between them, and Palance reminded himself this was not just another gig. He began unpacking the car, and Kyle blocked him.

"You take care of your guitar. I'll do the rest."

"Sure?" Palance asked.

"Sure."

"Oh, my God," Jilly said, walking up to them. "You're a mess. Come with me."

"It's not that bad," he told her.

"*Not that bad*," she repeated. "Do you hear that, Mom? *Not that bad*. It's a good thing you're getting married. Heaven knows you need someone to take care of you."

"What would I do without you, Jilly?" he asked.

"This," she said. "This is what you do. Unbelievable." She found a brush in her purse and fussed with his hair. "Come inside, and when Kyle is done, make sure he comes, too. Don't you dare look at Elise. I'll make sure she goes somewhere until you look like a proper groom."

"Who died and made you . . ."

"Your fiancée, almost your wife, when she made me her maid of honor," Jilly told him.

"But I'm the groom; don't I get any say?"

"You can say, 'I do.' Otherwise, smile and look pretty."

"I'll do my best. Where do I go?"

"You go to the room inside, third door on the left, and you be polite and friendly to Elise's dad."

"What about Kyle?" Palance asked.

"He has his own chores. Turn around," she told him, pulling a lint roller out of her purse and cleaning his tuxedo. "Elise is going to have her hands full with you." Jilly was glowing. Palance made a mental note about the odd behavior of women at weddings. "I'll take that," Jilly said, pointing to the guitar.

"No, you won't. I don't care what else happens, I keep the guitar."

"Fine, keep the guitar. Just get your ass in there and clean up. Here, turn around," she told him and continued to brush him with the lint roller. "You'd better take this with you," she said, handing it to him. "Kyle will know what to do."

The white marble was effervescent, and though he was not a religious person, Palance knew this was a sacred space. He clicked his tongue to check the acoustics. They rang with a sharp, natural reverberation. He wanted to sit and play his guitar. Opening the third door on the left, Palance saw his future father-in-law. They'd met only twice before, and this was their first time alone together.

"Hello, Mr. Fyelander," he said, extending his arm. "How is Baltimore, sir?" He watched as the man winced in mistrust.

"You're taking my daughter," he said. "And Baltimore is Baltimore. Always has been, always will be. You, however, are taking my daughter."

Palance wanted to tell Mr. Fyelander that, actually, he was going to *give* Elise to him, but he knew that wouldn't fly. Elise told Palance she resented anyone *giving her away*, though she was still conventional enough to want the traditional ceremony. It was the first time Palance really understood, telling his bride-to-be that he loved and would support her in whatever decisions she made. He attended the required tastings. He compared invitations, centerpieces, silverware, and linens until his head spun, each time rewarded with a look more endearing than the last.

"Sir," Palance said, in all sincerity, "your daughter has chosen to live here with me in Chicago, and it is my great pleasure and responsibility to make her as happy as possible. You have my word that we will visit you in Baltimore, and you will always be welcome in our home."

George Fyelander looked Palance straight in the eye for a full minute before a faint smile creased his lips. "I will trust you, young man, to keep to your word. I love that girl more than I loved my wife, rest her soul. Cross her, and you've crossed me."

"I'll do my best," Palance told him, eye to eye.

Kyle burst in, flustered, as if he'd been flung into the room. "Ten minutes," he announced, breathing heavily. "Do I look alright?"

"You look like you're the one on the block," Mr. Fyelander told him. "No one will be looking at us anyway. Once Elise walks down the aisle, she'll be the center of attention. "Better get used to that," he said to Palance.

"It's almost time. Do you have the rings?" Palance asked Kyle.

Kyle looked smug and patted his jacket pocket. "Safe and sound."

Palance heard music playing. He took his guitar out of the case and put the strap around his neck. His palms began to sweat, and his heart raced.

"You'll make a fine husband," Mr. Fyelander said. "A bit of nerves is a good sign. Marriage does not encourage complacency."

Palance paced the room, not daring to look at Kyle, much less Mr. Fyelander. In the old days, he would have made his way to the car and driven off until the sun went down and rose again, putting distance between himself and . . . he couldn't identify what he was running from.

"Anything wrong?" Kyle asked Palance.

"Leave him be," Mr. Fyelander said. "I damned near wore out a pair of shoes on my wedding day."

There was a knock on the door. "Two minutes," a voice called into the room. Palance quickened his paces and grasped the guitar tightly.

Kyle tapped Palance's arm. "It's time," he said, and the three men walked slowly and silently outside, where the wedding coordinator guided them behind the temple. Palance looked up, saw the lake, and felt the sun warm on his skin. He handed Kyle his guitar and told him to guard it with his life. Kyle took the guitar, and Mr. Fyelander wished Palance luck, walking down the hill to wait for his daughter.

Looking at the crowd of guests, some seated, others still milling about, Palance felt his heart pound. There were relatives he hadn't seen for years and many of Elise's relatives he'd never met. Ben and Dennis looked odd in suits and ties. The wedding coordinator directed Palance and Kyle to a small open area surrounded on three sides with flowers.

Palance saw Jason and breathed a sigh of relief. It took a great deal of persuasion. Elise was against it at first, but Jason had mostly sobered up, and was now an officially Ordained Minister of the Universal Life Church. It allowed the three of them to join forces once again. Palance embraced Jason.

"Places to go," Kyle told them. "Things to do."

"Hey, man," Palance said to Jason, "I'm glad you're doing this."

"You're the first one to let me. Don't worry. I won't screw it up," Jason said. "I hear you wrote a song for the occasion."

"Had to. You got the lyrics, right? This is the biggest thing in my life so far."

"I've got the lyrics. Is this bigger than the Whispering Screams?" Jason asked.

"The Screams didn't last that long," Palance said. "This better."

"We're still here," Kyle told him.

The music swelled into a Bach cantata while Palance's mother slowly made her way down the aisle, turning right at the front and taking a seat in the corner chair. Kyle came next, with Shalini, Elise's maid of honor, on one arm and Jilly on the other. A few people hooted. Palance kept an eye on his father's guitar nearby.

The music changed tempo, and Palance turned to the back of the aisle. Elise appeared on her father's right arm. He had never seen her as beautiful and graceful. Her father stood straight and tall. Elise was wearing a diaphanous white dress lilting in the lake breeze. Palance was mesmerized.

Everything decelerated into slow motion. Palance heard his breath amplified to the point of distraction. He traced the slight movements of Jason's nostrils. Elise moved toward him. She and the music stopped a few inches away, an exquisite silence punctuated by the waves, the scent of flowers, and the vision of his bride before him.

"Marriage is a journey," Jason began, in a voice Palance had never heard before. "A journey begins in a moment, this moment, and continues on, not merely for one lifetime, but for two. Palance Heller and Elise Fyelander have chosen to entwine their lives together as two roses wrap themselves around each other, each retaining their individuality, yet woven together to form a fabric unique to their relationship.

"This is not the beginning. Their relationship began before now, and it is certainly not the end. It is a moment in time, and in this moment in time, they stand before us, on this sacred ground, before family and friends, to pledge their vows to each other. Elise, will you speak your vows to Palance?"

"Palance Heller," Elise said, "I vow to support your dreams and your journey, to love, honor, and cherish you, and keep you in line when necessary. I vow to harmonize with you when I can, to celebrate our joys and mourn our losses together."

"Palance, will you speak your vows to Elise?"

"Elise, I thought I knew what love was, but then I met you, and I understood what love could be." Palance had to choke back tears. I vow to work to maintain a harmonious relationship. I vow to love, honor, and cherish you, to always be kind, and to support and care for you as long as we both shall live."

"Before we continue, and join this couple in holy matrimony," Jason announced, "Palance has a song for the occasion."

Kyle handed Palance the guitar. Palance turned toward Elise, cleared his throat and sang: *I don't remember the first time I loved you, I can't imagine the last, I don't remember the moment the dice were cast. But in a moment will be forever, moments slip away. But I will love you until the end of days.* Elise's eyes watered over. *And in this moment in time, two hearts beat in rhyme, two songs, two melodies aligned; two souls, two harmonies entwined.*

A single tear rolled silently down Elise's cheek, and Palance saw a look in her eyes he had not seen before. *The days that follow may seem uncertain, as the years unwind. You cannot look beyond the curtain, only look behind. But in this moment, we'll build a lifetime—who knows what we'll find? Here and now I speak my promise, always to be kind.* Their eyes locked as he sang the chorus again. *And in this moment in time, two hearts beat in rhyme, two songs, two melodies aligned; two souls, two harmonies entwined.*

And in this moment in time, in this moment in time, in this moment in time . . . entwined. There was silence now, and the wind and the waves. Palance handed the guitar back to Kyle.

"Do you, Elise Fyelander, take Palance Heller as your husband, to have and to hold, until death do you part?"

"I do," she said, taking the ring from Kyle and placing it on Palance's finger.

"And do you, Palance Heller, take Elise Fyelander as your wife, to have and to hold, until death do you part?"

"I do," Palance said, taking the other ring from Kyle and placing it on her finger.

"Then by the powers vested in me," Jason told them, "I have the prestigious and undeniable honor to pronounce you husband and wife."

Palance cupped Elise's face in his hands, kissing her, only dimly aware of the crowd before them, applauding. Jason guided them gently back down the aisle. Palance and Elise gripped hands as they walked.

Elise whispered in his ear, "Thank you for the song—it's beautiful."

"Not as beautiful as you."

On this night of firsts, Elise blushed beet red. "Thank you, husband," she said.

"Thank you, wife," he said, and they were caught up in the ceremonial pageant, the endless reception line with introductions to relatives they barely knew. Envelopes were stuffed into Palance's breast pocket. Palance worried about the guitar until Kyle told him it was safe. Mr. Fyelander reminded him, "I meant what I said, young man. She's my baby; you'd better take care of her."

"Yes, sir."

"Call me 'George,'" he said, without looking any less ferocious.

"Yes, sir—George."

Mr. Fyelander slapped him on the shoulder and stepped over to embrace his daughter in a bear hug. "You tell me any time this interloper gives you trouble."

"I can handle him, Daddy," she said.

The wedding photographer herded them to various locations around the temple and grounds, along with family and members of the wedding party. Palance couldn't recall smiling so widely and often. He wanted to take Elise's hand and run, but instead they were escorted to the white tent, where toasts were about to begin.

"I have known Elise," Shalini began, "since my second year in undergraduate school, when I was first chair in the orchestra, and she was second. I didn't notice her until she did the unthinkable during my junior year—beat me out for first chair. I have been plotting my revenge against her ever since, and now I am here to exact that revenge."

"You didn't tell me that," Palance whispered to Elise.

"So now," Shalini continued, "with Elise getting married, I will encourage Palance to get her pregnant as quickly as possible and keep her out of the competition." The guests roared with laughter, and Shalini had to wait to continue. "However, what I also need to say to Palance is that he married a treasure and that he should count his blessings every day of his life that he has that treasure, and treat my best friend accordingly. Okay?"

"Okay," Palance replied.

Shalini walked over and hugged Elise first and then Palance, whispering in his ear, "Don't mess this up." She kissed him on the cheek and walked back to her seat.

Kyle began tapping on his glass with a fork until everyone joined in. Palance took Elise in his arms and gave her a kiss fit for a Hollywood movie. Kyle began: "I've known Palance since we were running around together in short pants, and, I need to tell you—it wasn't a pretty sight. But really, I've had the privilege of being Palance's bandmate and friend for more than twenty years, and I have to tell you, he can really be a pain. When he isn't a pain, which isn't often, Palance is one of the most creative and kindhearted people you would ever want to meet. Despite his good qualities, Palance is not the easiest guy to commit to anything outside of his music, so the fact that he chose to marry Elise tells me she is a very special woman. I wish you both health and happiness, and a long and beautiful life together. Congratulations."

The guests again tapped their glasses, and, this time, Elise stood up, pulled Palance to her, bent him over, and kissed him for more than a minute. Afterward, Palance announced, "I am a very lucky man."

After speeches by Elise's father, Palance's mother, very tearful, and Jillian, sarcastic as ever, the wedding planner announced that food would be served in the adjoining tent, and all were welcome to partake, inviting Palance and Elise to enter first. Friends of Elise played the dinner music: flute and guitar, of course. Elise took his hand, and he followed her.

"So, what do you think, Mrs. Heller?" Palance asked Elise.

"We talked about that. I'm still Ms. Fyelander."

"And yet, you are a married lady."

Elise put down her plate, took Palance's out of his hand, and set it on the table. She pushed him against the wall and kissed him for what seemed like an eternity, until the guests applauded, and then pushed him away. "Married, maybe," she told him. "But a lady? I don't think so."

"Good—then I won't be disappointed."

Palance and Elise barely touched their food. Between toasts, they held hands and gazed at each other. After dinner, the wedding planner announced that Palance and Elise would have their first dance as husband and wife. The guitar and flute were joined by piano, bass, and drums, and the band played "Can You Feel the Love Tonight?" from *The Lion King*. Palance took Elise gracefully into his arms and held her close.

"Why, Mr. Heller, you can dance," she told him.

"Don't tell anyone. It'll be our secret."

"It was your secret."

"You, darling," he told her, "are going to have to keep my secrets now. I have a reputation to maintain."

"You *had* a reputation. Now you have me, and, more importantly, I have you."

The wedding planner announced the Mother and Groom Dance. Palance kissed Elise, walked over to his mother, and offered her his hand. She followed him to the dance floor, where he took her in his arms, and the band played "Sunrise, Sunset." The tears in her eyes wet his own.

"I'm proud of you," she told him. He noticed laugh lines around her eyes.

"I'm proud of you, too. It couldn't have been easy."

"You are a lot of things, Palance Heller, but easy is not one of them."

"Was I worth it?"

"We'll see," she said.

The wedding planner announced a Father-Daughter Dance. Palance expected to see his father glide across the dance floor with Jilly in his arms but instead watched Elise and her father on the dance floor. The afternoon and evening flowed by quickly, the wedding planner conducting, with Kyle and Shellie riding herd over it all. There were pictures, more toasts, and more dancing. Palance had to sit down for a few minutes. He was used to being onstage, not on the dance floor.

Friends and relatives pulled Palance and Elise apart. Elise's Uncle Winston advised Palance not to give in too much, too early. His Aunt Abbey, whom he hadn't seen since grammar school and didn't recognize, told him to keep his own friends. Someone he didn't recognize at all insisted he keep his options open. Palance walked away before finding out exactly what that meant. All he wanted was to be alone with Elise. He'd made reservations at the Orrington Hotel for the next two nights, and Palance looked forward to walking on the beach, eating at their favorite restaurants, and having her to himself.

He looked for Elise but couldn't find her. A tap on his shoulder turned out to be welcome relief, as Jason stood next to him, shaking his head back and forth.

"Married, huh?"

"You should know. Rumor is you had a part in it."

"If you need a little help from your friend, I've got some in the car."

"Haven't come that far, have you?" Palance asked.

"A long way, actually. Someday we'll sit around and tell stories."

"I'd like that. Someday soon. When we're alone."

"You haven't shared it all with the missus?"

"Yeah, but I don't think she wants to hear it retold. You're a part of me, Jase. Always have been, always will be. You had me worried for a while."

Jilly hugged Palance from behind. The last time she hugged him this long, they were kids. She was strangely silent. Taking his arm, she walked him down the hill to the street, and, together, they looked out toward the lake.

When there was a lull in the traffic noise, she spoke to him slowly and deliberately. "See that sailboat out there, the big one?"

"Uh-huh."

"I always thought we were supposed to sail like that, as a family. Something I read once, I can't remember what, but I thought we were supposed to sail around the world."

"Mom can't swim," Palance reminded her.

"I know, but that didn't seem to matter. I thought it was because Daddy died. Otherwise we would have set off on our big adventure. I thought he robbed us of that."

"He robbed us of everything," Palance said. "He was supposed to teach me to play the guitar."

"You learned anyway."

"Not the same," Palance told her. "All my life, I've been trying to live up to something, and I don't even know what it is."

"Maybe you found it in Elise," Jilly offered.

"Elise is wonderful, and I don't deserve her, but it's not her. I still don't know what it is."

"I admire you, Palance. I was so young when Daddy died. I admire you."

Palance kissed his sister tenderly on the cheek and told her not to get too mushy. He put his arm around her and squeezed her shoulder before he let her go. Palance looked up to see Elise walking toward him.

"I've missed you," he said.

She reached up and kissed him tenderly. She lay her head on his shoulder, wrapping her arms around him.

"When can we get out of here?" he asked.

"Too much for you?"

"I want to be alone with my wife."

"Soon," she said. "We still have to cut the cake."

"Stay close," he pled as his mother came up to them.

"You look so much like your father," his mother told him. "You act like him, too."

"I wish I had known him better. As an adult," Palance said.

"You didn't have a chance."

"I wonder what it would have been like if he had lived."

"I asked myself the same thing for years. Then I decided to get on with my life. I don't know what it would have been like. I wish we'd all had the chance to find out. But you get what you get, and he was your father for eleven years. What did those years mean to you?"

"Everything," Palance said.

"What else could you want?" she told him, kissing his forehead and brushing back his hair.

"Time to cut the cake," the wedding planner told them. Palance and Elise followed her, and Palance thought how nice it would be to walk these grounds without all the hoopla, this time of day, at dusk, just the two of them waiting for the stars to appear. Instead, they were herded to a seven-layer, butter-cream-frosted cake with small dolls representing them: a bride and groom perfectly still and solemn.

"Do not smash cake in my face," Elise warned him.

"It's your favorite. Chocolate with raspberry filling."

"Let me nibble a bite. Do not smash it into my face."

"Or?" Palance asked with a devilish smile.

"You'll be wearing the whole cake home."

"Will I?"

"You will."

"I'll let you nibble a bite. I never thought I'd be this happy."

"What's making you so happy?"

"You. When I saw you walk toward me down the aisle," he told her.

Palance cut a small piece of cake and held it out to Elise. She took a bite and Palance put the cake down, and allowed Elise to feed him. He wiped some frosting with his finger, spread it across her lips, and kissed her, licking it off while the guests cheered behind them. Elise reached for the back of his neck and engaged him in a long, deep kiss.

"I love you, Mr. Heller."

"I love you, Mrs. Heller." Elise winced but continued the kiss. "Just for tonight," she said when the kiss ended.

"I have something to say," Palance's mother announced at the microphone. "First, I would like to welcome Elise into our family and let her know how delighted we are. I would like to congratulate Palance for making one of the best decisions of his life. Thank you, Elise, for accepting his proposal. I have always been proud of my children—Palance, Jillian, and now Elise—and I wish you all long years of health, happiness, and joy." Elaine began to cry softly and added, "I love you, Palance. I have always loved you, from the moment you were born. I always will."

The rest of the night was a blur of well wishes and emotions. Palance felt overjoyed and overwhelmed. Elise flitted in and out of view as groups of friends and relatives absorbed and released her. Palance tried in vain to find Jason. Of everyone there, Jason was his closest friend. Jason appeared, offered an impish grin and a handshake, and then disappeared like the magician he had always been.

Palance walked into the night air, almost bumping into Elise as she gazed out at the lake, a vision in white. He looked out with her, noticing how the sky changed over the lake, increasing in contrast and deepening as it expanded over the water.

"Mistress," he said.

"Very proper. Not necessary."

"You still scare me a bit," he told her.

"I'm the one who's scared," Elise replied. "I'm the one who plans everything. You're the one who flies by the skin of your teeth, and I just signed up for that ride."

"Copilots," Palance told her.

"Then don't call me 'Mistress.' We're a duet."

"What will you call me?" he asked.

"The question is not what I will call you. It's when, how. and for what purpose. I have something in mind now, but it requires we escape from here. Not now, but soon."

"I'm ready whenever you are."

"What are you ready for?" she asked.

"For the depth, the breadth, and the wonder of you. For the future, whatever it holds. For the nights to come upon us and blanket the world with darkness so that we alone are all that exist in the world. For the dawn to break the darkness and illuminate our path. For the wind, rain and snow to remind us of our humanity. For the madness of the city to remind us who we are and to thrust us together. For the waters of the lake to heal us and wash us clean. To share all of this, and more, with you. That's what I'm ready for."

Entwined

I don't remember the first time I loved you,
I can't imagine the last.
I don't remember the moment
The dice were cast.

But in a moment will be forever,
Moments slip away.
But I will love you until
The end of days.

C
H   *And in this moment in time,*
O   *Two hearts beat in rhyme,*
R   *Two songs, two melodies – aligned*
U   *Two souls, two harmonies – entwined.*
S

The days that follow may seem uncertain
As the years unwind.
You cannot look beyond the curtain,
Only look behind.

But in this moment we'll build a lifetime,
Who knows what we'll find.
Here and now I speak my promise,
Always to be kind.

Entwined

Chorus

And in this moment in time,
In this moment in time,
In this moment in time . . .
Entwined.

Reunion: A River of Arpeggios

Palance walked into the music store noticing the neat rows of sheet music and accessories. Squire, Yamaha, and Ibanez guitars and basses hung in perfect alignment on the walls. He expected chaos and clouds of smoke. This looked more like it was Kyle's store.

"Hey, J-bird," Palance called as Jason walked toward him in faded blue jeans and a Cream, *Disraeli Gears* t-shirt.

"Nobody calls me that anymore."

"I came to ask you a favor."

"Not dealing anymore. Only smoking a little weed. Now and then. More then than now. It's been over a month."

"That's not the favor." Palance looked around the store and nodded toward the basses. "Do you still pick one up occasionally?"

"No," Jason told him, waiting for a response. Palance looked disappointed. "Every . . . damn . . . day. I play every damn day. What's the favor? I think I owe you one."

"High school reunion in two months. I think we should play it. As the Whispering Screams."

"What about the uptight drummer?" Jason asked.

"I think we should talk to him together. A united front."

"He isn't going to be easy. He never was."

"It's okay. I've mellowed in my old age," Palance said.

"I hope he has." Jason took a Fender Jazz bass from behind the counter and plugged it into the Gallien-Krueger amp in the middle of the store. "Pick up a guitar. There's nothing fancy. I sell mostly to high school kids. You remember what a pain they are, don't you?"

"Hey, I had a best friend who was a royal pain in high school and beyond, but I think he's straightened himself out now." Palance found an Ibanez guitar, similar to his, and plugged it into a Marshall amp.

"Don't bet on it. I still raise hell occasionally. Only now, I've got a business to run, and it's kicking my ass. Hard to get good help. To tell you the truth, I could use a partner. Let's run through some of the old stuff. See if we remember anything."

Palance flashed back to when he and Jason began playing together, when Jason's bass lines first meshed with Palance's voice and guitar. There was magic in the music, and it was still there.

They rambled, feeling each other's rhythms and tempo, then ran through an old set list; U2 and Van Morrison songs, and Palance's originals, "Too Old to Be So Young," and "Breakaway."

"I wouldn't be who I am without you, Jason. You know that."

"Quit being sappy. I won't take that crap from you."

"Then let's keep playing."

"You're just stalling. You don't want to risk Kyle saying, 'No.'"

"You're right."

"Okay, then," Jason said, putting down the bass. "Let's close up shop and go see him together."

"Shouldn't we call him first?"

"Now you're thinking like Kyle. Man, you need to be around me more. Loosen up. Did I mention I could use a partner?"

Kyle was living at home after college, working at an accounting firm downtown and planning his wedding to Shellie. Kyle's parents had talked them both out of Minnesota. His black Honda Accord was sitting in the driveway. Jason let Palance ring the doorbell. Kyle's mother, Shirley, opened the door. Her deadpan expression did not change for Palance. She frowned at Jason.

"I'll see if Kyle is available," she told them. She let the screen door close on them.

"*Is available*," Jason mimicked.

Kyle came down the stairs. "Have either of you guys heard of a telephone?"

"Telephone? Hmmm," Palance looked at Jason. "I think I've heard of one, but I can't quite place it. Have you heard of them?"

"No," Jason said, "I don't believe I have."

"Let's go outside," Kyle told them. My Mom is still pissed at both of you." He looked at Jason. "Especially you."

"Persona non grata," Jason said. "I'm almost tempted not to provide you with the most excellent offer, which is the object of our appearance. I am deeply offended."

"I didn't mean . . ." Kyle stuttered. Jason broke out laughing.

"Dude," Jason said, "do you have time for lunch with a couple of old bandmates?"

"Why not?" Kyle said. "You look good, Jason."

"And I don't?" Palance said.

"Where do you want to go?" Kyle asked.

"Somewhere we can get drumsticks," Jason said.

"You mean wings?" Kyle asked him

"Close enough. Buffalo Joe's it is!" Jason announced.

"I'll meet you there," Kyle told them, getting into his Honda.

"Of course," Jason told Palance. "He won't be seen on the street with the likes of us."

In the car, Jason told Palance to let him do "the ask." "I've got this. He hasn't changed a bit."

Palance ordered the Buffalo Chicken sandwich with the Cheddar Chips Elise wouldn't allow him if she were there. Jason ordered the Suicide Wings. Kyle ordered the Char Chicken sandwich; no mayonnaise, no fries, and a Diet Coke.

"Sensible," Jason remarked. Kyle glared at him. "So, Kyle," he asked, "what's the most fun you've ever had?"

"Spending time with Shellie," he answered.

"What about before that? Before college."

"You want me to say 'the band,' Don't you?"

"It's true, isn't it?"

"You guys were a pain in the ass," Kyle told them. "*You*," he told Jason, "were a giant pain in the ass. You wouldn't believe the flak I got from my parents about you. I'll hear it again when I get back. But yeah, it was fun."

"How would you like to relive those days? This time I promise to be less of a pain in the ass. I'll bring the sound system. I'll set it up. I'll even drive myself to the gig."

"What gig?" Kyle asked.

That's the sweetest part," Palance told him. Tenth high school reunion. Back at Stephen Tyng Mather High School. Back where it all began."

"I'm not a drummer anymore," Kyle told them. "I'm a working man."

"Can we talk you into it?" Palance asked. "One gig."

"I've got work and a wedding to plan. I'm going to propose."

"Sorry, man," Jason told him. "You're not my type. Are you coming to the reunion?"

"I'll be there. I don't know if *you'll* actually make it, but I'll be there," Kyle answered. Palance," Kyle continued, ignoring Jason, "We should hang out sometime. Just the four of us. With the girls. I've told Shellie all about you. Go out to dinner or something."

Jason leaned back and smiled, as if he knew something. "Okay," he said.

"What's that supposed to mean?" Kyle asked.

"I'll see you there," Jason answered. "At the reunion."

"I'm not bringing my drum kit."

"I didn't ask you to," Jason said.

"Okay," Palance told Kyle. "I'll call you tonight when Elise gets home. We'll set it up."

Kyle got up from the table. "Looking forward to it." He looked over at Jason. "I'll see you at the reunion. *If* you show up."

"Oh, I'll show up. I've changed. Have you?"

Kyle walked away.

"Why did you give up?" Palance asked. "We might have been able to talk him into it."

"Talk to Shellie. Let her know what a great drummer Kyle was."

"Why?"

"Girls like drummers. I'm guessing even girls like Shellie. If Shellie likes drummers, Kyle might decide to become one again."

"Think that'll work?"

"Worth a shot."

Elise was a little too eager for this.

"It's just dinner with Kyle."

"And Shellie. I never get to meet the wives, just the musicians. I'm not one of the boys."

"Never thought you were," Palance said. "I don't kiss the boys."

"Shellie sounds interesting. She works at the Oriental Institute."

"As a business manager," Palance said.

"Put down your guitar, and grab my purse. We're going to be late."

Walking out the door, Palance reminded her they were trying to talk Kyle into playing at the reunion. Elise smiled. "I want to see where it all started," she told him.

Elise and Palance drove up as Kyle maneuvered his Honda into the precise center of a parking space. Palance pulled in next to them, got out. and opened the door for Elise.

Elise hugged Shellie and Kyle. Shellie responded warmly. Kyle took a step back.

"It's nice to meet you both. Kyle doesn't talk much about the past," Shellie told them.

"Past is past," Kyle chimed in. "No time like the present."

"You sound like a cliché," Shellie told him.

"The truth will set you free," Elise responded, laughing as they sat down. The waitress handed them menus. "You're a musician, too?" Shellie asked Elise.

"Guilty as charged."

"So, tell us about yourself," Palance asked Shellie. "What do you love besides this joker?" he said, gesturing toward Kyle.

"In college, we went on a dig and found dinosaur bones in Montana," she told him. Her eyes lit up. "It was amazing. Bones and fossils from sixty-five million years ago. I held them with my own hands. And I like to dance," she said, laughing.

"So, Kyle," Elise asked. "Now that you've given up music, what do you love?"

"Shellie, of course."

"Of course," Elise answered. "But what are you going to do while she's in Montana digging up dinosaur bones and other fossils?"

"He's going to become an old fossil," Palance chimed in.

Elise had a mischievous look on her face. "I'll bet your parents have video tapes of you playing your drums," she said to Kyle. "They have some of the band you guys were in, don't they?"

"Speaking of digging up old bones," Kyle responded.

"Oh, Kyle," Shellie told him. "I've got to see those."

The waitress came over to take their order.

They asked for guacamole and looked over the menus.

"Kyle, when was the last time you picked up the sticks?" Palance asked.

"There were practice rooms at school. Every once in a while . . . when I got too wound up . . . I would head over there."

"You never told me," Shellie commented, looking quizzically at Kyle.

"I never told anybody."

"Mystery man," Elise remarked.

"My mystery man," Shellie said.

"No mystery," Kyle replied. "The Camarones Caribe sounds good," he said in his best Spanish accent.

"What's that?" Shellie asked.

"Coconut Shrimp."

"I'm going with the Pollo Relleno. That's chicken," Shellie said. "I'd like to see that."

"Well," Kyle told her, "If you order it, you'll see it in a few minutes."

"Not that silly. You. I'd like to see you."

"I'm right here."

"Play the drums."

"I'm going to have the skirt steak," Elise interrupted.

"Sounds good to me," Palance said. "You know, Jason has drum kits in his store. All set up and ready to go."

"If I'm going to play, I'm going to play my own," Kyle insisted.

Palance looked him in the eye. "I thought they were all packed away."

Sheepishly, Kyle replied, "Just packed in their cases."

Palance looked at Elise, who nodded. "You know, Shellie," he said, "Jason and I are going to play at the reunion coming up. We need a drummer, but since Kyle doesn't want to do it, Jason thinks he can find someone."

Kyle glared at Palance.

"Kyle," Shellie exclaimed, "you have to do it." She reached over and held his face in her hands. "I'm going to be so proud of you. Even more than I am already."

The waitress brought over guacamole with a basket of chips and took their order. Shellie couldn't keep her hands off Kyle, who looked simultaneously embarrassed and annoyed. Palance dug in to the guacamole, and Elise, nibbling on a tortilla chip, looked extremely satisfied.

"It's ironic," Jason told Palance on the way to Kyle's house. "He thinks he's the logical one. We've got a room in my store with a sound system and drum set all ready to go. But no, he has to have *his* drum set, so the only place we can practice is his house."

"Don't tell him," Palance warned. "He'll argue and won't be happy until he wins."

"Who cares if he wins?" Jason asked.

"We do," Palance said, "If Kyle ain't happy . . ."

"Nobody's happy," they both said together.

"I could've found a drummer. A better drummer," Jason told him.

"Wouldn't be the same."

They walked up to the familiar house carrying their instruments and amplifiers. Kyle opened the door and let them know his parents were out of town. Palance and Jason breathed sighs of relief.

"It's not that they don't like you guys . . ." Kyle began. Jason and Palance laughed. "Okay, they can't stand you. Hey, is it okay if Shellie listens in? She's stopping by after work."

"Why not?" Palance said. "She works in a museum. She's used to old relics."

"Everything's set up downstairs. No smoking," Kyle warned, looking at Jason, "anything."

Palance and Jason set up their instruments.

"I've been practicing," Kyle stated.

"Of course, you have," Jason smirked.

Palance plugged his Ibanez guitar into his old Peavey amp. The heads on Kyle's drum set looked new, and the cymbals were polished. "I may be a little bit rusty," Palance announced. "I've been playing acoustic for the past few years."

"You did fine at my store," Jason told him. "Shut up and play."

Kyle banged his drumsticks together, and they played "I Still Haven't Found What I'm Looking For." Jason and Palance both looked at Kyle when they'd finished. "You *have* been practicing," Jason told him.

"Somebody got Shellie all excited about this thing," he accused Palance.

"Hey," Jason countered, "If some girl was all excited about me, I'd be thankful."

"You're not me, Jason," Kyle reprimanded.

"Hell, no. Speaking of which . . ." he began as the doorbell rang.

"I'll get that," Kyle said, glaring at Jason.

Women's voices were talking and giggling. Kyle came down the stairs with a blonde and a brunette clunking after him. He gave Jason a smoldering stare and quietly whispered to Palance, "I swear, it's like high school all over again. I thought he had grown up."

Kyle shook his head as Jason asked, "It's okay if they listen, right?" He nodded toward the brunette. "This is Samantha."

"Sam," she corrected him, coming over to kiss him on the lips. "And this is my friend Emily. We'll be quiet," she said to Kyle, who was glaring at them.

Kyle shook his head and went back behind his drum kit. "Let's run through Pal's originals," he said.

"Shouldn't we find some chairs for Sam and Emily?" Palance asked Kyle.

Kyle got up, walked to the closet, took out two folding chairs, and without saying a word, set them up against the wall. Back behind his drum kit, he announced, "Too Old to Be So Young." He banged the drumsticks together, and they launched into the songs Palance wrote before Kyle left for Ithaca.

Jason admired the precision of Kyle's percussion. Kyle respected the creativity that Palance had in spades and how Jason's bass lines flowed effortlessly. Sam and Emily whispered to each other between songs.

Palance took charge and ran them through "Smells Like Teen Spirit," "One," by U2, "Walking in Memphis," and some older stuff: "Born to Run," by Springsteen, and "Tales of Brave Ulysses," by Cream. The last one took all their chops. Palance noticed the way Jason looked at Sam.

"How do you know them?" he asked Jason.

"We've been dating. Off and on."

"Both of them?"

"Just Sam."

"How long?"

"A while."

"Come on, J-bird. How long?"

"Almost a year," he said.

"Let's take a break," Palance said. "I think we've got this."

They heard the front door open and footsteps above.

"Can anyone use a cup of coffee?" Kyle asked in an uncharacteristic gesture of hospitality.

"I can get it, Shellie said, coming down the stairs.

"I've got it," Kyle told her. "No big deal. I'm going to make coffee."

"Really," she asked.

Jason introduced Sam and Emily to Shellie while Kyle started the coffee.

Shellie whispered into Kyle's ear. He sat down while she got out coffee cups, cream, and sugar. She finished making the coffee, and, while it brewed, she disappeared with the two other women into the living room.

"Girl talk," Palance said.

"You know what they're talking about, don't you?" Jason remarked.

"Us, of course," Kyle answered.

"So, what *is* going on with you and Sam?" Palance asked Jason.

"It's pretty serious."

"Serious enough I should write you guys a wedding song?" Palance asked.

"Don't rush me," Jason said. "But I was serious about wanting a partner for the store."

"I heard you guys are pretty good," Shellie said, walking back into the kitchen with Sam and Emily behind her.

"I'd like to hear some more," Emily told them. "I might be able to help you out. I'm an event planner. Corporate gigs. Pretty tasty."

Kyle appeared distressed. "I only agreed to one gig." He looked at Shellie. "I don't even remember agreeing to *this*."

Sam moved behind Jason and put her arms around his neck.

"Let's get this show on the road," Emily told them. "Chop, chop. Time is money."

As the women marched them down the stairs, Palance turned to Jason and Kyle. "Okay, boys," he said. "Let's put on a show."

Behind the drums, Kyle counted off, "One, two, three, four," and they launched into "Breakaway."

The women appeared conspiratorial. Later, at home, when he and Elise were getting ready for bed, she mentioned Shellie had told her that Emily was a corporate events planner.

"Good for her," Palance said.

"You just smile and look pretty," she replied. Palance didn't answer. He was used to being baffled.

Palance walked into Mather High School almost ten years to the day after graduation, his Ibanez in one hand and his amplifier in the other. Elise carried the Larriveé. She had been moody lately, and Palance was on edge. Behind them, Jason wheeled in the sound system on a dolly with Samantha by his side. In the gym, Kyle was sitting behind his drum kit, already set up on the risers, tuning the heads. Streamers and banners welcomed back the Class of 1994. Enlarged pictures from their yearbook hung on the walls.

"Cutting it a little close," Kyle told them.

"We've got two hours," Jason said. He and Kyle rolled their eyes at each other.

Palance and Jason set their instruments and amplifiers on the risers. Jason found an electrical outlet and plugged in power strips, duct taping them to the riser, and plugging in the amplifiers.

Palance and Jason set the speakers on their stands. "Do you want help?" Kyle asked.

"We're cool," Jason told him.

"You always were the 'cool ones,' weren't you?" Kyle remarked.

"You made us cool," Palance told him.

"You thought I was a nerd," Kyle retorted.

"You were a nerd," Jason told him. "That's what made us cool."

"Huh?" Kyle exclaimed.

"You took care of the gigs," Palance said.

"You took care of the sound system," Jason added. "You got us there. You got us home."

"You got us our first gig. We'd still be practicing in the garage if it hadn't been for you." Palance told him.

Jason looked Kyle in the eye and nodded his head. "You did it, man. You're to blame. You made us cool."

"And I'm the nerd?"

"Cool nerd," Jason said.

"Well," Kyle said to them, "Let's see what we can do here. If we don't screw this up too bad, maybe we can do another gig someday. Shellie likes this part of me. I blame the two of you."

Jason finished setting up the equipment while Kyle walked back to his drums.

"Are you sure you've got this?" Kyle asked Jason.

Jason flipped a switch, and the amplifiers and sound system came alive. Jason and Palance tuned their instruments, and the band ran through three or four songs. People began to wander in. Some looked familiar. Palance recognized others, though he couldn't recall most of their names. Mr. Claussen, who taught chemistry, recognized Jason and shook his head at him. Kyle saw Shellie and went to talk to her, letting her know Elise and Sam were by the vending machines.

Mr. Newsome, the music teacher, walked up to Kyle. After a few minutes, he walked over to Palance and told him he looked familiar.

"I went to school here. Never took band, though."

"No, that's not it," Mr. Newsome told him. "You look like someone I used to teach. Played the violin, and then switched to guitar. That's when I lost him."

"Lost who?" Palance asked.

"Alan. Alan . . ."

"Alan Heller?" Palance asked.

"That was the kid's name. You look just like him."

"He was my father."

"Hell of a violinist. Give him my best, would you?"

Palance was too shocked to answer as Mr. Newsome sauntered away. He knew his father had gone to school here, but not that he played the violin, or was in the orchestra.

Palance opened the Larriveé case and pulled out a song to play at the end. It was about what music meant to him. He wished his father could be there to hear it. He hoped Jason and Kyle would approve. And Elise. Lately, she didn't approve of much. He didn't know what had gotten into her, and he was getting tired of walking on eggshells around her.

He put the paper back in the guitar case and secured the case on stage behind his amplifier. He looked toward the door as Beth walked in. She was wearing a blue off-the-shoulder slit gown, her hair long and falling in curls. She took his breath away. He wondered if he'd made a mistake letting her go. Palance left the stage and embraced her, fighting the urge to kiss her on the lips. She released herself from Palance's embrace quickly. She was on the arm of his former classmate, Benjamin somebody, who sat across from him in Spanish class.

"You look beautiful," Palance said to her.

Ben reached over to shake his hand. "Hi," he said. "We were in Spanish together. I'm Ben. I guess you knew Beth." Palance realized, in that moment, that Beth had never mentioned him to Ben, never told him that he was her first, never played him her song. He barely heard her words, mesmerized by the sound of her voice. She told him she and Ben were engaged to be married.

Palance managed hesitant congratulations, excusing himself to head back to the bandstand. He watched from a distance as the room filled up. Beth was mingling, paying no attention to him, as Jason walked up.

"Blast from the past?" Jason asked.

"The past is overrated," he replied.

"Yes, it is," Jason told him. "How long until we go on?"

Palance was about to tell him that he had no idea, that he was waiting for Kyle to let him know, when he realized that this was *his* gig, something he should be used to by now, and he looked at his watch. "Fifteen minutes," he told Jason.

"She does look pretty," Jason said.

"Who?" Palance asked, trying to appear nonchalant.

Jason nodded in Beth's direction.

"Yes, she does."

"Any regrets?"

Palance's mind traveled quickly from Beth's Sweet Sixteen party to their night in the park, through dates and road trips;

the way she felt in his arms, her warmth and laughter, the feelings that grew between them; through visions of her sitting and listening to him play music in coffeehouses, and late nights sharing stories and secrets.

"Not a one," he lied, watching Elise walk back into the gym in her red satin dress. He marveled at Elise's confidence, her certain steps, and prayed this moody phase wouldn't last forever.

"I'm ready to see my man perform," Shellie said.

Beth and Ben walked up, and Palance introduced Elise to them.

"This is my wife, Elise," he said to Beth. "Elise, this is Beth and her fiancé Ben." His disdain for Ben was evident in his voice.

"I was a year behind them in school," Beth told Elise. "I grew up with Kyle. Palance and I hung out together for a while."

"Really? When was that?" Ben asked.

"It's good to meet you," Elise said to Beth, gracious to a fault. "Tell me how you and Ben met. I want to hear all about it." She positioned herself between Palance and Beth.

"We knew each other in high school. Not well," Ben answered. "She and my sister Holly were in the same grade. I heard about you guys back then," he said to the band. "Holly said you guys were cool."

"Very cool," Elise agreed. "Did Palance tell you we're married?"

"How long?" Beth asked.

"One year," Elise told her. "Couldn't be happier," she said. Stepping back to put her arm around Palance's waist, she kissed him on the lips. "I'll let you boys get ready," she added, walking toward Samantha and Shellie, with one backward glance at Beth.

"Let's do it," Palance said to Jason and Kyle. Jason strapped on his bass while Kyle walked back to his drums.

Donna, who headed the reunion committee, welcomed everyone. Kyle banged his drumsticks together. They played R.E.M.'s "Losing My Religion" and watched couples pour onto the dance floor.

Palance focused on the music, quickly syncing with Jason and Kyle. They found their groove, taking cues from each other and moving through the set list. Elise sat at a table with Shellie, who gazed at Kyle without blinking. Samantha went onto the dance floor, by herself, and Palance watched her move freely and gracefully. She passed Beth and Ben, who seemed natural in each other's arms, and Palance felt a sense of unease.

They played mostly covers, the same songs they did in high school. That's what this night was all about. Dread rose in him as memories came flooding back: his father's death, feeling adrift, abandoned, and betrayed as he recalled his mother forcing him to remove his father's guitar strings. He looked back at Kyle and Jason in between songs. "Let's do some originals," he said, and launched into "Too Old to Be So Young," and then "Breakaway" and "Icarus." At the end of the set, Palance announced a short break and walked outside to get some air.

He sat down on the front steps of the school to collect himself. Closing his eyes, he felt someone sit next to him, and assumed it was Elise. He opened his eyes and saw Beth.

"Ben is visiting with some school friends. He won't miss me."

Palance felt caught in a vortex between the death of his father and this moment.

"I know I was cold to you, but I didn't know how to react. I didn't know if you were mad at me or . . ."

"Why would I be mad at you?"

"I should have reached out, or let you know," Beth told him. "I was young. I was mad at you for not following me to Madison. That's why I never told him about you. He gets jealous."

"Jealous of me?"

"He would be if he knew. I was so in love with you. Palance. I still have feelings for you." She placed her hand on his knee.

"I'm married."

"I know, but I knew you were going to be here. You and the band. That's why I talked Ben into coming."

"To relive the past? That's what these things are all about."

"Maybe more than that. What do you like about Elise? Why did you marry her?"

"She knows me better than I know myself. She's amazing."

"Am I amazing? You used to think so. I still listen to the song you wrote for me. Especially when I'm feeling lonely."

"You have Ben."

"It's not the same. That song still does things for me. To me."

"Things change."

"How much have you changed? Do you still have feelings for me? If you asked me right now, I would run away with you."

"Where would we go?"

"We could go on the road together. Live like nomads. Be young and wild again."

"I did that. It gets old. Things are more complicated now. It's one thing to be twenty on the road. Thirty is different."

"It's just a number."

"You don't know how badly I want to kiss you," Palance told her. Beth leaned in, and Palance turned away. "What do you miss the most about being with me? About being young?"

"So many possibilities. Everything was open. We could be anyone we wanted to be."

"Who do you want to be?"

"I want to be that girl in the park who made love to you. I want to live in the moment."

"Can't you do that with Ben?"

"He has all these ideas about who he is. Who I am. I want to take you now and go back to the park where we first made love. I want you to hold me in your arms and tell me how you'll take me on adventures and show me the world."

Palance closed his eyes and tried to imagine a life with Beth on the road, back playing gigs every night and driving all day. "When I was on the road," he told her, "I spent most of my time in the car and the rest in cheap motel rooms."

"Then at least hold me, just for now. You said this reunion was about reliving our past. I want to relive it now, with you."

Palance put his arm around Beth's waist, and she laid her head on his shoulder.

"I was young then," she told him.

"I was young, too."

"Too old to be so young," Beth told him.

The two of them looked at each other. "I need to get back onstage," he told her.

"I know, but I'll never forget you," she said. "You were my first. I'm glad about that." She kissed him on the cheek, took him by the hand, and led him back into the school. "Play me my song," she asked as she let go of his hand.

Palance walked back to the stage, where Jason and Kyle were already in place. Kyle shouted out, "Almost Saturday Night," and Palance fell in line, singing and playing his part. For the next forty-five minutes, they ran through the set list, including Beth's song. Palance could see her gazing at him, and he felt unstuck in time.

"One more set to go, buddy," Jason told him.

At the table, Shellie engulfed Kyle in her arms, laying her head on his shoulder. "You are amazingly awesome. I'm going to come to all your gigs."

"All my . . . what gigs?" Kyle asked.

"We'll talk. I want to see you like this more often."

Palance told Elise he was feeling lost. He needed to find steady work, but couldn't see teaching in a university or any classroom. "I don't know what I can do."

"You can run the store with me," Jason told him. "Fifty-fifty," he said.

"Are you serious?" Palance asked.

"Dude, I've been dropping hints for the past three months."

"What could I do there?"

"Sell instruments, change strings, give guitar lessons. Give me a damn day off."

"I can do that?"

"You can do that, and more."

"What more?"

"You can finish the gig," Kyle told him. "It's time."

"I can finish the gig," Palance repeated.

They played the last set including two encores to standing ovations. For their last song, they chose Don Henley's "The End of Innocence." Jason and Kyle high-fived each other, and Palance asked Jason, "Can you leave the sound system up for a while? There's a song I want to play for you, Kyle, and anyone who will listen."

"Sure, buddy," Jason told him, noticing the crowd thinning out. "I meant it about the store. Fifty-fifty. I could use the help."

"Do you need us?" Kyle asked.

Palance paused, looking pensive. After a minute, he shook his head. "No—not for this." He walked back to the stage with a folding chair, sat down, and adjusted the microphones for himself and the Larriveé.

Palance started slowly and tentatively, and then picked up the tempo.

Some days rise into crescendo, some days ache, like broken strings.

People who remained turned around. Some gave final hugs to former classmates and left. Those who stayed moved closer to the stage. Elise held her breath. From the back of the room, Beth looked directly into Palance's eyes.

Some days glide into glissando, some days howl and some days sing.

Those remaining listened intently. Beth smiled, and Elise let go of the breath she had been holding. Jason and Kyle grinned. Shellie looked at Kyle with admiration and awe.

I have lived my life through music, through the grace of harmony.

Some of the people who were on their way to the parking lot drifted back into the room. Even the janitors and cleaning crew, ready to man their mops and buckets, armed with garbage bags and sweep brooms, came in to listen.

Like a river of arpeggios, flowing out into the sea.

Palance finished the song. He heard applause and the sound of footsteps leaving the gym. He turned around, put the Larriveé back in its case, snapped the latches shut, turned off the sound system, and began packing up. Jason and Kyle walked up to the stage to tear down the equipment.

Palance looked to see Beth smiling at him as Ben guided her toward the door. Elise came up; she embraced him and kissed him. "This is who you are. I love you."

"I've got to pack up," he told her.

"I know. You pack up. I'll meet you outside." Elise walked toward Samantha and Shellie.

Samantha turned to Elise as Beth and Ben walked out with the rest of the crowd. "Do you want to go somewhere and get a drink?" she asked.

"I can't," Elise told her. "I'm pregnant."

A River of Arpeggios

Some days rise into crescendo,
Some days ache like broken strings,
Some days glide into glissando,
Some days howl, and some days sing.

C
H I have lived my life through music,
O through the grace of harmony,
R like a river of arpeggios
U flowing out into the sea.
S

Some days rest upon a tonic,
Some days sound in different keys,
Some days ring out their harmonics,
Some days follow, some days lead.

Chorus

Some days rise up in ascension,
Some days slide like a trombone,
Some days cry vibrato violins,
Some days call in truer tones.

Chorus

Some days rise into crescendo,
Some days ache like broken strings,
Some days glide into glissando,
Some days howl, and some days sing.
Some days howl, and some days sing.

Chapter Fifteen

This Guitar

I t was two o'clock in the morning, and Palance couldn't sleep. He and Jason were expanding the store. He'd just put in an order for a dozen high-end guitars, and now he wasn't sure he could sell them. He had four lessons set up in the morning, and they had a gig with Kyle tomorrow night. They decided to rename the band The River of Arpeggios. It fit them now, better than the Whispering Screams.

Palance went downstairs and pulled the Larriveé out of its case. He tuned it and started playing, amazed at his life. His own home and family. His own basement. A music store that came with connections to friends, to the past, and to the future. He took out the song he had been working on. It was almost complete.

When the song was finished, Palance sat in the basement in silence, his own tools mixed with those of his father. He gripped his guitar and closed his eyes. Time passed, and he heard faint cries. Palance gripped the guitar by the neck and carried it upstairs.

In the nursery, Palance laid the guitar against the wall and picked up his son. He carried him to the rocking chair, sat down, and began to rock, humming a lullaby. In a few minutes, Alan quieted down and was sleeping peacefully. Palance laid Alan back in his crib and sang him the song he had written. When it was done, he sat in the rocking chair, watching him sleep; then he went back down to the basement, where he placed the Larriveé back in its case on the shelf. Palance went upstairs for the night to lie down next to the woman he loved and settle into his dreams.

This Guitar

This guitar is your guitar,
to travel with you near and far,
it's so large and you're so small,
one day you'll be big and tall,
so for the time, I'll hold it close,
you're the one I love the most,
and when it's time to play these strings,
they will sing.

All your dreams are all my dreams,
I hope that they will all redeem,
they're so large and you're so small,
one day you'll be big and tall,
so, for the time, I'll hold them close,
you're the one I love the most,
and when it's time to live your dreams,
live your dreams.

I wish that I could promise you,
sun and moon and starlight, too,
cloudless skies and summer days,
fireworks so bright ablaze, in
summer nights that never end,
to be shared with loving friends,
who dance with you in endless song,
until the morning comes along,
but all that I can promise you

is that my love is always true,
and everything I have is yours,
to have, to hold, to love, and more.

This guitar is your guitar,
to travel with, near and far,
it's so large and you're so small,
one day you'll be big and tall,
so, for the time, I'll hold it close,
you're the one I love the most,
and when it's time to sing your song,
sing your song.

About the Author

ary grew up in Rogers Park, a neighborhood on the north side of Chicago, where he was influenced by a love of writing, literature, and music. When he was a young child, his mother asked him if he would like to take something to bed with him. He asked her what he should take. His mother said, "Something you really like," so he took a record album to bed with him.

While in high school, he was fortunate to discover the No Exit Coffeehouse near his home, where he was introduced to folk and blues music, poetry and jazz. A string of musicians came through the coffeehouse, including Steve Goodman, John Prine, Bob Gibson, Michael Smith, Jim Brewer and Art Thieme.

While quickly learning that poetry and folk music were not the best ways to support himself, Gary never stopped writing poetry, stories, and songs, and learned to play the guitar. After a brief career as a sound engineer, Gary worked designing and building electrical controls, later going back to school and earning a master's degree in community counseling. It was during this time that he began writing *River of Arpeggios*, only to discover that a career in community mental health left little time or energy for writing. After his recent retirement, Gary picked up the novel where he left off, and found a renewed energy for writing and playing music. He is currently working on a second novel, *Leda & the Swan*, as well as a book of poetry, and is considering publishing a collection of his short stories. He works part-time as a psychotherapist.

Gary resides in McHenry County, Illinois, thirty miles northwest of Rogers Park, with his wife, Sherry, their dog Carly, and two cats, Mr. Tucker and Heather. He hopes you enjoy his work as much as he enjoys writing.

* 9 7 9 8 9 8 5 2 9 1 3 0 8 *